Possible...

FIRST EDITION

International ISBN: 978-0615520209 (Paperback)

Published by:

Monkey Queen Publishing
P.O. Box 52
Hampton, New York 12837

THE SPACES IN BETWEEN

By

Mary Martin Holland

*Where the realms of
truth and fiction
quietly align...*

DEDICATION:

This book is dedicated to
all my relations,
both present and passed.
May we celebrate the beauty
of our own existence,
and the beauty in all creation,
and may history smile
warmly on the choices
that we make.

PREFACE

The Spaces In Between delves headlong into the unseen connections that shape our reality. Suppose the rules of physics were to shift without notice, and all of the rulebooks became obsolete?

As known forces battle unknown forces, the war breaches the threshold of Loretta's family home. Her makeshift band of strangers prove both raw and enchanting, and will capture your imagination, if not your heart.

Amid waves of fear and turmoil, each faction is struggling to identify the truth. With right and wrong now blurred beyond all recognition, a more primitive system has arrived at the forefront.

When answers begin outweighing the questions, humanity is faced with the ultimate decision....

Get ready for a thrilling adventure unlike any you've known, and welcome to *The Spaces In Between!*

THE SPACES IN BETWEEN

PART I
"FACES IN THE CROWD"

x

"LORETTA'S LIGHT"

Spirit don't rest once the crows take flight, recalls Loretta, lifting her favorite mug from its hook beneath the cupboard. Though she'd dismissed many of the old woman's ramblings, grandmother's words seem to visit quite often these days.

Cradling the pottery in her worn and weathered hands, both stained and etched in their lifetime of service, she gets lost for a moment in the swirl of the steam. Images spill from her memory like photos from a shoebox, and she allows herself to revel for a moment in the happy times when all was right with the world.

The charm of an August evening is hard to resist, and the fireflies soon coax her out to share the evening. Seems the creak of the screen door has awakened her Henry from his easy chair dreams, and Loretta hears familiar sounds of bedtime in the making. As Henry pads off like a sleep walking bear, she eases into the old porch rocker next to Momma's red geranium.

Wrapped snugly in the comfort of their forty-odd years, she turns her gaze to the blanket of stars stretched high overhead. This is definitely her patch of sky – familiar and dependable, and inside she's certain that it knows her too. Nestling down into the worn wicker, her eyes come to rest on a particularly bright spot above the old horse barn. It's mesmerizing, really ... until it's too late.

1

Loretta doesn't hear her favorite mug shatter as it strikes against the geranium pot, yet the sound rattles through Henry like a sonic blast. Stumbling out of bed, he fumbles for his glasses. He can see her through the screen door, an eternity away. A knot forms in the pit of his stomach as she just sits there, slack jawed and fixated, oblivious to the fact that she's soaking in a puddle of tea with shards of glass around her feet.

"You all right, Loretta?!" Henry hollers, striding across the floor at a pace he hasn't known for quite some time.

He can hear the panic in his voice, but can do little to hide it. *Please, Loretta,* his mind begs, heart nearly leaping from his chest. Life without her is not something he's willing to consider, so he shoves the screen door open and moves quickly to her side, taking his wife by the hand. A single tear rolls down Loretta's cheek, and all she can do is just stare.

The raging ball of fire is screaming through the darkness, and within seconds the air starts to crackle all around them. Ripping through the front yard with a deafening roar, it sends shudders right down to the bedrock, and similarly, straight to the bone. When the sizzling settles, along with the dust, the couple is left speechless in the wake of the firestorm.

Perhaps it's curiosity, or something else entirely, yet Henry can resist no more, and staggers to the far side of the smoldering abyss. A steaming trench of scorched and naked soil yaws open before him like a gaping wound. Peering beyond the ragged edge and deep into the void, a slow smile creeps across his face, as Loretta joins him cautiously from the opposite side.

His expression obscures the boundaries between serenity and wonder when the truth slowly dawns in his eyes. She's just about to ask him, when Henry mouths the words, "I love you," and drops suddenly and lifelessly down into the pit.

Loretta scrambles blindly over the freshly churned earth, desperate to breath him back into this world. She thumps his chest repeatedly and presses her warm mouth to his, until his lips are too soon cooled, and dear Henry joins the night.

Her heart wrings out like a blood-soaked towel, drenched and drained and permanently stained. Kneeling over the body of her one true love, she strokes his hair and smoothes his cheeks, and wails from the depths of her being.

As she wipes the tears from her swollen eyes, Loretta raises her face to the stars. With fear and exhaustion both circling, she ponders if she'll ever again know the comfort she had known just an hour ago.

"ONLY JONAS"

"Hmmph."

Mornings are just reminders of a crumbled past, and evenings an omen of darkness yet to come. The days seem longer now – now that there's nothing to fill them. Twenty-four hours quickly splinters into some eighty-six thousand seconds spent whirling from drama to distraction and back again.

Physically, his health is exceptional, yet Jonas invites death to join him on a regular basis. One cigarette, one frustration, one angry thought at a time, he extracts every ounce of joy like a surgeon removing a cancer.

His disdain for life is palpable, permeating, until it grates on the nerve endings and forms an icy film around your heart. At first you don't notice; it's still you, just crisper, perhaps a bit more cynical. Yet the comments, the sideways glimpses, the slow twisting of ideals is insidious, creeping, seeping like smoke into the crevices of your psyche.

He didn't get here on his own – no one ever does. Jonas can recite his list of evildoers as easily as the alphabet, by rote and with proper inflection. His stage so abounds with ghosts from the past that he has neither the time nor the energy to nourish his present. Each new face that enters his world is but a shadowed reflection of some earlier pain.

Why should I care? Jonas waxes rhetorically. *Caring breeds weakness, and the weak don't survive. I'm no fool. The world is full of wolves and fools, predators and prey. I refuse to be prey,* he thinks, sucking down the last fiery drag of a de-filtered cigarette.

Grinding out the grisly stub into an ashtray that hasn't tasted water since his third wife left, Jonas begins obsessing over a frayed bit of cuticle on his left index finger. He picks and tugs and gnaws at the nail bed until it's raw and bloody, then moves for a short time to the dry patch along his hairline, before finally arriving at his nose and that persistent dry bit that demands second-knuckle spelunking to get the job done.

How quickly civilization slips away when confronted with solitude. Sadly, Jonas and the ashtray have more in common than the endless barrage of nicotine they quietly consume. Together they covertly experiment with the boundaries of acceptable hygiene. Of course, the ashtray has no choice in the matter.

Jonas picks through the charred butts, reclaiming scraps of tobacco from the discarded embers. Light, ultra-light, menthol – it doesn't really matter. In fact, he considers himself an aficionado, a connoisseur of sorts, able to correctly identify the exact brands contained in each noxious concoction. How dare you pester the Wizard with questions or facts?! Pay no attention to the man behind the curtain!

Tossing the filters into the trash, he twists up the plastic sack and struggles to withdraw the bag from its ancient container. Grunting, swearing, and thrashing about, he not only dislodges the bag, but also tears an enormous hole in the side, which spews four days of rotting debris across the kitchen floor. The ensuing tirade invokes all the high drama of an Oscar winning performance, and elongates the clean up to nearly fifty minutes. The day's entire schedule consisted of taking out the trash, so when it's all said and done, at least it was exciting.

Upon returning from the dumpster, he twists another smoke from the remnant pile and fires it up. Hunkered on the edge of a dilapidated stool, he rests for a moment alongside what used to be the breakfast bar. Smoking like a convict or someone who's lived on the streets, he sits there, hunched and shielded against imaginary elements, a self-imposed prisoner within the walls of his home.

He stubs them out when they burn his lips or fingers, and not a moment sooner. Inserting the singed digits into the comfort of his mouth, he forgot about the garbage on his unwashed hands and retches all the way to the bathroom. Turns out he had spent very little time there lately.

However, the situation proves inspiring, and Jonas decides to exert himself beyond his usual two-part bathing system. With weeks between actual showers or submersions, he has adapted a sponge bath method that, in addition to brushing his teeth, involves no more than two body parts per day. Yet today, he can even smell himself, so it seems a full-body wash is finally in order.

Shutting off the shower, he can hear the telephone ringing, and seconds later the answering machine kicks on. *Blah, blah, blah, who is it?* he wonders, standing naked and dripping as he listens for the automated drone of a sales call. The mere sound of Lizzie's voice can echo through the decades, and it always makes his heart skip a beat. Lizzie is Jonas's first born, and one of the few people on the planet who can still make him smile.

"Hey, Pops! This is number one, and I'm really havin' fun!" she chants in familiar fashion. It's a personal exchange shared since childhood when Jonas had assured her that being a big sister would be fun. He's not quite sure how that panned out in the long run, but either way, the words have endured.

While not many things will cause Jonas to clamber from the shower, Lizzie is at the top of that list. Snatching a towel from the bar, he wraps it around his torso and yanks open the door. He can still hear her talking, so he hurries down the hallway toward the kitchen in hopes of catching her before she hangs up. Yet as Jonas clears the refrigerator, a truly sickening sensation grabs him by the belly.

"THE CONFLICTS OF CADENCE"

Her silence is only a forerunner to the formal click and hum of the true disconnect. Cadence simply shakes her head, and tosses the phone with disgust.

It appears Mother has discovered some fatal flaw in her brother's latest fiancé, and now has her in the crosshairs. Her twisted sense of propriety has been a blight on her children for decades, with countless suitors rejected for the perfect illusion.

With thirty in the rearview growing dimmer by the minute, her gallery of prospects has thinned down considerably. Now her ovaries cringe as the fifty-something reruns eye her from the outskirts of their first-wife social gatherings. Lately, she finds herself suppressing the urge to bolt when it's suggested that she cradle yet another mewling newborn.

Strolling across the crisp white marble, she pulls open the refrigerator door and pours herself a glass of sun tea from the pitcher Maggie left. Lemon slices bob cheerfully amid the ice cubes as she tops it with a fresh sprig of mint and heads for the lanai.

The staccato of Italian leather sling-backs against smooth slate contradicts the soft, rolling landscape, so she casually slips them off and tosses them aside. Stretching her bare feet against the cool of the stone, she pops and cracks her toes until each appendage can fully absorb the reality of their freedom.

Running a lazy finger along the sweaty glass, she ponders the analogy of her toes with her life. Expensive cages are still cages, and she feels like a prisoner in her gilded life. It's all about serving the money. The right people, the right organizations, the right affiliations – everything revolves around keeping and growing their precious money tree.

A coolish breeze rolls up the valley from the river down below carrying scent memories laden with prepubescent joy. For a few short years, children are allowed pleasure without pressure, and she longs for the liberty to roam paradise again.

Startled by the sound of the telephone, she topples the glass of tea and watches motionless as it shatters on the tiles below. Bile rises in her throat as she surveys the splintered bits of crystal while listening to the voice of Aunt Mattie reminding her of this evening's obligation.

By the time she's finished cleaning up the mess, it's nearly five o'clock, and time to start preparations for another dreaded fundraiser. One would think she'd be inured to the process by now, yet the thought of making small talk with so many Botoxed faces is almost more than she can bear. Duty calls, however, so she retreats to her dressing area, dons the image of an heiress, and waltzes down the staircase promptly at seven.

A tuxedoed driver awaits, and whisks her to the gala with all the style anticipated for a woman of her station. The evening is predictable, cooing at digitized prodigies, handing off a substantial donation and engaging in trivial conversation until she can manage to excuse herself for another champagne.

Following what amounts to her fourth introduction to someone's clearly gay son, she snags a full glass from a passing tray and ducks out the nearest service entrance. As she pushes through the doorway, she sees a gentleman in chef whites has beaten her to the punch. With a hefty sigh, she resigns herself to rejoining the festivities and ponders a plausible excuse.

"I won't bite, you know," drips off his tongue like summer honey as their eyes find each other. "At least not hard," he adds, and once again offers her the back of his head.

Rebuking his insolence would certainly be in order, yet she's intrigued by the tug of his begrudging smile. Cadence is contemplating just how long it's been since she shared the company of a man, much less a *real* man, when her revelry is rudely interrupted.

"In or out," he states without turning around, "or we'll both get busted."

Her inner debate is short-lived. Stepping onto the cement platform, she leans against the railing and ponders the damp curl that overlaps his shirt collar. In silence she observes him, appreciating every fiber of that taunt white cotton stretched across his shoulders. All at once conscious that her jaw is agape, Cady regains her composure and quickly drains the glass.

"You're welcome to sit," he suggests, pulling a towel from his waistband and spreading it out beside him. To her pause, he replies, "Unless of course, you're a bitch, in which case, I rescind my invitation."

The entire monologue takes place without him ever facing her, which she finds highly appealing. He will not dignify her unless and until she dignifies him. With a rush of defiance, she steps over the towel and delicately lowers her linen-covered derriere onto the cement step. Reaching down beside him, he retrieves a reasonably full bottle of bubbly and freshens her glass without asking.

"So, are you from around here?" Cadence asks, once again shifting control. Peering over his shoulder with a raised eyebrow and a smirk, the gesture itself clearly mocks the implication. He does, however, offer a reply.

"Spent much time in the city?"

As they recount wild nights spent club hopping, Cady finds herself teetering precariously along the edge of recklessness. The more she considers her obligations, the more she resents them, and with each glass of champagne, she can feel her inhibitions slipping quietly away. By the time they reach empty, the charm of his smile and thrust of his wit have fully engaged her, and she feels helpless to escape her own desire. Clutching his shirtfront with manicured nails, she draws his lips to hers in a deep, consuming kiss.

"So you *are* hungry," he smiles, wiping silvery wetness from beneath her lower lip.

A knowing smile appears on the waitress's face as she watches them disappear into the storeroom. There is little need for thought or conversation as their inner animals spring into action. Frantic fingers roam each other's bodies in search of softness and hardness, before finally settling into the powerful wetness of unadulterated passion. Their thick, hot union soon coaxes both to a shuddering climax, leaving them breathless in the wake of their lust.

Collapsing into one another, they bask for a moment in the glow, yet awkwardness quickly ensues as each shuffles to regain their clothing and composure. Cadence dresses in silence, then plants a parting kiss on his lips and heads toward the door.

"Michael," he whispers as she reaches for the latch. "In case you ever wonder."

With a coquettish smile, she blows him a kiss and leaves him to dress with nary a word. Thankfully, the restroom is just around the corner, and she is able to ease past the other guests without attracting their attention. Straightening herself, she reapplies her lipstick and a dab of perfume before returning to the fundraiser to say her goodbyes.

Back in the limo, the driver's nostrils flare as he observes her through the rearview, and as the flush rises on her cheeks, so does the dark glass between them. Alone in the sanctity of her private chamber, she squirms with the knowledge of her illicit affair, and secretly revels at her boldness.

Yet beyond the defiance and well past the guilt, Cadence can hardly avoid contemplating the obvious risk.

"AURORA BOREALIS"

Aurora awakens sweaty and breathless, tangled in illusions, both present and past. She gropes the unused pillows and seeks out the bathroom light, before choking down the fact that he's not coming to bed.

A frustrated sigh escapes her lips when she realizes it's been less than an hour since she crumbled and gave up on the day. *Oh, but he gave up on so much more*, she argues in her head, as if she could somehow rationalize the defeat. His or hers is barely the issue. Decades between them, and now this. There'll be no trophy, no gold star, and no lifelong companion in the middle of the night.

However, tonight there *will* be tequila, she decides, climbing out of her king-sized bed and absently pulling on a pair of his socks. *Medicinal purposes,* she affirms, snagging a sleep-inducer from the well-stocked liquor cabinet. Wrapped in a hand-woven blanket, she lumbers out to the front porch and slumps down onto the bench.

Uncapping the bottle, she rests it on one knee and stares out across the desert. The stars are magnificent, even through her dimmed-down perspective, and she gets lost there for a moment in the comfort of the sky. Tranquility is fleeting, however, as a burst of flames pierces the eastern sky and scorches a path straight down to earth. By the time it reaches ground, well beyond the horizon, Aurora is aware of every hair on her body. Her eyes are glued to the now darkened scene as her retinas reflect the image now permanently etched in her psyche. Hoisting the bottle to her lips, Rori gulps down a good double shot.

"If that's not going down in flames, I don't know what is," she declares, as coyotes begin howling somewhere off in the distance. Their mournful sound soon rattles loose the tears, melting her anger into salt until all that remains is the raw. The crux of this argument has been replaying since that first light-hearted conversation some twenty years back.

We were on our way home from that restaurant…what was the name? We loved that place! We drove that rusty, old piece of crap and it died right out front in the middle of the road! What was the name of that place? Ryan would know, she surmises, wiping fresh tears on the blanket. Tossing back another shot, she remembers a million thoughts, just like yesterday. She laughs through the tears, recalling how little they thought it all mattered, sheltered as they were in the confidence of youth. *Who knew we'd outlive invincibility,* she laughs sardonically.

They've shared these same rooms, on too many occasions, all the while remaining locked behind emotional walls that could rival the Great One in China. Somewhere along the line, they were alienated by principle, each one retreating to their separate outposts. It's not so much that they've changed, as gnawed down to the bones of their differences, while starving for a taste of the same.

We've been unplugged for so long, she confesses to herself. *So disconnected, I can barely feel him anymore. I miss "Us," and I don't even know where we went,* admits Aurora, just as the coyotes take to growling and yipping somewhere out beyond the halo of her porch light.

Clutching the blanket around her, she thrusts the bottle up over her head and howls out a tribute to all things wild - at least within earshot, anyway. With a smack of her lips, she screws the cap back on the tequila and sets it down beside her.

Off in the distance, there's more tussling, and then he's rushing her, charging out of the darkness like a freight train. This wasn't the introduction he was hoping for, yet this is certainly the moment. So with the pack at his heels, he runs headlong for the light, breaching the wilderness for a taste of humanity.

Impaired being a foregone conclusion, Rori's afforded little opportunity to react before the flying fur ball knocks her to the floor.

"THE THUD OF REALITY"

"Let us begin at the beginning," recollects the old astronomer, as Emanuel looks down at his watch. Overlooking the obvious slight, the senior man settles back into his chair, confident the details will soon capture the younger man's attention.

"Centuries back, there was an ill-regarded prophet who was banished from the Church under charges of impurity," he continues, peering over the rim of his glasses until their eyes finally meet.

"*'Hailing in a ball of fire, it will rain down in the spirit of man,'*" he quotes in his best Charlton Heston. "Cryptic, eh? Yeah, we've never really understood it either. The date, however, was very specific – it was slated to arrive on 17 August, century unknown. Of course, the Church being the Church, our astronomers have been diligently searching the skies ever since."

"So are you saying that it actually happened?" Emanuel prompts him, now somewhat engaged.

"Yes, we believe it has," the old man nods with a sad but knowing smile. "We're still awaiting confirmation, but we saw her touch down. Which brings us to our second set of numbers – six-six-six. There, I said it," he spits, as if rinsing the words from his mouth. "Some suggest that's why they banished him."

"The numbers?"

17

"Well, it certainly didn't help.   Nor did the second half of the prophecy when he predicted that exactly six months, six days and six hours from impact, *'Humanity itself will divinely realign.'*"

"What do you think he meant by 'realign?'"

"Your guess is as good as mine," the old man admits. "But someone had better get this thing figured out, because the clock is ticking, my son. The countdown is on," he advises, resting a hand on the younger man's shoulder.

His words land loud with the thud of reality, and Emanuel can only sit there in silence as he absorbs the full weight of a potential apocalypse.

"COOKIES"

"Hello…"

The voice not only surrounds him, it passes through him like a warm breeze, and immediately reminds him of cookies.

"I like cookies," Justin volunteers. "When Mommy makes cookies, she lets me lick the bowl!"

"She's a very good Mommy," affirms the voice, in that delightfully permeating fashion.

Adults sometimes find this form of communication disturbing, yet children and animals find it quite familiar and even comforting.

"DECIMALS AND CROWS"

The buzz of the alarm clock is somewhat soothed by the aroma of coffee wafting from the kitchen. Blinking his eyes, Grant switches off the alarm and struggles to hold the glimpses of his daybreak dream. Grabbing a notepad from his bedside table, he jots down the remnants before they evaporate.

"Grandmother, stones, crows," he scrawls in the barely legible script of dawn. The fragmented images are disturbing his orderly sense of the day, so he stumbles into the bathroom to rinse away the psychic debris. Days can be challenging when he can't shake off the dreams, so he does his best to rally a good game face.

The fact that he'll be meeting Mirabella for lunch goes a long way toward fortifying the day. With the warm shower spilling over his neck and shoulders, he feels himself gradually returning to a semblance of normal. He gives thanks for programmable coffee makers, as the day becomes more succulent with each inhalation. By 7:15, he's ready to face the world.

Rush hour through downtown could rival Daytona, yet there's nothing like the adrenaline of a high-speed chase to get your juices pumping. After maneuvering through the high-rise district, he pulls into the designated lot and flashes his parking pass to the uniformed attendant. It will take his remaining ten minutes to cross the seven lanes of traffic, navigate the security checkpoints and ride the elevator up to accounting. Grant enjoys the precision of perfectly aligning the decimals of his day.

Nancy looks up from the reception desk to exchange morning niceties before the telephone reaches that scandalous third ring. Liz is busy checking emails when he arrives at her workstation, yet spins around to greet him with a rundown of the day.

"Can you move my one o'clock with Saylor to two? I'm having lunch with Mirabella," he offers in response to the unasked question.

"I'll give it my best shot, Casanova," she grins, handing off a stack of telephone messages, in addition to the updated figures for the morning staff meeting. Liz is the consummate Assistant – organized and efficient, with a witty sense of humor. She likes what she does, and it shows. Since Grant's promotion to Director, Liz has been a true blessing. She knows the ropes, knows the folks and her negotiation skills could put a U.N. ambassador to shame.

Stepping into his office, Grant takes a seat behind the desk and prioritizes the pile while donning the prerequisite headset. The beauty of a headset is mobility, so after dialing the four-digit extension, he strolls over to the window and pulls open the vertical blinds.

21

A slow prickle develops along the back of his neck as each tiny hair stands at attention. Perched on the windowsill, just beyond the glass, stories above the metropolis, sits one shiny black crow. Eyes reflecting like midnight pools, it stares back at him, waiting, until Grant slowly taps the button and disconnects the call.

"TRAVELING SHOES"

A murder of crows arrived this morning, which is just a tad unusual out here in the desert. One or two would not have warranted a second glance, yet Aurora can count at least nine of them pecking around the front yard. The dog watches in silence, curious to discover if they've located some tantalizing dead thing that he may have overlooked. He's settled in rather nicely since his bizarre entrance, and quickly established that he's staying for life.

Aurora smiles at his doggish daydreams, yet intuition keeps drawing her back to the crows. One strolls close enough to look her directly in the eye before pumping its wings and catching a ride on the next current south. Grabbing up her walking stick, she heads out into the desert, under the close supervision of her four-legged friend. While their walk was intended for flying with crows, her companion soon bolts from the path in favor of chasing shadows in the afternoon sun.

Familiar with her piece of the desert, Aurora simply follows along, allowing his instincts to guide them. He's a good dog, and she's grown attached to him already. Hasn't decided on a name yet, yet she guesses one will come to her in time.

Blazing trail, the dog suddenly starts barking and jumping around just a few feet ahead of her.

Although her first thought is *rattler*, she keeps walking. *The dog's not afraid...*

Why she steps blindly around that prickly pear cactus will entertain her for a lifetime, but that's exactly what she does. And there, on the other side, lying in wait against the now disturbed sand . . . rests the biggest gold nugget her eyes have ever seen!

Now fool's gold is plentiful around these parts, and she knows it well. This is not fool's gold. Her heart begins racing at the sight of it, as she snatches it up from the ground. With some spit and a shirttail polish, the nugget cleans up rather nicely. Holding it up to the light, the grin starts above her navel then spreads well past the limits of her flesh.

"You are one *amazing* dog!" she beams, petting and patting the dancing dog. "I'd say you've more than earned your keep," she laughs, bending down to hug the fur around his neck. He licks her face as she croons in his ear and praises his excellent find.

Ribbons of purple and orange intertwine with the horizon as the sun dips below the mountains and whispers a velvety good night. It's time to head home while they still have some light, so she tucks the rock in her pocket and walks toward the base of the mountain. She spots her friend Joe in the distance, out gathering medicinals from the desert floor. His relatives have inhabited this valley since the beginning of time, and he walks in quiet harmony with *all that is* and *all that was*. He says *what will be* is beyond him, then winks and invites them to join him for a fire.

Rori surprises even herself by accepting, as she hooks her arm in his and they walk toward the house. With a practiced hand, Joe soon rallies a crackling fire that sends embers shooting high into the sky. As they sit watching sparks attempt to dance with the stars, he plucks a thought from the sizzling air and poses it gently before her.

"So what do you know about crows?"

Her startled expression speaks volumes, so Joe begins sharing the stories of his grandfather, and his grandfather before. Their lore casts crows as keepers of the truth, knowers of unknowable mysteries and guardians of the sacred law. They are said to travel between worlds, carrying a knowledge as deep as their midnight eyes. He tells her that the appearance of crows signals change on the horizon, and suggests she pay attention to her dreams.

Old Joe has been having some dreams of his own, and just this morning he dug out his traveling shoes.

"LEVI THE HAPPY-GO-LUCKY"

"Hey, Brand, what's good today?" asks Levi.

"It's all good, every day," she replies from the working side of the lunch counter.

The two grew up together right here in this same small town, just like generations before them for nearly a century. Farmers and "Slaters" both working the land, trading sweat for satisfaction and a handful of coin. As children they played, then fought, then kissed, and their history is as comfortable as an old flannel shirt.

"In that case, I'll have a cheeseburger deluxe, a small onion ring, and…"

"A medium mocha shake," she chimes in, finishing his sentence as she writes up the order. "No pickles."

"No pickles," he grins.

They realized long ago that they were far better friends than anything else. If the truth be told, Brandi's penchant for piercings and tattoos scares him just a bit, and on more than one occasion he's witnessed the bloodying effects of her wit on those who've done her wrong. Yet her compassion and loyalty are unsurpassed, and she'll make an incredible nurse when she finishes school.

She serves up the order on a bright red tray, yet snatches it back when he reaches for it, all the while eyeing the front pocket of his jeans. He smiles and shakes his head at her subtlety. Digging deep, he pulls out a handful of change and drops it into the tip jar resting on the counter. Grinning like a Cheshire cat, she doles out the obligatory thank you and finally releases the tray to his custody. There's a mid-afternoon break between customers, so Brandi wanders out from behind the counter to join him at the table.

"So what's up tonight?" she asks, snagging a couple of rings off his plate.

"There's a band playing over at Hog's Breath," he offers, avoiding commitment.

"What time?"

"Somewhere between nine and ten, I suspect."

"Anybody going?"

"I'm headed over to Zeke's after chores, so we'll see what's up from there," he shares, deciding to offer up the details before she drags them out with those vicious blue nails.

"You won't make it," she states with a tone. The expression is purely Brandi, and with that one look, every ounce of her d isgust and impatience is clearly conveyed.

"Why you givin' me stink eye?" Levi spouts defensively.

"You know."

"What?"

"You'll go over to Zeke's, sample whatever crap he's serving up for the day, you'll take less, he'll take more and you'll end up babysitting his ass until he passes out. Long and short – you won't make it."

Her eyes are flat and emotionless as she levels him, casting him naked into the blazing light of a bitter truth. With little taste for her harsh reality, he shoves the tray and stands up to leave.

"Whatever," he grunts, barely looking at her as he distributes his trash into the recycling bins.

Brandi gets up from the table and straightens herself a bit before planting her right fist directly into Levi's bicep.

"You know I still love you," she offers begrudgingly, the twinkle having returned to her eyes.

"I know," he sniffs, shuffling his feet in the dirt. "You just want me for my body."

"Shut up!" she exclaims, "I'm waiting for tips from these geezers! I need more green to get me someplace warm!"

"Sick 'em," he teases, walking away. "Maybe I'll catch you later," he calls back over his shoulder.

"Yeah, right. When French fries float from heaven."

"PERFECTLY LIZZIE"

"How's his 2:20?" Liz volleys in the back-and-forth negotiation of executive scheduling. The week-at-a-glance calendar is fully displayed when a call comes through on her second line.

"Can you hold a sec, Gayle?"

It's more of a statement than a question, and considering the hierarchy of their positions, Liz doesn't wait for an answer before flashing to the next line with a well-applied smile.

"Accounting, Liz Breslen, how may I help you?" her voice simply floats like heady magnolias, sweet and clean and everything you could hope for. Though the professionalism remains, there is a sudden shift in countenance, as a glimpse of sadness intrudes without warning.

"Just a minute, Peggy. Let me take care of this other call and I'll get right back to you."

Liz pauses for a moment, draws a deep breath and then carefully places the smile back on her face.

"Thank you so much for holding, Gayle," she practically sings, "Will 2:20 work for Saylor? Terrific. It's a date then, 2:20 in Mr. Fontaine's office, projections in hand. You're the best!" she adds warmly before clearing the line.

A few seconds pass as she tries to overcome the dread, then Lizzie opens the line to her pustulent past.

29

"So, wassup, little sis?" she inquires, feigning levity in hopes that the news will be good.

She listens intently for several minutes, jotting a few notes on the pad near her phone. Once the facts are all relayed, she pens a heavily-lined box around the writing, which is reinforced several times over, and then fortified with thick, dark triangles. Order. Boundaries and Order.

By the time the call has ended, the cramping has already begun, so she forwards her phone to Nancy and excuses herself to the restroom. Unfortunately, that calm, cool exterior is underwritten by a chronic case of IBS. Irritable Bowel Syndrome is a dirty little secret arguably held by many a great over-achiever. She relies on Imodium® chewies to keep her functional, and a well-cut suit to cover the rest.

Secured behind the black marble partitions of the executive washroom, Liz doubles over, gripping her mid-section and rocking to and fro until the wave subsides. Drawing a long breath deep into her body, she blows it out slowly in an effort to release the painful spasm. After repeating the technique several times, she attempts to stand fully erect.

A glance at her watch reveals there are just forty-five minutes until Friday is over. With some lipstick and breath spray, she's back in the game. When it comes to appearances, the Jones' have nothing on *this* Breslen.

She retrieves her messages from Nancy and heads back to the office for their end-of-day briefing. With the dread that sent her reeling now basically in check, she collects the necessities along with her favorite purple pen and rounds the corner to his office. The door is open, yet she politely drums her nails across the surface to gain Grant's attention.

Looking up from the day's figures, he smiles and invites her to join him. Painfully aware of her organs, Liz gingerly lights on the guest chair, and tries her best not to wince in the process.

Grant definitely enjoys getting lost in his numbers, yet has never been able to escape his intuition, and something is definitely amiss with his assistant.

"You okay, Liz?"

"Just dandy, thanks for asking," she replies, without missing a beat.

"Alrighty then," he answers, not believing her for an instant, yet accepting her cue to move things along. "Well, how about we close out the week and see what the weekend holds."

The mere thought of the next few days brings a fresh pang to her twisted innards, so she gladly sets about the business at hand. They coordinate schedules, prioritize their projects and decide on an action plan for the upcoming week.

By the time they finish, it's nearly 5:00pm, yet both appear willing to linger. Neither, it seems,

31

is all that anxious to abandon their clean, structured environment for the challenge that awaits them beyond these walls...

"WHEN OLD AND NEW FRIENDS MEET"

Joe pitches their belongings into the back of the pickup while Aurora closes up the house. She whistles for Gold Dog to come in from the desert. It's been four days since the crows arrived, one less every day, leaving exactly five days to get wherever it is they're going.

The dog climbs in between them on the wide, bench seat, with the agreement that Rori share the window and her lap. Joe shifts the truck into gear as all five of the crows take to the sky . . . and so the pilgrimage begins.

Crows as a navigational system demands quite an assumption of faith, yet they prove to be courteous traveling partners and remain in unison to avoid misdirection. Less could be said of the radio programs spouting news of the wars and the murders, and of the bombings, the divas, and the socially shunned. Henchmen capitalize as the frightened become more fearful and as circumstance tests faith.

"Appears the storm is coming," Joe comments, switching the channel from their fretfully static commentary.

Aurora finally tracks down some tunes on the dial, and they decide to stick with higher frequencies for the duration of the trip. Twilight marks the close of day for five tired crows, two humans and a dog, so they pull off the highway at the next vacancy sign that features both a room and some food.

Four crows await them come morning. Together they count up the miles while counting down the crows, until just two days remain.

Dawn arrives with high winds tossing timber like trashcans, and forces two weary crows to take shelter. So as the power lines tremble and the lights flicker out, Rori and Joe stand poised at the window watching as chaos unfolds.

The howl of the wind becomes quiet by dawn, and they're greeted with the calm of a picture-perfect day. Emerging from the shelter of their battered motel room, they find a solitary crow perched atop the pickup truck. Her eyes are bright and lively as she gratefully devours the bread that Aurora has brought her.

Anticipation sparks the air, charging their senses for a much-needed success. Having lost a day to weather, both are fairly certain there will be plenty of ground left to cover.

Their guide has caught some tailwind, and Joe is racing every one of those horses corralled beneath the hood. Soon the shadows are stretched out before them, pulled long by the afternoon sun as they weave their way through back roads in pursuit of one highflying crow. They get a bit nervous when the weeds have grown tall between the tire tracks, yet those black wings beat on against the now darkening sky.

The road disappears into a dense row of trees that borders the meadow on the eastern side. Joe is first to notice the distant silhouettes – a two-story to the left and an old barn on the right. Passing through the line of foliage, they arrive at an aging farmhouse. And there along the ridgeline, stretched out along the peak, rest eight waiting crows who are quickly joined by the ninth. It seems they have arrived.

Gold Dog is first to bound from captivity, lunging for freedom with every dog breath in his body. After relieving himself in several locations, he commences with the primary inspection, in accordance with his dogly obligations. A woman appears in the doorway just as Joe and Aurora are climbing the steps.

"Can I help you?" she inquires, leaving the screen door between them.

"Yes. My name is Aurora, this is my friend Joe, and that curious fellow over there is Gold Dog," she offers, by way of introduction.

"That's an unusual name for a black dog," Loretta ponders aloud, stepping from the shadows to get a better look.

And so the conversation begins, and soon Loretta invites them inside for a nibble and a sip. Before long she is telling them all about her Henry and the incredible flaming chariot that took him

35

away. She tearfully confides that she still feels him with her, just as clearly as she can feel them, yet he's stronger now, like when they were young. Joe assures her that he died a good death, and that time will never keep them apart.

As her eyes well with remembrance, Gold Dog steps in for a nuzzle that nudges its way to her heart. Within a few minutes, Loretta disappears into her bedroom, only to return with a plastic grocery sack. The contents are rather bulky, with points and sharp edges protruding in every direction. She sets it gently on her lap, cradled in the apron she wears tied around her waist.

Nervous, she seeks their eyes around the room until she's practically ready to burst. Hands resting lightly on top of the bag, Loretta draws a deep breath and finally lets loose with her secret.

"SEAN OF THE MOUNTAIN"

The fragrance of cherry wood is dense in the air as a practiced hand glides over the newly-sanded surface. Smiling, Sean extracts a fresh pad of steel wool from a plastic bag and begins the final finish. His current creation looms an imposing seven feet, and is more than just a treat for the eyes. The rich textures and wide curving arches invite both fantasy and wonder.

Made entirely of wood, the structure features two reverse seats that appear wrapped like a rosebud in a tender embrace. The union is sacred and palpable; life and death divinely intertwined. His choice of form and finish were chosen maintain the essence of the wood, accentuating each delicate grain in relation to the whole. With the lightest of touch, he presses steel to wood and wood to steel, quietly courting the truly divine.

He claims there's an exact second when the soul of a piece comes to life, which is precisely the moment when his work is complete. And so he lingers, stroking the grain from here to beyond, breathlessly awaiting each instant of truth.

The process is pure seduction, and universal in nature. Some know it as grace, and some simply lust after it in every possible sense; yet at the core, each of us knows. More than a thought, more than an emotion, it's a deeper kind of knowing that resonates throughout with unmistakable clarity.

Without a doubt, grace is the only addiction worth pursuing.

Yet even passion peaks and recedes, and his muscles are beginning to ache with the strain. A glimpse at the window reveals the light is also dwindling, so he steps outside to enjoy the last remnants of sunset that are strewn across the sky. Shades of purple and orange silhouette the mountains and a crow calls out from the branches overhead.

Closing his eyes, the images of shadow and light are etched upon his eyelids while he envisions himself soaring with the crow. They ride gentle currents as the wind guides them high above the treetops and deep into the darkening sky. Through his mind's eye, he witnesses a tiny star twinkle to life, as if for the very first time.

His flight is interrupted, however, when the cool night breeze penetrates his flannel and sends shivers down his spine. Anchored back on terra firma, he realizes that the sunset has now faded, and steps back inside his shop to pack it in for the night.

At home in the cabin, Sean kicks off his pre-tied boots and immediately heads for the fridge. Cold one in hand, he settles back into a kitchen chair and sifts through the day's stack of mail. Amid the collection of sales flyers and credit card offers springs a hand-addressed envelope bearing his favorite postmark.

Tearing open the seal, his eyes dance across the page as he ciphers his way through the message, with the tiniest of stars reflecting in his smile.

"BONE DOG"

Atop piles of pillows and crisp white sheets, a stuffed animal named *Bone Dog* patiently waits beneath hospital fluorescents for the return of his "bestest" friend.

"CADY'S ESCAPE"

Generations of wealth have taught them to sacrifice, and many a lamb has fallen along the way. Her own dear father left this earth far too early, and under a shroud of rather questionable circumstances. So now it's Cadence's turn to withstand the pressure of her family's expectations.

Perched naked atop her porcelain throne, she surveys the opulence of her spacious bathing suite. Rose-colored marble covers the floors and gilded mirrors reflect her in whichever light she chooses. Standing, she crosses the wide expanse and shuts down the stream to the oversized tub.

Soft music is playing in the background as she sinks below the surface of her steaming floral bath. The fragrance of lavender seeps into her pores, and she prays for the relaxation that has eluded her for weeks. While the warm water eases her aching muscles, it does little to relax the knot between her ears.

After staring up at the stained glass ceiling, she closes her eyes and lets the colorful images dance behind her eyelids. As escapes go, this one's pretty good, yet the temperature eventually cools, and she's forced to leave the comfort of her watery cocoon.

Stepping from the tub, she sinks into a seemingly bottomless mat that envelops her feet like a luxurious cloud. Wrapping herself in an enormous bath sheet, she steels her resolve, and proceeds with the business at hand. It's rather hard to fathom that her entire future can be resting on the countertop beside the commode. Yet there it is, plain and simple.

Heart beating at a wild crescendo, she resolutely strides across the floor and wraps her long fingers around the device. Facing the mirror, her inner and outer worlds are colliding, and a single tear rolls down her cheek. The moment of truth has arrived.

Her whole body begins to tremble and her eyes travel down to her tightly clenched fist. With tears now streaming, she blinks them away, willing herself back into focus.

Reality strikes swiftly and she drops to the floor in a shuddering mass. Rocking herself against the cool of the tiles, every critical word that mother ever spoke is violently assaulting her brain. Amidst the storm of condemnation, as Cady cradles her head in her hands, the tiniest thought sparks into light – she's not alone.

The baby growing inside of her is such a brilliant example of hope for the universe, and maybe for Cadence, as well. With that one thought, whole worlds begin to shift. Possibilities begin to form and take shape, and that layer of cynicism that's been disguising her heart is replaced with sheer radiance, the likes of which she's never known.

Gripping the counter, she pulls herself vertical and applies some cool water to her face. As she pats away the droplets, an entirely new woman stares back in the mirror. For a long while she just watches, hoping she won't disappear, then eventually decides to get started on the day.

She selects items from the fridge that include every food group, and enjoys a heartier breakfast than she's consumed in many years. It seems the dread that overcame her has now taken a backseat to a delightful sense of optimism that is completely unfamiliar. Sipping at her orange juice, she gazes across the landscape, imagining a life she had not yet considered.

Maggie arrives for the day with several bags of groceries, and Cadence uncharacteristically joins her in putting things away. Historically, conversation between them has been minimal and has centered primarily on household items. There has been the occasional mingling of pleasantries, yet it has never been her practice to assist with daily chores.

"You seem to be feeling particularly chipper this morning, Ma'am," Maggie states, shielding her bewilderment.

"I'm pregnant, Maggie, and you're the first to know," Cadence blurts out, although carefully avoids any eye contact.

Stunned, Maggie's mind races with questions as she fumbles for an appropriate answer.

"I guess I'm not quite sure what to say," Maggie offers truthfully.

"That's okay. I think I just needed to say it out loud."

"Have you seen a doctor yet?"

"Not yet. To tell the truth, I'm not sure what I want to do. I don't even want to think about how mother will react," confides Cadence.

The housekeeper stretches her arms out wide and Cady gratefully accepts the motherly embrace. Maggie offers a tissue to accommodate the tears, and affords her employer some simple advice.

"Sounds to me like you need time to sort things out," Maggie reasons, brushing the hair from Cady's cheek.

"You know, Maggie, you are absolutely right," she sniffs. "Some thinking time away may be exactly what I need." As ideas start to surface, the fire ignites in her eyes, and that same wild spirit steps up to the plate. "Now that you mention it, with just a few phone calls, I can be outta here today!" she exclaims.

With more resolve than she's felt in a very long while, she summons a driver to take her to the airport. Packing several bags, she decides to leave her cell phone on the counter and provides Maggie with instructions on where she can be reached.

Armed with a new-found authority, Cady peers over the top of her favorite sunglasses and sets her perspective in a brand new direction. The airport is fairly quiet, so she moves through the checkpoints with relative ease. Ticket in hand and forty minutes to spare, she pops into a small restaurant for something cold to drink.

A few people are scattered around the booths sipping coffee, and one curious old woman appears to be staring. Cady dismisses her as yet another airport oddity, grabs a counter stool and orders a small cranberry juice from the waitress. The cup is soon empty and diversion time is over, so she gathers up her luggage to leave.

"'Scuse me, dear, would you have just a moment?" the old woman asks as Cadence starts toward the door.

Normally, she would have ignored her as just another panhandler and kept walking; yet today, she stops, at least for a moment.

"Is there something I can do for you?" she inquires.

"Or I for you," the woman smiles, and motions an invitation to join her in the booth.

Although more than a bit skeptical, Cady surprises even herself and accepts the invitation. Tossing her bags onto the seat ahead of her, she slides across the shiny vinyl and settles into an indentation left by millions of previous bottoms.

Just as the "don't talk to strangers" dialogue is replaying in her head for the umpteenth time, she looks up to find the most smiling eyes she has possibly ever seen. With that one look, all trepidation melts easily away, and the two women connect in a way that Cadence would never have thought possible.

Clearly the woman who emerged from the mirror this morning views life from a whole new perspective, and on many more levels, it seems. All too soon it's departure time, so she says her goodbyes and collects her belongings. Extending a hand to her newfound friend, Cady senses an odd-shaped object being pressed into her palm.

"This is for you, dear," she states, and her gentle words pierce Cadence straight through the heart.

"LEVI'S LAPSE"

Brandi's been saving up money all summer long for her first real adventure out into the world. School starts again in September, and this will be her final semester, so she's determined to take this trip while she's still a free woman. Tomorrow she'll buy the ticket that will take her someplace warm – with sandy, untamed beaches that are a long, long way from home. Small towns can be delightful, yet when options are limited, they too can need escaping.

Others sometimes choose a more desperate escape, like Zeke, for instance, who is bent on getting lost inside tonight. He intends to ride that wild pony until one of them breaks, and there will be no deterrent to his efforts. Seems a guy knows a guy that knows a guy that knows Zeke, and that guy stopped by earlier today with a very small package.

The sound of a pounding bass seems to have alerted all but the most hearing impaired, so by the time Levi arrives, the party is well underway. "Z" greets him at the door with some smoke and some fire and an icy brew to squelch the flames. And the games begin. At the rate Callie's going, she'll have her clothes off by nine, and it looks like ol' Stu may be our lucky winner this evening.

Lola's practically lying on the table, yet just before her eyelids achieve total darkness, she rallies enough to snort another line, so we won't count her out just yet. Zeke and Lola have been an item for quite a while now, yet spend most of their time living on the surface. He capitalizes on her oral fixation, and covertly, she does too. Hard telling whether the demons are nipping at their flesh or if the truth is eating its way out, but they're tied by their mutual discomfort, and for now that's enough. Let's call it a union of convenience that keeps them from dying alone.

Marlie's in the corner philosophizing, and Sam's doing his best to hold onto his beer and a thought at the very same time. It's Friday night in small town, and contrary to popular belief, boredom and excitement can walk hand-in-hand here just like anywhere else. More a function of cerebrum than circumstance, people tend to court the experience that most suits their perspective.

And so it follows that our friend Zeke, master of cynicism and purveyor of doubt, has once again discovered the monotony of symbolic celebration. Another party for the sake of partying has left him restless and irritable, so he snorts another line, downs several shots straight from the bottle and shoves his tongue down Lola's throat.

Apparently his tequila has offended her schnapps, and Lola's gag reflex opts to settle the argument. Had his senses been intact, he may have noticed at first retch, yet such is not the case, and Zeke's mouth becomes the unwilling receptacle for what remains of Lola's lunch. It's a nasty display that triggers a regular spew fest. Callie runs for the bathroom, while Z claims the kitchen sink. Marlie attempts to comfort Lola who immediately launches into an apologetic crying jag, which is doing little to atone for her original sin.

Wiping at his mouth with the back of his hand, Zeke eyes Lola with such venom that Marlie plants herself between them and volunteers to drive her home. Barraging them with a string of curses, he waves them off while they practically drag Lola out the front door and pour her into the backseat of Sammy's old car.

Callie is sobbing into Stu's chest as he offers a nod to Levi and Zeke, and escorts her out to his waiting chariot. The excitement of the evening has sobered her up a bit, yet not so much as to regain her senses . . . and far be it from this red-blooded American male to miss *that* opportunity. So at least old Stu gets to play savior tonight as he gallantly whisks off the last of the babes.

Levi parks himself in a kitchen chair and pulls another around for Zeke. The two sit there in silence downing shots until all images of the last hour are completely eradicated. They raise a toast to brotherhood, to small towns, to liquor, and to anything else they can think of as they pour straight alcohol down open gullets.

With his one lingering brain cell, Zeke manages to recall the delivery that came his way this afternoon. He disappears into the bedroom to retrieve a jewel-sized Ziploc from his dresser drawer before staggering back out to the table.

"Snort, smoke or go for the gallery?" Zeke asks, referring to the hypodermic in his opposite hand.

"Whoa, man, I gotta milk cows in the morning," Levi declares, doing his best to hold back the nausea now curdling at the back of his throat.

"Well, this here's a little something special from my friend down south," Zeke tells him, as he lays out the necessary equipment and prepares for his first solo flight.

"C'mon Z, let's just go down to the Hog and pick us up some strange," he suggests, hoping to interrupt the inevitable.

When it's clear that Zeke won't be diverted, Levi retreats to the truck to wait for his friend. His stomach is still churning, so he lights up a cigarette and cranks up the music in an effort to clear the image of the needle from his brain. Moments later Z pulls open the truck door and melts into the seat beside him. His skin is ashen and reminds Levi of one of those creepy figures from a wax museum.

Turning away from his crippled co-pilot, Levi decides that in light of Zeke's condition, he'd best focus on getting them down mountain. By now, it's nearly 11:00pm and the moon is shining high above the ridgeline. A doe carefully steps to the edge of the road, then thinks better of crossing as their headlights crest the hilltop.

Every bit of his attention is focused on driving, so Levi doesn't even notice when Zeke's eyes roll back into his head. It's not until he hears the gagging that he realizes his lifelong compadre has slipped beneath the surface. Shocked and frightened, he jerks the wheel, and in the blink of an eye, they're off the road. Luckily they've reached Miller's meadow, and simply drop into the drainage ditch which brings them to a stop.

By now, Zeke is convulsing. Saliva and God knows what are gurgling from his mouth, and he appears to be choking on his tongue. Levi leans him forward and slaps him on the back, yet is absolutely clueless about what to do next. Frightened tears are streaming down his face and all he can think to do is run for help.

"Z!" he chokes out, "Z, I'm going for help! The truck's stuck! I'm gonna run down to the bar! I'll be right back! Don't you f---ing die, man!"

Instantly sober, Levi runs like the wind, a picture of grace as he flies the quarter mile to the base of the hill. He reaches the parking lot just as Brandi is leaving the bar, and there's no one in the world he'd rather see. In an instant, they're in her car and then at the truck, and she's wiping Zeke's mouth to initiate procedures.

Levi stands back helplessly, watching from some distant place inside, in awe of her ability, grateful for her knowledge. She's breathing, she's pounding, she's checking, she's breathing again.

It's hard to know exactly how long it continued before the night air came calling, yet death will not be mistaken, despite all conviction. Steeling herself, Brandi turns back to Levi, takes him by the shoulders and tells him the words he most needs to hear.

"He's gone, Levi. He's gone, and he's not coming back. I've done all I can, and we need to call 9-1-1. Listen, I can smell you from here," she tells him, "and unless you're ready to answer a whole lot of questions and probably turn over your license, you'd better get the hell outta here."

By now Levi is a basket case, as detached from the world as an escaping balloon. Brandi can tell he's "shocky," yet in no condition to deal with EMS, much less the police. Her mind is whirling, and she's truly thankful that she had no taste for beer tonight. Dropping her voice, she speaks slowly and clearly while reciting his instructions.

"Levi, you need to go to my house. Cut through the woods and don't let anyone see you. Do you understand?" she asks, raising his chin until their eyes meet.

He nods limply, then looks away, more forlorn than she's ever seen him, but his feet need to be moving – right now. Physically turning him around, Brandi nudges him gently in the direction of the woods.

"Hurry, Levi! Go to my house, get in my bed and wait for me!" she calls after him.

He raises his hand in acknowledgement, then manages to pick it up to a trot before disappearing into the woods. Brandi opens the left door of the truck and with one smooth move, pulls Zeke's body into the driver's seat. She positions his feet and presses his fingers around the steering wheel. As an afterthought, she pulls her sleeve down over her hand and manages to shift the truck into gear before dialing the necessary digits.

"HMMMM....."

"I've lost her behind the escalator. Are you pickin' her up, Ted?"

"Not yet. I've got a blind spot over here ... about twenty feet. She should be showing up any second now... I think I've got her... Maybe... Yes! Yes! We've got her back. The subject is now under surveillance."

"ONCE UPON A STRANGE DAY"

Unlike the other passengers on her flight, Lizzie does not welcome the well-polished monologue announcing their arrival. There is but one leg left before her final destination, and already the cramping has begun. Popping an antacid, she returns her seat to the upright position and attempts to find that quiet place her therapist describes.

Beyond the window glass, the day outside is brilliant, yet none of that seems to reach inside her disillusioned shell. It's amazing how quickly the mere thought of home can disassemble the bricks of her well-constructed life. Still, she strives to be the dutiful daughter, regardless of the consequence exacted on her bowels.

The landing is uneventful, and within minutes Lizzie is negotiating the throng of people clotting the wide corridor. So accustomed to the frenzy of airport travel, she is half way to her connecting flight before recalling the significant layover. Shifting her gaze, she scopes out the nearest restroom and adjusts her course accordingly.

Entering the Ladies Room, several women stand poised at the sinks, yet she pays them little mind in her search for a stall. Grateful for liners, she pulls one from the dispenser and settles onto the seat gripping her midsection in a now familiar fashion. When the wave finally passes, she collects her belongings and re-enters the room.

An elderly woman catches Lizzie's eye in the mirror and turns around mid-lipstick to face her.

"Are you alright, dear?"

"Yes ma'am, I'll be fine," Lizzie answers automatically, as she reaches for a paper towel.

Pale and drained, she dampens the towel and presses the coolness to her forehead and cheeks.

"Have faith, my dear," the woman offers.

It has been so long since Lizzie's allowed anyone to glimpse her inner world, that now, before a complete stranger, her walls begin to slip. Tears spill from her eyes faster than she can blot them away, so she leans over the sink and just lets them roll. The woman remains at her side all the while, patting her back and whispering quiet assurances until the storm subsides.

"There, there," she says, handing Lizzie several squares to blot her eyes.

"Thank you," she sniffs, accepting the tissue. "You've been so kind."

"No thanks needed," she states. "In fact, I have something for you."

Reaching deep inside of her well-traveled bag, the woman withdraws what appears to be an object folded into the heart of one time worn hand. As once-graceful fingers slowly unfurl, Lizzie's eyes grow wide with true amazement.

Cradled in her palm rests a stone that would surely be the prize of any jeweler. While the color would be difficult to describe, it practically dances with light to the point where one might wonder if it's actually alive. She looks into stranger's eyes with astonishment, and then down again into her outstretched palm.

"Can I touch it?" she asks with all the wonder of a child.

"Of course you can," the woman chuckles, "It's yours!"

"No!" she exclaims in shock and disbelief, "How can that be?!"

"Trust me," the lady assures her, placing the stone in her hand, "It's yours to enjoy."

Dumbstruck, Lizzie stands staring in awe at her wonderful gift. Staring down at the treasure in utter delight, she is overcome with a state of pure joy. The sensation is both unfamiliar and disarming, and momentarily captures every bit of her attention. Suddenly, Lizzie remembers her manners, yet looks up to find her benefactor has completely disappeared. Gathering her bags, she hurries out to the corridor, but the stranger is nowhere in sight.

Tucking the stone in her purse, she proceeds toward the appointed gate, all the while searching the crowd for her favorite antique angel. Without a name or destination, the chances of tracking her down will be slim at best, yet she maintains a wary eye along the way.

57

Within a matter of minutes, Lizzie's demeanor has gone from that of gum on the sidewalk to resting on that infamous *Cloud Nine*, which she is now quite certain they encountered somewhere in the vicinity of 18,000 feet.

Peggy is waiting just beyond the security, and from the expression on her face, the heavens are about to let loose. Perhaps she can hug some joy into her sister before it's time to leave. Ninety minutes ago, Lizzie would not have thought that even possible. Who knew she was but one thought away?

Crossing that imaginary line from secure to unprotected, Lizzie wraps her sister in a heartfelt embrace that would be worthy of peace in the Middle East. Swaying to and fro, she can feel Peggy's tears streaming hot against her neck, and holds her baby sister even tighter. It's not until her sister's shoulders stop heaving and she resumes normal breathing that Lizzie finally comes up for air.

"If I'd known there'd be flooding, I'd have worn higher heels!" she teases, in her best femme fatale.

Holding Peggy's face in her hands, she looks into her eyes and shares the only truth they'll ever need.

"We can do this."

Peggy searches her sister's eyes for some sign of misgiving, yet there's none to be found. The avoidance has become exhausting, and Liz just can't run anymore. She started this journey riddled with doubt; the gift of a stranger afforded her faith; and now the pain in her sister's eyes has solidified her resolve. Some way, some how, she will pull what remains of this family back together - for one, and for all.

"SECRET BLESSINGS"

By the time Eleanor disconnects the call, her head is spinning so fast she might actually vomit. Swallowing hard, she attempts to choke down the lump that has formed in her throat. *It's finally happening. I always knew it could, and now it really is... What the hell am I going to do?* she wonders in desperation.

Bridgette agrees to entertain Hannah while Ellie tidies the house and shops for the dinner. The elaborate meal takes the remainder of the day, and it's four o'clock before Ellie can retreat for a shower. As the warmth of the water soaks into her flesh, she actually breathes for the first time since receiving the call.

The lack of time cuts back on her obsessing, yet this afternoon, on several occasions, she could feel her carotid pulsing. Combing back that rebellious clump of hair for the third time now, she smoothes on some lipstick and stands back to admire her reflection. A polished and powerful woman is staring back from the mirror, and Ellie invites her to stay for the evening.

With a few last minute preparations, the cooking portion of the meal is finally complete. The hot stuff is heating, the cool stuff is cooling and the appetizer is expertly arranged on a shining silver platter. Bridgette and Hannah are building castles out of Lego's when the doorbell rings, and Eleanor's heart jumps straight into her throat. *Just breathe,* she reminds herself while walking toward the door.

The man on the porch proves immediately endearing, as he greets her with flowers and a gregarious smile. Cool confidence in action, he reaches around her midriff and draws her in close for a fluid embrace. His charisma is disarming, and Ellie is caught off guard when she once again experiences that indescribable warmth. Despite all misgivings, she finds herself smiling and laughing and truly welcoming Elijah into their home.

Bridgette and Hannah are anxiously waiting in the background for their formal introductions, and Ellie is quick to oblige. Elijah is wholly enchanting as he greets them with a bow, extending his hand first to Hannah, who he twirls around like a princess before placing a polite kiss on the back of her hand. Bridgette receives the adult version, followed by a gentlemanly buss on the cheek.

To the left of the foyer is the kitchen, and to the right, the formal dining room opens into an expansive living space, which has been carefully designed for entertaining. The back is the play area, while the front of the room has been arranged for adult conversation, complete with leather wingbacks and an antique divan. Elijah takes a seat on the sofa, where he is promptly joined by their petite social butterfly, who proceeds to engage him in lively conversation.

Ellie excuses herself to the kitchen for drinks and hors d'oeuvres, leaving the three to get better acquainted. She uncaps the white sparkling grape, selected with Hannah in mind, and centers it on the serving tray, along with stemware for three plus one sippy cup. Laughter from the living room is encouraging, and puts a spring in her step as she returns to the group.

"Who wants bubbles?"

An exuberant Hannah is practically bouncing with excitement, and is happily enjoying her grown-up drink when Eleanor returns with the appetizer. The crystal bowl contains a zesty lime spread, and is surrounded by water crackers and paper-thin cucumber, all topped with thin curls of the tangy green rind. Fine dining is art, and her execution is flawless.

Bridgette prepares a test cracker for Hannah, who they have meticulously groomed to be a fearless sampler. Her eyes widen a bit as the sweet combines with the tart and the crisp, yet she offers up an enthusiastic nod, prompting laughter all around.

"So," begins Ellie with veiled curiosity, "What brings you east, Elijah?"

"We were invited to play the Palace Theatre, and when I heard through the vines that you were living up here, well, how could I resist?" he asks with that engaging smile that always left her squirming.

"I have to admit, it was quite a surprise to hear your voice after all these years. It's sooo good to see you, I had nearly forgotten," she genuinely reveals. "And how is your darling Genevieve?"

"Genevieve," he explains to Bridgette and Hannah, "is my beloved saxophone. She sings so sweet and low, you'll swear there's an angel inside!" An expression of pure delight washes over him at the mere mention of her name, and he enjoys a temporary visit to a world that's all his own. Back on solid ground, or carpet as the case may be, he turns to the ladies and asks, "Would anyone care to meet her?"

Back from the car in a twinkle, Genevieve in hand, he soon fills the walls with such heavenly sounds. A little Coltrane, a bit of Max Davis, and a finale of *Wild Thing* by the Troggs, just to make Hannah giggle. Following the impromptu revue, they adjourn to the dining room to partake in the meal.

The simplicity of the Shaker table is offset by the elaborate Faerie Garden now enjoying center stage. Being Elijah's first experience with faeries, Hannah explains the story behind her living miniature as Bridgette and Eleanor begin serving dinner. Gram's wooden bowls are perfect for the raw green bean salads, and they're far more forgiving than glass. The wee one is happily nibbling on a pile of raw string beans, mostly because they're crunchy and she thinks they're fun to eat.

The entrée arrives to oohs and aahs, as Ellie rests each breathtaking display onto waiting charger plates. Baked boneless chicken breasts are infused with fresh apple cider, dabbed with butter, and sprinkled with an aromatic blending of pepper and herbs. For a side dish she's prepared a fragrant jasmine rice dotted with fresh corn and red bell peppers, and seasoned with just a dash of cinnamon and chili. Julienne squash and fresh snow peas have been sautéed with a hint of mint, then garnished with a dollop of sweet creamery butter to perfectly balance the plate.

"So my dear Bridgette, tell me all about your life," Elijah inquires between a sampling of savory bites.

"Ah, where to begin…" she ponders.

"The beginning, the middle or the present are just fine," he assures her, with a grin.

"Well, the short version reads, historical fiction writer, while the longer version may take centuries," she jests, winking at Hannah who is already playing with her vegetables. She's dismissed from the table before boredom takes hold, and is happy having tea with Mr. Bear while the others enjoy some grown-up conversation.

They share stories and reminiscences, nostalgia and dreams, and strangely enough, by the end of the meal, all are now truly acquainted. Both ladies are pleasantly surprised, although Elijah typically anticipates the best, of himself and of every situation. Whatever it is, it's working for him, as both Eleanor and Bridgette agree while retrieving coffee and desserts from the kitchen.

"Treat time, Hannah-Banana!" Ellie hollers toward the living room. "Dessert then story time," she informs the sleepy-eyed child as she clambers back up into her chair.

Spiced apple parfaits layered with custard and cream are a scrumptious conclusion to a wonderful meal. With a promise of kisses, Hannah agrees to say goodnight, and Bridgette ceremoniously escorts her up to bed. With a grin and a wink, Elijah adds a goodly splash of social lubricant to all of their coffees.

"So, Miss Eleanor," he prefaces, slowly stirring the spoon in his cup. "Drastic changes since last we met. Are you happy?" he asks, searching her eyes.

"Very," she answers in all honesty. "What made you look me up after all these years?" she finally inquires, all the while preparing for the line drive that could make or break the game.

"Ran into some mutual friends, and one had your phone number. Said you lived back east now. Bridgette seems wonderful. Yet I have to ask," he whispers cautiously, "Did I do something wrong?"

"What on earth do you mean?"

"Well," he pauses, choosing his words carefully, "We shared a night, you moved east, and now you're with a woman – a great woman – but a woman nonetheless. Are you following me here?" he whispers discreetly, glancing back over his shoulder.

"Completely. You were marvelous. You *ARE* marvelous. It's just that Bridgette is Bridgette. I'd love her no matter," she assures him. "You have no idea how special you are to me."

"How's that?" he wonders, considering their complete lack of conversation.

"What do you think about Hannah?"

"She is *adorable* incarnate, and a joy through and through," he raves, "Yet what does she have to do with…." His sentence trails off as the gears of his slightly foggy brain realign. Clearly, he'd never speculated.

"I didn't want to hold you responsible for a night of too much wine and too little protection. I'd moved east before I knew, and I wasn't sure how you'd feel, and then there was Bridgette. And the rest, well…" Reaching across the table, she takes him by the hand. "You have no obligation, yet you're welcome to get to know your daughter, if that's something you wish to consider."

Out in the living room, beneath the coffee table, an effervescent glow suddenly radiates out through the cracks of Genevieve's case.

"DELICATE THUNDER"

The first things to catch Carlie's eye as she turns off the pavement are the beautiful cairns erected on either side of the drive. Blue morning glories lacing throughout the stonework create an explosion of color as they climb toward the sky. Beyond the cairns, the dirt driveway quickly disappears into a spectacular wood, so meticulously groomed it literally sparkles with life. A beam of sunlight slips quietly through the canopy to illuminate the ground pine spread across the forest floor.

Flashes of childhood skip through her brain like smooth stones dancing over water. Countless hours spent amid the trees inventing fantastic games to champion some wicked and shadowy foe. Sean has been her hero since the beginning of time, and as Carlie rolls up on the old homestead, she's glowing from the inside out.

Topping the porch steps, she spots a note tacked to the front door - *"MEET ME AT THE PAW!"* Life with Sean has never been dull, and she can feel a rush of adrenaline charge her senses as she sets out across the meadow in search of her brother. The anomaly known as Wolf's Paw consists of four stone spires that burst through the earth as if clawing their way from the inside out. Each imposing appendage is eight to ten feet wide and twenty to thirty feet long angling out from the

67

ground to a height of twenty feet or better above the slope.

The Paw itself rests a good fifty feet below the wood line, emerging from a clearing that is both windblown and stubbled. A vast panorama lies stretched out before her, as a tree-lined vista reaches for infinity and that indiscernible horizon where the mountains touch the sky.

"Adventure awaits," ripples through the air, perhaps more felt than heard.

The words spark a sense of wonder she's been missing for too long. Spinning on her heels, Carlie spots Sean leaning against the grandfather of all pine trees, and her heart simply leaps. Closing the gap between them, she pulls him in close for a giant bear hug that could rival any grizzly.

Once the flourish of greetings has subsided, he ushers her by the elbow out beyond the monoliths. Sheltered from the wind, rests a smaller, flatter stone perched like a dewclaw on the foreleg of the beast, and with just two easy steps they're on top. Plunked down side-by-side on the stone's surface, legs dangling over the edge, Sean pulls open a waiting sack and produces their makeshift lunch. The cheddar, the bread, the apples and tea may as well be a feast to the famished Carlie.

"Whoa, whoa, take a breath, woman!" he teases in an attempt to slow her down. While she has no idea what awaits, he is absolutely certain she will not want a lump in her stomach. The speed eating has given her hiccups, and she can't help laughing at herself as she guzzles the tea to wash down the bread, while of course, he continues to goad.

"Well not every host requires their guest to hike up a mountain before dinner!" she exclaims.

"Touché," he replies, "I'm glad to see you haven't lost your edge. You're going to need it," he states, with mischief in his eyes.

She studies him for a moment with a sideways stare looking for clues to his cryptic exchange. *What is he up to?* she wonders, running through a mental list of possibilities. Guessing has always been half the fun, so she breaks off a piece of cheese and chews on them both for a while.

"I suppose rock climbing would be a bit too obvious," she speculates, gazing in his direction on the off chance that she's right. His expression confirms her foregone conclusion, so she wastes no time in moving on to the next possibility. "Mountain biking? You could have them stashed around here someplace," she reasons, scouting for potential locations. Exhausting her multiple-choices, she concedes to the surprise, and closes her eyes in anticipation. "Okay, what is it?" she asks, as he maneuvers behind her in secrecy.

Slowly removing the windbreaker from his knapsack, he carefully raises it up, then drops it unceremoniously on top of her head. She gasps and jumps and nearly topples from the rock, until he laughingly rescues her from that uncertain fate.

"There's your clue!" he blurts, scrambling out of reach before she clobbers him. With a devilish laugh, he leaps to the ground and begins dashing full speed for the Paw.

"I'd hurt you if it didn't mean I'd have to drag your butt down this mountain!" she threatens in mock anger.

Disappearing behind the Wolf's little toe, Sean is still laughing when he picks up the pack he'd stashed there earlier. God he's missed this! Alone so much of the time, he'd forgotten how great it can be to have someone around. Especially Carlie. Life can get lonely on the cutting edge. She knows him and she gets him, and that feels good, really good. Stepping back from the other side, he hoists the pack up onto his shoulder and returns to his sister, who's just zipping up the jacket.

"So what is it, Mister?" she demands, looking all official with her deeply furrowed brow.

"Okay, okay, alright already!" he exclaims. "If you must know, I've been planning this for months. You and me, Adventure Girl, are you ready?"

"Bring it, Mountain Man!"

As Sean begins withdrawing harnesses from the oversized pack, Carlie gets that puppy dog look, with her inquisitive head all cocked to one side. Her face lights up upon seeing the colorful canopy and her heart begins to race with the thrill. Choosing the patch of ground just below the wood line, he stretches the rectangular chute out above the Paw, and aligns the risers and brake chords in preparation for flight.

She is practically squirming with delight by the time he plunks the helmet on her head. Next comes the harness, which she hikes onto her shoulders like a vest, whereupon he buckles her in and adjusts her leg straps for running. Bestowing her with gloves and glasses, he secures his own helmet before attaching his harness to the risers. Once suited, he puts the spreader bars in place, and finally connects the two harnesses for their first tandem flight.

Together they run downhill into the wind until the colorful kite inflates overhead. The lines are all in place and working properly, and the weather conditions appear prime for flying, so with a few last instructions, they're off! The expanse of stubble between them and Wolf's Paw quickly disappears until they are running full-speed toward the looming precipice. Fear teeters on the brink of exhilaration as they charge headlong toward the edge of the giant abyss. Just when their feet and their hearts and the wind come in sync, they are lifted gently from the earth and are embraced by the sky.

Once breathing resumes, Carlie is positively awestruck. This is a bird of a whole other feather.

The wind in her face gives her courage, and before long her heart has slowed to a healthy jog as she absorbs the sensation of absolute freedom. A hawk soars off in the distance, riding the same gentle current that now carries them high above the valley. Each savors the ecstasy of their exquisite reunion – with themselves, with each other and with the earth, the wind and the sky.

Unbeknownst to either of them, a crow is watching from the treetops as a long awaited glow illuminates the sky. It is here, in the midst of this most sacred harmony that a delicate thunder echoes through the universe.

"QUIET TIME"

It's best Justin's mother never know that he saw absolutely everything. The chrome grill of the 18-wheeler screaming down upon them, the sickened expression on the face of the driver, the ferocity of steel crushing steel into unnatural contortions… None of this will fortify her for the challenges ahead.

"THE WHIMSY OF SCARECROWS"

Grant arrives home on Friday night to find a message from his Grandmother. "Grant? This is your Maimie. I'm half way there, and I'm meeting all sorts of nice people! Maybe I'll travel more often! Okay then, I'll see you 'round six. Bye, bye." He sets down his briefcase and looks up at the clock. It's already time to go. A quick glance around to make sure the place is in order, and he's back out the door to the airport.

With the exception of photos, the stylish apartment reflects very little sign of his humble beginnings. Of course, success has come at high cost, which he, like others, never supposed would be *time*. In the weeks since Gramps' passing, the quandary of Maimie has consumed his thoughts both day and night. He can support her financially, of course, has been for years, yet finance isn't really the issue.

Speeding down the interstate, his mind is reeling. *At her age, she just can't live there by herself. The house and property are way too much to maintain, and I'm not comfortable hiring people from here. If she sells the house, there's that new senior living community just a few miles south of the farm. She'd know people. Or she can come up here and live with me, and we can look into some local care facilities a bit down the road.*

74

Anxious fingers are working to release the knot at the base of his skull when he spies the airport exit. Checking the dash clock, he congratulates himself on achieving an ETA of exactly nine minutes, leaving a full six to reach Baggage by ten after. Precision can be such a beautiful thing.

Unfortunately, tailwind had not been factored into his equation, and Loretta is already standing at the curb with her bags. Flustered and apologetic, Grant is talking fast and moving faster as he collects her things and starts back toward the car. *Why isn't she moving?* he puzzles in her direction.

"Grant Fontaine! I raised you better than that!" she reprimands him sternly. "Now set that stuff down and come give your Maimie a squunch! Where *is* that gentleman I sent off to the big city?" she inquires up toward the sky.

Setting the bags back onto the sidewalk, he turns to her with arms spread wide. Obedience aside, his heart is truly leaping for its ultimate reward. Some hugs are cursory, curt and sanitized, while others can be jovial, and served up with a twinkle. Yet Maimie's hugs ... Maimie's hugs are legendary. She has a way of reaching people, and within seconds she has found him as well.

Arm in arm, they walk toward the car, each with a bag in one hand, while Loretta regales him with stories of her first solo flight. The conversation continues on down the highway, until, during a momentary lapse in conversation, he hears her hungry stomach rumbling up a storm.

"Maimie, you must be starving! Mirabella has been experimenting all day with some sort of *Southern Fusion* cooking, she calls it, but if you want to stop and get a snack on the way, we can do that," he offers conspiratorially, lifting an eyebrow in her direction.

"Oh, no, no, I'll be fine," she assures him, albeit a bit prematurely for her very next thought. "Is the airport far from your home, dear?"

"Almost there," he smiles. *Still doesn't miss a trick,* Grant observes, and for this he is entirely grateful.

As they enter the apartment, an amazing combination of aromas comes wafting toward the doorway. Spearing the last pineapple chunk into its jerk-seasoned hush puppy, Mirabella rests it on a serving platter and hurries out to join them. She appears around the corner wiping her hands on her apron, and the sight of her stops Lorretta in her tracks.

She's the ninth! Immediately struck by the young woman's presence, she is more certain than ever before. Without a word, Loretta opens her arms, and Bella steps naturally into the heart of her embrace.

"Maimie, Mirabella. Mirabella, Maimie," Grant chuckles, somewhat disarmed by their intimacy. While they might have waited for an introduction, he is pleased nonetheless with the heartfelt reception, and sets about delivering the luggage to her room.

"It's fitting that I'd find you here," Loretta smiles, shaking her head. "I can't tell you why you need this, but it belongs to you," she confides, slipping the final stone into Mirabella's palm.

The moment the crystal comes in contact with her skin, Bella senses a shift deep down inside that causes her to grab onto the back of the sofa. Loretta feels it as well. Once both women regain their balance, the facets of the stone begin to shimmer, and then they start to glow, until the whole room is brilliant with the sparkling light. Loretta's eye's well up as she recalls her dear Henry bathed in that radiant light.

"Perhaps it's best if you tuck that away for now," she suggests, hearing Grant's footsteps echo down the hallway.

Mirabella slips the stone into her pocket, and employs all the grace she was born with to remain casual. Excusing herself to the kitchen, she leaves Grant and his mysterious Grandmother to enjoy each other's company, while she prepares them a taste of sweet tea.

The hush puppy combination is served with a creamy cucumber dip that she's flavored with mint leaves and pineapple juice. One bite and Loretta declares herself "fused" and wanting for a full explanation on "Fusion Cooking!" Having struck upon one of Bella's many passions, the lively exchange carries them on through the meal, and before they know it they're retiring to the living room for warm herbal tea and some fresh mango cobbler.

Grant compliments Bella on the incredible meal as he helps carry their plates to the kitchen. Although they've only been dating for a short time, in his mind, they fit together like reports and graphs. One describes and one simplifies, although which is which can perplex the best of minds.

By the time they return with dessert, Loretta has nodded off in the chair, exhausted from a long day of travel. With a touch to her arm she awakens, quietly aware she's been caught red-handed, or –eyed, as the case may be. Bestowing both with kisses, Loretta bids them good night and promptly retires for the evening.

"Those are some lovely roots you've come by," Mirabella observes, as she and Grant snuggle down into the plush sofa cushions.

"Yeah, Maimie's something special, that's for sure," he smiles, temporarily wading through the treasure trove of happy thoughts she'd so lovingly instilled.

Maimie and Gramps had always been there for him, especially in the years after the highway took his parents. Although alcohol had clearly been a factor in the accident, that portrayal does little to capture the essence of his mother or the courage of his father. His memories may be fragmented, them having departed at such tender age, yet the mere thought of them invokes a smile and the spirit of life in the making.

"She gave me something wonderful," Bella confides, fetching him back from his reverie. Wriggling her fingers into the pocket of her jeans, she produces the gleaming crystal and displays it before him on her outstretched palm.

As the inevitable wonder overtakes him, his breath catches slightly and holds. Awash in the splendor of its beauty and form, his harmony is soon dispelled with the beckoning of crows, gliding unbidden on the updraft of his psyche. Instinctively steadying himself, Grant draws a deep breath and begins inner preparation for the quake that's yet to come.

The Spaces In Between

PART II
"THE FALLACY OF STRANGERS"

PART II
"THE FALLACY OF STRANGERS"

"SOMEPLACE WARM"

It's a good thing Levi paid for the week, because when he awakens hours later, he's well into his second night. He now has exactly six days and five nights to forget that his best friend is dead.

With a bit of fast-talking, Brandi managed to convince the authorities that Levi had left on vacation that very night, and, against her best advice, had entrusted his pickup to Zeke. She knew them all, and they knew her, and all things considered, it seemed pretty clear that the death was an overdose. So after significant questioning, ample documentation and a death certificate signed by the coroner, they transported the body and cleared the scene.

And so goes the life of one Ezekiel Jones. He was a friend, a son and a brother, an addict, an abuser and a thief, and would have been a million other things between his cradle and his grave, had not this life been so rudely interrupted. Brandi made it less than a mile before puking, then spit, wiped her mouth and drove the rest of the way home.

Making good on her lie, she piled a devastated Levi into her car, along with all of the cash she'd been saving, and delivered them both to the airport, while a barn-full of Holsteins stood chewing their cuds. As it turned out, the first flight south included a substantial layover, yet beggars can't be choosers, so Levi was forced to bide his time.

The farthest he'd ever been from home was three hours by car, so in addition to watching his best friend die, the entire experience has proven a bit much. He finally broke down on the floor of the airport, leaning against the windows, waiting for his plane. Lots of people noticed. Many looked away. Some even escaped to other sections.

Loretta saw him. She knew that pain. It was still fresh in her heart, and she could no more turn away from that boy than abandon herself, so she walked over to him and offered her hand. Levi was confused at first by the gesture, yet as she stood there in front of him, the light began to shine.

Grasping her hand, he rose to his feet and stared down at the old woman in astonished disbelief. She just nodded, wrapped her arms around him and held on until the pain inside him exploded like a nuclear blast. He cried and he sobbed and then he cried some more. And there she stood all the while, at the heart of it, holding him tight until his tears were reduced to a trickle. She rocked the boy in her arms until the man appeared, and then planted the stone in his hand.

Which is exactly where he finds it on awakening, tucked beneath his pillow at some anonymous motel. The air conditioning is practically frosting the windows, which is a serious attraction 'round these parts 'bout now. It's a nice enough room, he suspects, although he's only stayed in one other motel. Spying a binder on the nightstand, he's grateful to find a listing of restaurants, most of which appear to deliver.

After several minutes of considering, he picks up the receiver and calls for a pizza. The voice on the other end is heavily accented, and may well be the sweetest sound that Levi's ever heard. Jillian says they're fixin' to close any minute, and deliveries have stopped for the night, but if he's willing to pick it up at the office, she may just be able to drop it by on her way home.

Levi promises to be waiting out front with cash in hand, along with a well-deserved tip. Brandi trained him well. Glancing in the mirror, it's hard not to notice that he looks like hell, and if the truth be told, he's not exactly nose candy either. Southern girls may not be attracted to *Eau de Bovine,* so with Jillian in mind, he jumps into the shower and hopes for the best.

One last swipe with the comb, followed by just the right amount of mussing, and he can actually recognize himself again. Although Brandi gave him far more cash than he has any intention of spending, it's comforting to know there's enough, and tomorrow he'll venture out for some supplies. Retrieving his clothes from their pile on the floor, he throws them back on, snatches up the room key and sets out to meet his sweet Jillian.

The man at the front desk suggests that the men's room off the lobby has a contraption that sprays you down with aftershave. Holding his breath, he takes a shot to the face, then pats off the excess for strategic distribution. Levi doesn't consider himself much of a lady's man, yet that's hardly been an issue for the ladies. Giving himself the once-over, he reminds himself he won't be meeting any ladies in the men's room, and swiftly pulls open the door.

A sand-filled ashtray and an artificial tree serve to separate the long, vinyl benches that line the wall beneath the windows. To the left by the restrooms, is a worn and dingy countertop that holds empty displays for the Continental Breakfast. To the right, the entrance is flanked by a rack of brochures on one side, and newspaper vending machines on the other. For some reason, the sight of the newspaper brings his thoughts around to Zeke, and the expression on his face when Jillian walks through the door is somewhat different than the one he had planned.

"You look like somebody just shot your dog," she states, quite profoundly.

"I've had better days," he answers, clenching both his jaw and his will to prevent further spillage. Conjuring his finest country smile, he slowly seeks out her eyes before giving voice to the obvious, "You must be Jillian."

"That'd be me," she affirms, mildly amused.

Levi reaches for the pizza, yet it's clear from her stance that their first transaction will be financial. *Again with the custody battle*, he thinks with just the hint of a smirk.

"You can't blame a girl, out here at night with strangers," she explains, like he'd spoken aloud.

"Oh, no! Please! I'm just grinnin' 'cuz I know better," Levi confides, smiling sheepishly as he hands her cash for nearly double the order.

Handing over the pizza, Jillian pulls out a wad of small bills and begins counting back change from her tips.

"I don't need change."

"Are you sure? That's one healthy tip," she says, pausing midway through her count. As he's nodding his head, she flashes him a gorgeous smile, and in that delightful southern accent says, "Thank you. Thank you very much." As a further courtesy, she engages him in some light conversation. "So, what brings you down here?"

While the question is innocent enough, it's one that Levi is completely unprepared to answer. Following a rather awkward silence, he finally stumbles onto a vague enough response, "I just had to get away," he offers lamely, wishing all the while he would happen on some brilliance. "It's my first time down here, so if you happen to know someone as nice as you, I could sure use a tour guide," he ventures hopefully, all the while shifting his gaze between her eyes and his shoes.

Maybe it's the combination of cow crap and cologne that finally makes her trust him, but she agrees to meet back here tomorrow. Walking to her car, Jillian just smiles and shakes her head, feeling all at once crazy and intrigued.

To Levi, however, she is a vision in the moonlight, shining as brightly as hope itself.

"A Piece of the Grail"

Elbows resting on Loretta's kitchen table, Aurora cradles the stone in her fingertips, examining it against the daylight. The luminosity is absolutely brilliant – clearer than sunlight between her and the window. She decides to tackle this like any good mystery - analytically, considering every possible factor. So far she's exposed the stone to a variety of physical conditions to gauge its reaction, yet wasn't at all surprised to find they'd had little affect.

If they have, as she suspects, been "delivered," their purpose may have little to do with the tangible world. Her suspicions are leaning toward a whole different plane. She can feel it. Yet despite her best intentions, the truth will only unfold as it will, and no amount of force or resolve will hasten the ebb or the flow.

Gold Dog is asleep at her feet, dreaming of night things and the sniffing of stones, just as Joe is climbing from the shower upstairs. A few minutes later, he arrives in the kitchen, clean, dressed and ready to explore. While Aurora opts to stay behind, Gold Dog is more than happy to accompany him.

Inhaling the rich scent of September, Joe fills his lungs with the splendor of the season, passing one to the next in such glorious procession. Beauty lives here – in the soil, in the trees, and across the grassy meadows that lie stretched on either side.

It's a very different beauty than his desert home, and his heart feels awake and alive. Traveling shoes are good. There's no question in his mind where he's going.

It seems Henry's body had barely left the ground when the armed investigators arrived to "secure the debris field." Much about them had disturbed her, someplace down deep in her soul, so Loretta held onto her secret, and quietly held back the stones. They finally left three days ago, disgruntled with their findings and driven off by the storm.

Yet, when our motley crew pulled up out front, Loretta had looked into their eyes and into their hearts, and welcomed them into her home. That evening she produced the grocery sack, and from it she withdrew nine sacred crystals, which immediately lit up the room. Joe offered up a prayer. Gold Dog sniffed the pile and committed to memory the scent of cosmic dust. Aurora sat silently with tears in her eyes, while Loretta simply nodded, secure, at last, in her choice of companions.

Yet out beyond the window glass, beyond the trees, beyond the light, a fifth set of eyes watched from beneath branches well-laden with crows. He lingered there in silence until the final light fell dim, then waited one more hour for the house to fall asleep. Under the cover of darkness, he crept from the vehicle, and stealthily crossed over the lawn. The crows came cawing, swooping and diving, and alas, one member of the household had been listening all along.

As he peered through the living room window, gloved hands cupped against the glass, the man came face to face with one sneering, black dog. What began as a low growl, deep in Gold Dog's throat, rapidly erupted into a fierce, snarling bark that sprayed saliva all over Loretta's window glass.

Joe conquered the stairs in just a few bounds, yet caught only a glimpse at the edges of the shadows. Muddy footprints at the window revealed what they already knew, yet it was the sound that really gave them the shivers. Somewhere in the darkness, an ignition took hold, followed by the soft rumble of an engine rolling surreptitiously away.

With adrenaline still pulsing through their sleep-deprived brains, they sought to establish a solid course of action. The need to guard the crystals was becoming more evident with each new attempt at confiscation. So together they decided that this most precious, crow-guarded gift from the heavens must be hidden and protected, like a modern-day grail.

Each of them felt that the greatest risk was in keeping the stones together, and Joe presented an inspired idea to disperse them. Despite avid protest, Loretta insisted that she alone should choose the recipients, and left yesterday to visit her grandson, bringing with her all of the crystals but one.

Late last night, as Joe and Aurora returned from the airport, he thought he caught a glimmer out here along the trees. Gold Dog is certain of it, tied as he was to the porch rail while his family was away. Unaided by the tire tracks, he quickly leads Joe directly to the scene, and growls at the mere thought of that human, skulking about uninvited. Joe can make his own plans. Now that Gold Dog's got a good whiff, the wind will reveal that intruder if he ever attempts to return. There's an odor to malevolence that really pricks at the olfactories.

"RED EYE"

Elijah finishes his last set at the Palace beneath a choir of carved and gilded cherubs. Adorning pillars and archways, they stand in attendance to angels that gaze down from the rafters above. This week has transported him all over the map – geographically, emotionally and spiritually, as well.

From the gypsy-hearted traveler gifting the world with ancient stones, to the pixie-eyed neophyte secretly sprung from his very own loins, he stands encouraged in the company of angels and comforted by his sweet Genevieve. As the last fluid notes flow smoothly from her throat, the curve of her brass has enchanted them again. There's an energy that radiates from a satisfied crowd that can heal all the pain in your soul, so Elijah opens his heart to the magic and basks in the wave of applause.

Offering up his regrets, he foregoes the *after party* in favor of the next flight home. Needless to say, it's a bit of a red eye. By the time he touches down, his body is exhausted and more than ready to experience the comfort of his own sagging mattress. Of course, by the time he gets there, the scale has tipped and he's rallied once again, so he opts to unpack and absorb some of the time change.

At home, Genevieve occupies a customized stand, which keeps their lives interactive and musically charmed. Opening her case, out tumbles Loretta's precious stone, and he catches it up in one hand. It is truly beautiful. The light glinting from its many facets reflects around the room like so many dancing faeries. *Dancing faeries … Hannah….*

Dropping onto the bed, he's dazed with the very thought of her. Such a magical creature – she captured his heart at first twirl. He slips off his clothes to climb beneath the sheets and rests a sleep-craving head on his pillow. Clutching the stone to his chest, he soon drifts away, with fantasies of fatherhood whirling through his brain.

While admittedly semi-conscious, Elijah is relatively certain that he turned off the lights. Or can it be morning already? It seems like he's barely laid down. His eyelids feel like sandpaper when they finally blink open, yet snap to full attention in light of the circumstance. In the middle of his chest rests Loretta's ancient stone, right where he left it, tucked neatly in hand.

Spilling through his fingers, onto the ceiling and onto the floor, a brilliant light is flooding the entire room. His brain skips like a needle on vinyl, refusing to align with a particular thought. The initial sense is wonder, somewhere north of awe, then verges on fascination before giving way to fear. As his fear continues to manifest, Elijah bangs his fist against the bed, which promptly extinguishes the light.   Now with bleakness and blackness surrounding him, Elijah is absolutely certain he has never been more scared.

"LOST AND FOUND"

From her balcony overlooking the ocean, Cadence listens to the seagulls and breathes in the warm salt air. The detachment appears to have followed her south, and she realizes how familiar it's become. She's like an observer, an outsider, desperate to gain access to some illusive inner world.

Despite the lavish surroundings, she would leap out of her skin, if given the chance. The confines of this suite only increase her claustrophobia, so she plants a ball cap on her head, slips on her shades and decides to peck her way out of this shell. As the door closes behind her, the first chip falls away, and it's vibration resonates clearly throughout time and space. The day seems perfect for pushing envelopes, jumping fences and taking one giant leap forward for Cadence Merriweather.

While the rental car enjoys cutting-edge technology, the operator does not, so she ignores the GPS and navigates by intuition. Out past the beach zone and the tourist traps, she finds some beautiful farm country stretched all along a quiet two-lane road. Pausing at the intersection, she lowers the convertible top and heads out of town with the wind in her face.

Although the peanut fields elude her, she is tickled to identify the white-tufted cotton plants lining the roadside.   A curving creek is discernible from a distance by the lofty line of sentinel trees flagging its banks.   Spanish moss adorns the September branches like swaying sirens beckoning travelers to rest.

Whether it was her intention to stop becomes irrelevant when a jagged shard of road debris guarantees the visit.   The pierced tire threatens to send her car reeling, yet Cadence holds fast and maintains control.   Guiding the lame vehicle off of the roadway, she hobbles to a stop before killing the engine.

Poised in the drivers seat, she looks at herself in the mirror and recognizes that this is indeed one of those moments. She can feel it. Every so often in life, we are presented with an opportunity to claim our truth. She can press that call button and remain a pampered princess, or get her hands dirty and take care of this herself. If she's ever going to face motherhood, she should at least be able to face a flat tire. In that light, the choice is clear. It's time to make a stand.

Popping the trunk, she fully expects to see everything waiting. Why, she's not quite sure, as it wasn't there when the porter unloaded her luggage. *Okay, obstacle number one.* Within seconds she notices the pull key on the floor, and voila! *What the heck is that?* she wonders, staring down at the temporary tire.   As she removes it from the compartment, one highly manicured nail snaps off at the quick, yet with barely a yelp, she continues unabated.

A number of other parts have been included as well, so she removes them all, reviewing each to determine its purpose and function. *That must be the twisty thing, and that appears to be something like a jack, yet there must be some trick to make it work...* she surmises, staring down at the array of metal parts strewn across the trunk. *The book! All of them have a book! With a few instructions, I'll have this licked in no time!* she concludes.

Pleased with her insight, she slides into the passenger seat to examine the sought-after pages. Pressing the button to the glove box, Cady is immediately crestfallen. The compartment is empty, save for a few receipts from some previous driver. Slamming the door with a bit too much gusto, she stomps around the car to the driver's side, all the while casting a violent stream of curse words into that slow moving creek.

Emotions that had smoldered quietly for years are now sparking flash fires that erupt without notice. Gnawing at her torn bit of nail, she leans up against the door, and stares with contempt at the demon tire. *I can give those parts another look and try to figure it out, or I can press that button and be rescued. By money. Again.* Minus instructions, "Plan A" seems fairly questionable, yet the thought of "Plan B" makes her want to throw up.

Churning fears and doubts that have transcended generations, Cadence kicks frustrated pebbles at her deflated albatross, as the older model compact car approaches from the opposite side. Lost in thought, she overlooks the moment when they cross the centerline. Just as sunlight fills the void between two fast-moving clouds, one startled driver stomps down hard on the brakes.

With the glare off the river, they could have missed her completely, yet everything happens for a reason, you know. Salty tears are stinging her eyes when Cadence finally spots them. They're walking fast in her direction, two of them, their young faces awash with both fear and concern.

"Are you okay, Ma'am?" he asks, in a familiar sort of drawl.

"Something in the road," she stammers, no more able to identify the object than she is to fix the damage.

"Yeah, we saw it," he agrees, motioning with his chin toward the mangled offender, a heat shield off a catalytic converter that is now riding bareback somewhere down the highway. "You look like you could use some help," he begins, glancing nervously from her eyes to the ground just beside her.

Cadence is stunned and finding it difficult to speak, and suddenly she's sprouting a flood that may well raise the water level of the river down below.

"Ma'am, I'm sorry," he pleads, grown more anxious with her tears. "This will just take a minute." Striding toward the back of her car, he returns with a tire iron clenched squarely in the grasp of one sinewy right fist.

Cady closes her eyes and breathes in until her lungs are filled to capacity, then slowly exhales as the oxygen seeps into her body. *What turn of fate has brought me to this moment? To this option I had not even considered?* Wiping her face with the back of her hand, she opens her eyes and smiles. The young man is kneeling down on one knee, and spinning lug nuts off her tire with the greatest of ease.

His lady friend is squatting down beside him, obviously familiar with the drill, as she feeds and collects tools with mechanical precision. Cadence stands in awe of their ability, and studies the procedure like the scholar that she is. The task is completed in no time, yet with the simple twist of a wrench, entire paradigms have shifted for one slightly jaded lady who's now finding her way home.

"INSIDE OUT"

"Are you enjoying yourself?" he hears, from the inside, out.

"I like this one very much!" he replies enthusiastically. The puzzles simply occur at his beckoning, as his young, fertile mind masters challenge after challenge.

Today the big bird came to visit, and he petted his shiny, black feathers. Their eyes twinkled together for a while, and then he had to go. Justin is always happy to see him.

"ARE YOU AFRAID OF THE DARK YET?"

Although rivulets of water are trickling down the cleft between his buttocks, Jonas manages to clench his teeth and recoil his lips into what may technically be referred to as a smile. Essentially paralyzed, he's standing there in the kitchen, wrapped in a thin towel, quietly debating a secret addition to the pool of water collecting at his feet. His darling Lizzie has obviously lost her mind. It appears she has descended with Peggy, Warren and a complete stranger, and Jonas is grimly certain that one transparent pane won't hold them back for long.

Taking what time he can get, he turns away from the invaders and shuffles down the hall, pointedly failing to grant them admission, despite expectations and expletives. He grumbles loudly while pulling on his unintentional uniform of worn corduroys, a frayed turtleneck, a suit coat hailing from the days of yore and slippers that should have been laid to rest long ago. Mid-tirade, he yanks a knitted winter cap down over his ears and wraps a sad-looking scarf several times around his neck before stomping back out to the kitchen.

"Hey Dad," Lizzie greets him, having used her key. "You going somewhere?" she asks, commenting on the extra apparel.

"Took a shower!" he scoffs, disgustedly. "Could get sick!" he adds, as if it that were a widely accepted consequence of indoor showering. "What the hell's it to you, anyway? Any of you?!"

"Whoa, Big Daddy...Ease on up..." Lizzie croons, pulling her father into an embrace that remembers the magic of shared moments in front of the hi-fi swaying softly to sounds of the blues. In a heartbeat, she has him dancing to some far away tune, and for one harmonious instant the world disappears. For a moment, it's all okay – he's the man he truly is – beyond his fallacies and faults. Jonas enjoys one delicious mouthful of clarity, and then...

"Hi, Daddy," Peggy interjects, as she innocently attempts to join the celebration. She never knows the right thing to say or the right time to say it, especially around her father. Never has. Every time he looks at her that way, her heart shrivels a bit in her chest and that chronic bladder control issue rears its ugly head. Figures, her bladder would be her biggest defender, always allowing her an excuse from the room. Today, however, she's prepared, undergarments in place, and with the utmost courage, she asserts herself again.

"Daddy, we've been worried about you," she begins, with just the slightest quiver in her voice. "You haven't been yourself." She reaches for his shoulder, yet the chill is clearly tangible, so

103

she hurriedly withdraws.   Wincing from the emotional blow, Peggy takes shelter behind Warren and the stranger and begins licking those old, familiar wounds.

"Who the hell's this anyway?" barks Jonas, as a stray drop of sputum clings to the stranger's cheek.

"His name is Vincent; he's with our church," Warren relays as one fluid thought.

"Why's he here?"   The question is simple, yet the true implication is reflected in his tone. Jonas has been developing this tone since childhood, and the results are now menacing, the ferocity palpable.

"Believe it or not, I'm here to help," Vincent steps in, undeterred. He doesn't offer his hand, yet looks Jonas directly in the eye. "It smells in here. Peggy has already determined that there's barely enough food in the house to feed a rat, and I wouldn't be surprised if I found you sleeping under a bridge on my way out of town."

"Get out of my house!" Jonas bellows, pointing his arm toward the door. "Get out NOOOW!" he commands, thrusting the bulk of his venom at the stranger. Turning toward his eldest, his eyes demands an answer, "Lizzie?!"

"C'mon, Dad, let's you and me sit down here for a while," she suggests, casually ushering him through the kitchen toward the living room. "Maybe you guys can go for coffee? Perhaps a few groceries?" Lizzie's eyes are pleading, and Peggy does not require a second invitation to collect her entourage and escape to the comfort of anywhere else.

As the door closes behind them, Lizzie captures a startling glimpse of her father, and is grateful for the sofa when her knees begin to buckle. A lifetime of deflection had prevented her from seeing the fear behind his gruff tones and infallible sarcasm. Yet there it was, if only for an instant, and the truth was unmistakable. *How could I have been so blind?* she wonders, as the familiar slideshow tumbles through her brain at a slightly different angle.

"What the hell was that all about?" Jonas demands, yanking her back to their present dilemma.

With a shake of her head, Lizzie blinks back the moisture that has formed in her eyes, swallows the lump in her throat and tugs on him gently to join her on the couch. He begins to shake her off – *The nerve of these people!* – and then he looks into her eyes. Reluctantly settling onto the cushion beside her, he refuses to occupy more than an edge. Once his hackles have been patted down and his breathing returns to a semblance of normal, Lizzie readies herself for the conversation of a lifetime.

"Sorry it took so long for me to get here, Dad. Peggy's been worried for quite some time, but I just kept blowing her off, ya know?" Jonas shrugs his agreement with a bit of a chuckle, yet listens intently, heart melting in his chest. "But this time she sounded so desperate, and told me she had arranged an *Intervention* like on television, and literally begged me to come. So here I am. And God love you Dad, I can see why she called. Forgive me for saying this, but it appears ol' Vinnie wasn't too far off the mark. What's going on in there?" she probes gently, searching his eyes for an answer.

"What? So the old man hits a bad patch, don't we all?"

"Bad patch, eh – how's about a bad year?"

"Well, we have those too."

"Yeah, I suspect we do. What's say we call this one over?"

"Easier said than done," Jonas grunts.

"No doubt. Any ideas?"

"Christ, Lizzie, you think I'd still be sittin' here if I did?!" he barks in frustration.

"Point taken. Well, it's clear we've got to do something, Dad. I sure can't let you waste away while this place falls down around your ears, so let's toss a few ideas around and see what sticks, okay?"

"Go."

"What?"

"Ideas! Go. Start. Begin. What was your IQ?"

"Be good or you can go live with Warren and Peggy," she goads with a wry smile.

"All right, all right…"

"Okay then. Let's start with what's important to you."

"Obviously, not a hell of a lot."

"Well then, I guess things can only get better from here," Lizzie declares, offering him one of those patent smiles he loves so well.

With bonds renewed and alliances reinstated, the two set about masterminding a plan for the future. Lizzie watches the light return to his eyes as his mind engages and their hearts reconnect, and out in the entryway, just beyond their view, a brilliant light emanates from one unobtrusive handbag resting by the door.

"THE ROAD TO HELL"

Grant awakens from a restless sleep, vexed with fragmented questions that span the continuum. The jumble of thoughts are disjointed, even on paper, so he tosses the journal back into its drawer and plods thickly toward the master bath. Water always helps.

As her young man comes striding down the hallway, all washed, preened and expertly groomed, Loretta realizes that while he presents a striking image, Grant leaves little room for want or need. *Perhaps Mirabella will open that door,* she surmises, and looks forward to meeting her for breakfast.

"By the way," Grant opens, pouring coffee for both he and Loretta, "Bella showed me something last night."

"Ahh," she acknowledges, nodding her head.

"That's it? *Ahh?*"

"What do you need me to tell you?" she inquires, as their eyes interlock.

"You don't have to tell me anything," he retreats, albeit insincerely.

"Well then, I'll just go get ready. Remember your magnificence, Grant, and that the day is yours to celebrate."

And with that, she disappears, leaving him alone with his thoughts. He had heard those words every morning of his young life, yet somewhere along the road they'd fallen silent, and with them the concepts, as well. Deep inside, a long forgotten truth comes out of hibernation, and two rooms away, his grandmother smiles.

A cup of coffee later, Loretta emerges in her best, flowered frock, radiance spilling in every direction. Grant can only smile and offer her his arm as they exit the apartment to begin the celebration. He decides on the scenic route to the restaurant, wandering through suburbs dotted with senior living communities, and on several occassions points out flower gardens that just happen to border their grounds. Loretta simply nods and smiles, and enjoys the lovely ride with her grandson.

Rearranging the condiments for at least the third time, Mirabella shifts in her seat like a fidgety child. Grant has been planning this conversation since returning from his grandfather's funeral, and of course, she is here to support him. Of course, all this was well and good before she met Loretta. Now, she can scarcely imagine this amazing woman being tucked away with some cookie-cutter care.

Just seconds from a graceful escape, her eye catches Loretta's as they come through the door. The smile that follows is completely disarming, and Bella's reservations all but slip away. By the time she unwraps from Loretta's embrace, she's certain that all will be well in the world. The three of them settle back into the booth and order up skillets of their favorite design. Within minutes, the waitress delivers mouth-watering stacks of their tastiest foods, layered to perfection and smothered with gravy.

Once the yummy sounds have subsided, Grant downs one last swallow of coffee and searches for the best place to begin. Loretta is watching him from across the table. *Squirmed just like that in my own kitchen chair right before he told us he was leaving,* she recalls.

"The flowers at the rest home were beautiful, Grant, and I miss you every day of my life," Loretta begins, holding up a finger to stave off interruption. "I've taken care of everything. You needn't worry about me. A man and a woman are staying with me at the farm, and something tells me we're going to get along just fine," she concludes, enjoying another bite of her breakfast.

Momentarily derailed, Grants follows suit, leaving conversation to Mirabella, who adeptly fields the punt. "What a creative solution! I applaud your resourcefulness! I've heard an imaginative woman is rarely at a loss in this world," she adds with a wink, which endears her to Loretta for all time.

Confused and somewhat disoriented, Grant is beginning to see his Maimie with entirely new eyes. He had always seen her as sweet and perhaps a bit naïve, definitely thoughtful, though not much of a thinker. Rather unexpectedly, he is now coming to realize that a number of his assumptions have been terribly skewed. So much for good intentions….

"A MOUNTAIN OF SEAN"

Wiping his hands on a shop rag, Sean stands back and inspects the final finish on Carlie's wedding gift. He's crafted a beautiful drop-leaf dining table for them, designed after an antique he'd once seen. After eyeing it from ten different angles, he stands back, crosses his arms and finally revels in the moment of completion. It is a thing of beauty.

The halo from Carlie's stone casts a warm sheen over the shiny wet surface. It's the darnedest thing, that stone. Some lady she met in the airport just gave it to her! Only Carlie! The thing glowed 24/7 the whole time she was here, yet fell lifeless as soon as she left. Now it shines mostly while he's working, yet always grows dim far sooner than he'd hoped. His hours of research have yet to reveal its origin or classification, so he's taken to carrying it around with him, for a number of reasons, no doubt.

Slipping it into his shirt pocket, he flips off the light switches and steps into the night. The stars are especially brilliant this evening, and the Milky Way is blazing a spectacular trail. With the galaxy stretched out before him, he takes a moment to contemplate its black-hole heart that is continually birthing new stars into the sky. It's a divine connection that could shapes us from stardust, along with billions of others, so that we can experience this planet, this life and this time.

Mid-way through pondering, he notices his pocket is outshining the stars. Withdrawing the stone, he holds it flat in his hand and allows it to illuminate the trail that leads him home. Smiling, he thinks about Carlie and the new life she's about to begin. She deserves every happiness. Shaking his head, he drops the stone back into his pocket and walks inside the house.

The more he studies the specimen, the more curious it becomes. Understanding will only come through analysis, so he's started a journal to document his findings. Retrieving the book from the living room, he jots down the date, the time and location, and includes the notation "communing with stars." He hopes that with sufficient data, commonalities will begin to appear and he can determine some cause and effect for the shining.

Opening the refrigerator door, he is suddenly confronted with the reality of bachelorhood. Condiments, a scrap of lettuce and some milk that's far enough past date to make cheese, remind him that he hasn't been shopping since Carlie left. Rifling through the cupboard, he finds half a box of spaghetti, a can of pork 'n beans and chicken noodle soup left over from a cold. He grabs the can of beans along with four of the six slices of bread left in the breadbox along with mayo from the fridge, and begins constructing his favorite childhood delicacy – baked bean sandwiches.

His sister would make horrible faces and he would just laugh, smug in the fact that he wouldn't have to share. Now he wishes he had someone to share it with. He's been up here six years now, ever since the accident, and rarely, if ever, could he remember being lonely. Carlie comes to visit; he gets together once a month with the woodworkers; and Lenwood and Laurie, friends since forever, live just a couple of miles down mountain. Thinking about it, it's been weeks since he's seen them, going on months, if he's completely honest.

Healing had taken some time, as healing always does, and then he had his work. He thrived on connecting with each new idea, new concept, new project, and there was always the property. Generations of his family have worked this land – cleared meadows, built fences, groomed the forest to be strong and healthy – and every bit was undertaken as a labor of love. It's a tradition he's proud to maintain, yet it's what accompanies that pride that is his true reward.

At the heart of every action exists a state of absolute harmony, wherein each element of the process aligns with its optimum. And Sean has experienced that harmony enough times to have driven himself nearly mad in the pursuit. And that's probably the lion's share of why he doesn't leave this place.

He experienced it here as a boy – the magic of absolute synchronicity – and the flavor was intoxicating. He tried to find it as a young man, between a multitude of thighs, yet the harmony was fleeting, and only the heartbreak endured. Later, he sought it through chemicals, off the nail or on the rocks, but they only served as anesthesia for the bone-breaking crash that soon followed.

Now he can reach it most often through his woodwork or his work on the land. And that was all fine, great in fact, until the delicate balance was finally interrupted. Carlie's getting married, and therein lies the rub. And today he's feeling a bit chafed. Found himself reminiscing throughout the afternoon, as he lightly stroked the surface of her new family's table. She's found another hero, another confidant and friend, and tonight his heart is lonely and mourning days long past.

This place had been his salvation, yet he imagines in time he'll be leaving, and senses it might be sooner than later. That night sleep floats easily down upon him, beckoning his spirit toward the shared world of dreams. Guided by the light of an ancient stone, the white knight journeys forth into the misty unknown, alone but for the calling of crows.

"AND ON TO THE NEXT"

The cows were still waiting when Levi got home. Thankfully, cows are a patient lot, and he was not the only *milker* on the farm. Yet as a family enterprise, he had a number of co-workers who were all *very* interested in hearing his explanation.

The police showed up at the barn the morning Zeke was found dead of an overdose. Brandi left a message at his Mom's, although it was incredibly brief and seriously lacking in details. His brother had to go get his truck from the cop shop after they cleared out the body and gave it the twice over. The saving grace for Levi was that they all thought he didn't know.

Yet that's presenting its own challenges, which continue to test his limited skills as an actor. The police want a follow-up, his brother's ticked off that he up and went on vacation, and every time he sees his mother, she practically drills a hole right through him with her infamous stare. And he misses Zeke. At this stage, that feels an awful lot like anger, and he rants at him loudly out in the barn, between crying and falling apart.

Brandi stops by just after milking to steal him away for a ride. Our girl was raised to get back on the horse, so she wastes no time in driving straight to the scene of poor Zeke's demise. While Levi attempts to impale her with four-letter words, she drags him from the car, then pushes, pulls and tugs until he is standing in the exact spot where it happened. Despite his rocking and spouting, dancing and spewing, she aligns his chin with hers, stares him into looking at her, and gives him the funeral he needs in his heart. She holds him, there at the side of Mr. Miller's drainage ditch. Cradling her friend in her arms, she holds fast as he sobs for *his* Zeke – the one who had *lived* through so very much.

When he's all out of salt, and drained of all water, Brandi piles him back into the car and drives him on down to the bar. Lola has been honored with the coveted corner booth, yet slides over when she sees him, patting the vinyl for them to sit down. Her eyes are so swollen that Levi asks about the other guy. Shaking her head, she just reaches for him and pulls him down into her neck. They share a few tears and a really long hug, then she buys him a drink and the services begin.

Stuart is first to visit the booth, with Callie on his arm. Endlessly uncertain, he fumbles through an awkward hug as they offer their condolences. Marlie spies them from the pool table and practically runs across the bar, arms outstretched and waving as she throws herself into the booth beside Levi. She's so anxious to comfort him that she's talking in a continual stream, and by now he's simply watching her lips move. Sam stops by, as does the remainder of the bar, one after the next, sharing sympathy and beer until Brandi straps him in the passenger seat and finally takes him home.

He wakes up at her place, in his clothes, on the couch. It appears that Brandi's still in bed, yet sitting on the coffee table wait three aspirin and a bottle of water. Downing it all, he pulls the afghan up under his chin and rolls onto his other side. Some time later, he awakens to the sound of pans rattling in the kitchen behind him. Inching over the arm, he attempts to peek around the sofa while feigning asleep. Yeah right.

"Get up, you lazy bum! What do you think this is? Brandi's Stop-N-Flop?"

So she rousts him, by blame or by shame, and together they fix breakfast, a little heavy on the pork. Handing back whatever money was left over, he tells her about Jillian, about Loretta, and about the heiress he met by the side of the road. He paints a fine portrait of his adventures, and when he finishes the story, he tells her the rest.

They talk about his mother, about how she could always grill the truth out of them and could always spot a lie. Both are certain she'll force it out of him in time. He describes how lost he feels without Zeke, and how there really are nice people beyond the state line. The heiress offered him a job out-of-state painting barns that will pay enough to make a fresh start.

Or course, he won't leave 'til they're even, as if that could ever be true.

"A BIRD ON THE WING"

Elijah lays frozen in his bed, barely willing to breathe. The only sound he can hear is the pounding of his heart. Slowly reaching for the light switch, his eyes never waiver from the stone. Ghost images of a light now extinguished still dance in the memory of his tired eyes. Even after the room fills with electric light, the essence remains, imprinted on his soul.

Although the light had frightened him, its absence was the true definition of fear. The world never looked darker than the moment that brilliance vanished from sight. There was nothing gradual about it, and the separation seems painful, yet at some point before dawn, he finally falls back to sleep.

Morning arrives just a bit before noon, and it happens the kitchen serves breakfast all day. He's craving eggs this morning, over-easy and on top of the toast. Sipping at his orange juice, he wanders out front to collect his mail from the box. *Junk, junk, junk…what the heck?* The postmark is from his landlord, who lives just a continent away.

Sliding his finger beneath the flap, he extracts the letter. Skimming over the formalities, the primary matter quickly springs to the forefront - they've sold his house! Thirty days notice, with ten days now gone. Dumbstruck, he plops down on the sofa, and wonders when it went up for sale.

Removing the stone from the pocket of his robe, he turns it slowly around in his hand. "Tell me you're not at the bottom of this," he voices aloud with guarded disbelief.

As opposed to taking legal action, Elijah spends the next twenty days consumed with the business of relocation. His grandmother's house will be empty two years come spring, and all things considered, he may as well go east. Southeast versus northeast, but east is east, and it's closer than west. From the moment he makes his decision, the stone begins to twinkle, and his heart nearly weeps with delight. Something about its light is addictive, and the addiction rests deeper than any he's known. When it glows, he glows, and everything simply aligns, and when it goes dark, he feels such sadness and longing for its light.

It seems to enjoy lots of music, and of course loves his sweet Genevieve, so the gifted crystal becomes an unlikely third in their alternative family. Between parties and dinners with a decade of well-wishers, Elijah sifts through the plethora of what to take forward and what's best left behind.

Fame has certainly afforded him friends and acquaintances, not to mention a mountain of fans, yet years on stage have kept him somewhat alone and apart. At least that's how he's beginning to feel, now that fatherhood is no longer an illusion, but a living, breathing, dancing girl who has already captured his heart. She will definitely be an influence on his touring schedule, and her priority seems to be growing by the second.

Moving always comes with a side dish of soul searching, so he decides on a rental and gets ready to drive.

"AND THEN THERE WAS LIGHT"

Butterflies are floating lazily through the meadow of his mind, when suddenly he's surrounded with a most astounding light. He laughs right out loud as joy flutters all around him and through him, illuminating his spirit with the truth of all that is, all that was and all that's yet to be.

Dabbing at her tears, Lorna kisses Justin's comatose forehead, pats his tiny hand, and leaves her grandson with the gift of a beautiful stone.

"Drifting"

Despite their obvious differences, the connection between them is undeniable. Although neither quite understands it, the space between people involves so much more than distance. She greets him from the steps of an elaborate entryway, and welcomes him genuinely to her magnificent home.

Cadence is accustomed to offering the tour, having accompanied her mother on countless occasions since childhood. Levi, on the other hand, can't decide if it's a church or a museum. Noticing the bowed head and folded hands, she touches his arm in reassurance and escorts him to his quarters. Like the rest of Merriweather Hall, his room is outfitted with exquisite antiques, neither masculine nor feminine, yet unmistakably grand.

Depositing his ill-fitting bags into the room, they return to the kitchen where Maggie is just finishing up with dinner preparations. Of course, she loves him immediately, and wraps the young man in a "gi-normous" embrace that lifts him right up on his toes. While Cady invites her to stay, she graciously defers to a standing obligation, and exits the kitchen toward her car and her husband.

With neither Maggie nor Jillian between them, Levi's shyness comes quickly to the surface, as he shuffles his feet and stares at his shoes. And while Cadence was spoon-fed civility from birth, she was also weaned on condescension, which lately rests like a bitter pill upon her tongue. Yet as she wrestles to avoid treating him like a subordinate, Levi is doing battle with his own set of judgments. Despite their discomfort, the meal is delicious, and opens the door, as food often does.

"So what color am I painting your barns?" Levi asks, before the silence grows too awkward.

"The same, I suspect, although I hadn't really thought about it. They've been that color since I was a girl."

"Well, if that's what you like, then that's what we'll do!"

"If that's what I like…" she trails off, brain shifting into uncharted territory.

For several mouthfuls, he simply watches her, enjoying the progression of expressions that are crossing her face. An embarrassed smile appears the moment Cady realizes she's been drifting.

"You never knew you had a choice, did you?" he gleans, looking down to spare her dignity.

"I guess not," she acknowledges, to herself as much as him. "I suppose I'll have to think on that tonight."

Having finished their meal, Levi insists on washing the dishes, despite vigorous protest from Cadence. Finally she relents, if only to save his mother from the shame. Now it's her turn to watch, as he stands elbow-deep before the sink, and what she sees is a young man with insight far beyond his years. By nine, both are willing to call it a night, and she vows to have chosen a color by dawn. They agree to meet for breakfast and get an early start, and Levi grins at her version of early as they go separate ways at the stairs.

By the time Maggie arrives the next morning, he's up waiting in the kitchen – shat, showered and shaved. The housekeeper just smiles and shakes her head, and the two never lack for conversation until Miss Cady makes her way down the stairs.

When she walks through the door, they're both laughing as Levi relays a truly graphic tale involving a rope, a calf and a very large pile of manure. Wiping the tears from her eyes, Maggie serves them up two beautiful plates featuring omelets, croissants and fresh fruits with cream.

"So, I ask you again," poses Levi, "what color am I painting your barns?"

Thrusting her chin up into the air, she raises her fist in defiance. "Midnight blue!"

Levi applauds her decision, and gallantly stands to offer a bow. Maggie's chuckling in the background as Cadence nods and offers a queenly wave to her adoring subjects. Bubbling up from someplace deep within, Cady suddenly remembers her *Joy!* And beneath the rafters of that majestic home, two precious stones begin glowing in unison.

With breakfast now a delicious memory, Levi and Cadence set about the business of planning their project. The decision is unanimous

125

that he is to inspect the job before they proceed with any purchases. Of the three buildings, the horse and hay barns have been empty for years, and only the garage is still in use. There'll be some scraping, but all in all, they're in pretty good shape, so it's off to the hardware store for supplies.

Cadence suggests they take Levi's truck to more easily transport the paint, and with a nod of his head, he agrees. There's an odor to the cab that threatens to take her breakfast, so she quickly rolls down the window for a breath of fresh air.

It's best not to discuss it at the moment and tempt tipping the balance toward nausea, so they ride along in silence until Levi finds something suitable on the radio. To say the least, she's glad to arrive, and the salesman is happy to see them too. Buckets of blue paint and nearly a dozen brushes later, it's well past noon before they finally finish.

Baking in the mid-day sun, the odor has ripened to a full-blown stench, and Cady immediately retches upon opening the door. Thankfully she's running on empty by now, and withholds any further contribution to the smell. Levi is solemn as he climbs into the truck. Rolling down both windows, he simply waits there until she can join him, then fires up the engine and heads them back home. It's nearly half the ride before she can manage to speak, yet for the life of her, she can hold her tongue no longer.

"Forgive me, Levi, I don't mean to be rude, but what on earth is that smell?"

"Death," he answers flatly.

Cady looks at the expression on his face, or rather the lack thereof, and realizes he is completely serious. As he pulls the truck over, she bolts from the cab, with the retching now fully renewed. Once the vocalizing stops, he joins her, and together they occupy two large rocks there beside the road.

"What happened?" she asks tenderly, placing her hand on his forearm.

Levi pours out the whole tragic affair, much to his amazement. Although the story is sordid, and shocking, no doubt, Cadence connects with his pain and his loneliness, and feels only compassion for his poor aching heart. He continues to tell her about Brandi, and watches her eyes for any sign she might report them. When none appears, he tells her about the woman he met at the airport, and finally he shows her his beautiful stone.

Cady's eyes grow wide, and then wider, and then Levi is forced to carry her now limp body back to the truck.

"BLACK DOG LAUGHING"

Grant steers the rental car down the infamous dirt lane, swallowing hard against the lump that's now forming in his throat. This is his first trip back since the funeral, and it will be doubly strange without Gramps or the houseful of relatives. Instead they'll be greeted by strangers, and with that thought, he reaches up to massage that familiar knot at the back of his skull. Watching him, Loretta interjects.

"I bet you'll absolutely love Aurora's dog, Grant. You've always been a dog person, and he has such a personality!"

"Yes, I'm sure I will, Maimie," he admits, well accustomed to her *"think good thoughts"* position. *A positive approach allows for a positive outcome, while fear grows nothing but a garden full of weeds and leads to a hungry existence.* He has witnessed the truth of her theory on numerous occasions throughout his life, and if he ever proves it mathematically, he'll be forced to concede. Until that time, he worries more often than not, and placates his grandmother at every turn.

Loretta has been aware of his inner struggle throughout most of his life. His trauma over the death of both parents spawned a lifetime of planning to avoid every pitfall, and worrying that he had not planned enough. It's an unfortunate perspective that pre-supposes the worst. She's

128

watched it destroy too many lives, and in so many ways, that her heart truly aches for those she's lost along the way. Loretta summons up a glorious smile, and considers the infinite possibilities that Grant can find his way.

Mirabella cranes her neck in an attempt to see beyond the trees. "This is so beautiful, Grant! I can finally see where you come from!"

"It's a little piece of heaven," Loretta beams. "Our family has been here for almost 150 years now. Built this place on sweat, love and faith, and I bet this old house could stand here forever," she muses, as Grant pulls the car in beside Gramps' old pickup.

Blinking back the moisture, he switches off the ignition and gazes through the windshield at the old farmhouse. He rejects the image of Gramps standing in the doorway, and instead looks to the rooflines and below, distracting his mind with a list of repairs. By the time he collects himself, both women are already out of the car, so he quickly pops the trunk and grabs up the luggage.

Wearing his biggest, broad smile, Gold Dog bounds from the front door with Aurora and Joe close behind. They too are genuinely happy to see Loretta return home, safe from her journey as *Messenger of Stones*. A relieved Rory embraces her directly, followed by Joe, along with several serious nudges from her fur-bearing friend. Mirabella is delighted with the reception, and assumes the tradition of hugs all around.

Grant, on the other hand, is not quite so familiar, with his primary concern being Maimie's affairs. His initial impression is good, however, as Joe looks him square in the eye and takes hold of the heaviest bag. And frankly, it seems impossible to mistrust Aurora. She exudes such resolve and integrity that even her shadows are confident. Of course, Gold Dog is all that Maimie promised, with a personality as big as the great outdoors, yet there are details to discuss and decimals to be placed before Grant will declare that all is in order.

After enjoying a truly delicious meal, Grant settles back in his chair and initiates a very pointed conversation. Accustomed to working dinners consumed in conference rooms, he navigates easily from *prop talk* to *shop talk*, and moves quite adeptly to the bone of his contention.

"As financial advisor to my grandmother, it is important that I be aware of any arrangements or agreements between you. Have you settled on any form of compensation?" he asks, looking from Loretta to Joe to Aurora and back.

The entire table just sits there staring at him. There had been no such discussion, and truly none was needed.

"Have you met Gold Dog?" Aurora asks, hugging him and stroking his fur. Loretta and Joe simply chuckle, which Grant finds disturbing and rather offensive.

"Of course, I've met the dog," he begins in exasperation, before Aurora politely interrupts and spares him the apology.

"I tell most people that he was named for his heart, which is all but true, of course," she begins. Loretta shoots Grant a *"hush up and listen"* look, which settles him quickly back in his chair. "Gold Dog has a gift," she continues. "Some dogs sniff out people; some dogs sniff out drugs. Gold Dog sniffs out gold," she grins, and drops a hefty, leather pouch onto the table with a thud. "Go ahead," she offers, nudging at the bag.

Grant pulls open the drawstring and nearly chokes on his own saliva. It's near overflowing with shiny gold nuggets, straight from the earth, in all of their glory. Mirabella leans in and starts laughing. First it's a yuck at the surprise of it all, then it rolls into a hearty celebration of one gifted black dog.

With his fears allayed and a renewed sense of wonder, Grant can now listen to the rest of the story. Pulling the shades in the living room, Loretta invites everyone to join her for dessert, and a covert conversation on the state of the world.

"GOOD MORNING"

"Simply align with all that is possible, and all will be well in the world. Faith is all you need to find your way."

The voices seem to fade into the distance as Justin paddles through the swirling mist on his journey toward the surface. Popping through the veil between hither and yon, he opens his eyes to see Bone Dog resting right there beside him, where he's been waiting all along. It's a strange room, but there are cartoons on the television, so he snatches up Bone Dog and latches onto his thumb. His mother walks into the room with her coat and her purse, and he watches as she hangs them both neatly on the rack.

"Hi Mommy," Justin greets her quite happily, yet stops short when she stumbles, barely catching herself on a chair.

Rosalie can scarcely believe her eyes. Her baby is finally awake! After weeks in the coma, his prognosis had weakened, yet here he is talking and sucking his thumb! Swooping her son up into her arms, she rocks him and kisses him and squeezes him tight, until he quietly asks her when they can go home.

"DEW DROP INN"

Having delivered the armoire to the far side of the valley, Sean is officially free.

Freedom is not something he's allowed himself lately. Instead he's been committed to overlapping projects and internal obligations. Of course, he has traveled light years from the truly dark times, and has grown to accept his choices, for better or worse. Yet this illusive pursuit of true harmony has left him decidedly lonely and wanting for more.

An interesting concept: more. Got him in a whole lot of trouble once – for a decade or so. Yet more, like most things, is relative, and more harmony is still a star worth chasing. And chase it he has, through the mountains and the valleys, from the east coast to the west. So as the frost seeps into this good northern ground, Sean is heading south for the very first time.

His beloved mountains soon dissolve into prairies and flat lands before spilling into farm country and acre after acre of uprooted soil. The fields have gone dormant for winter, and lie quietly awaiting the nourishment of snow. Something about it touches him inside, so he sets about finding a place for the night.

As a dozen or so streetlights flicker to life, a well-lit invitation reads *Dew Drop Inn*. Wheeling into the dirt parking lot, he can smell the chicken 'n biscuits right from the road. A small bell is mounted inside the door announces his arrival with a melodious ring, and gathers the attention of all who will hear.

A woman behind the counter invites him to sit wherever he likes, so Sean chooses a booth with full view of the room. He's a bit late for dining with farmers, who rarely wait for roosters to begin their day. A couple of older gentlemen are seated at the counter, allowing a stool between them, as is socially proper.

The tables are standard issue, yet the booths appear to be handcrafted, and have probably been here forever. The wood has a deep honey finish that has warmed over time, as if in response to the countless meals shared in her presence. He snags a menu from its shiny chrome holder and carefully reads through the choices.

The Dew Drop specialty is down-home cookin' with flair, from the obvious chicken 'n biscuits with a side order of gizzards, to catfish, green chili grits and sizzling okra. The menu is well beyond his bachelor cuisine, and Sean is intrigued with the list of possibilities. At this point his stomach is willing to try just about anything.

"See anything you like?" asks the smiling woman with the apron and the order pad. Her eyes dance with a warmth that simply draws folks in for more, yet he's hoping it's the cooking that keeps 'em comin' back.

"Well I'm not really sure," he tells her quite honestly. "There's a whole lot of firsts for me on this menu."

"Well, I'm sure you've tasted a burger before," she chides, pointing to the appropriate section.

"True. But where's the adventure in that?" he asks with a smile.

"Adventure, eh? Well, what brings you to this part of the world?"

Sean explains how he set out this morning on his first vacation in years, and how the smell of her cooking drew him in off the highway. Her face lights up, of course, and with a little assistance, he chooses a meal, complete with all the fixings. Strolling toward the kitchen with his order in hand, she calls back to him over her shoulder.

"Oh, by the way, I'm Daisy, if you need me." And under her breath, "And Daisy if you don't," she reminds herself, wary of her instant attraction.

Daisy delivers a steaming platter, and he practically dives into her *Caribbean glazed chicken, southern fried rice* and *crackling corn salad*, until he's ultimately forced to come up for air. She chuckles from behind the counter, satisfied with the hearty reception. Ringing up Jessie and Mac, she thanks them both and bids them goodnight, then starts wiping down the counter for the night. The busywork allows her to observe him without being

135

blatant. She likes to watch him eat. Heck, she likes to watch him – *period!* And while she's not looking, Sean enjoys watching her too.

Despite his overfilled belly, he can't resist her *sweet potato pie with a pecan crust,* served with coffee, and company, if that's allowed. She explains that there's cleanup before the others can leave, and Sean correctly surmises that she carries the keys.

With a slow smile, he tells her that pie this good should never be rushed, and Daisy feels a flutter that she may not admit. The day's mess is set right amid giggles and grins, and the staff soon leaves them alone to turn out the lights. Embarrassed, and more than a little bit nervous, Daisy pushes through the kitchen door with a hot cup of tea in her hand.

"So, I gather my compliments should go directly to you," he opens, as she gracefully slides in on the opposite side. "That was the best meal I've eaten in years," he relays most sincerely. Slipping his fingers beneath her right hand, he raises it up until she can feel his warm breath on her fingers, then slowly lifts his eyes to meet hers. "Thank you for sharing your immeasurable talents."

For a moment he rests his soft lips against the back of her hand, sending tingles straight down her spine. For nearly an hour, they sit there, laughing and sharing more easily than either thought possible. Daisy glances up at the clock, and with the sweep of a hand, it's time for Cinderella to leave the ball.

"I've got a little guy waiting for me upstairs, and I'm pretty sure he'd *really* like you, so unless you're planning on staying for life, it's best that we call it a night," she informs him as her heart slowly sinks to the floor. "Let me grab your room key, and you can follow me up."

"My pleasure," rolls out a bit smoother than he had intended, so he draws a deep breath and reels it back in.

As the key slides smoothly into the lock, it seems their evening has drawn to a close, yet long before either is ready. He gently touches her cheek with his fingertips, lingering in hopes of an unspoken answer. When her wanting eyes meet his, he cups her face and draws her lips firmly to his. Their still-hungry mouths nearly devour each other until they're nearly lost in the electricity between them. Daisy can feel him hard against her body, as her inhibitions melt away inside her jeans.

If not for the sound of small footsteps overhead....

"Juvie"

Fast-forwarding through memories now decades past, Elijah crawls along the two-lane in an effort to locate the overgrown driveway. When he finally turns the truck down the narrow lane, he is shocked by the image of his grandmother's windows all blinded with patches of plywood. Of course it was necessary to protect them from the weather, yet it remains stark in the glare of the afternoon sun.

He throws the moving van into park in front of the wide front porch, then shuts down the engine and steps to the ground. With multiple moves to his credit, he has learned to position tools at the back of the truck, and the first order of business will be unleashing his car from the tow trailer. Removing the tire straps, he backs the car onto terra firma, unhitches the trailer and pulls it around to the side of the house.

When his tongue is sticking to the roof of his mouth, Elijah finally to stop for a drink. Grabbing a cold beverage from the bag on the seat, he downs nearly half of it before returning to the back of the trailer for his claw hammer. He is startled to find a visitor blatantly pawing through his belongings. A juvenile delinquent in perfect white boots is busy nosing through his stuff without so much as a second thought. She looks over at him, then casually turns away, as if his presence is irrelevant and doesn't phase her in the least. His first reaction is to laugh at her, or with her, he suspects, for surely she is laughing all the while.

Mounting the rear of the truck, he presses slowly inward at a smooth and steady pace, careful to avoid startling her. Reaching a hand in her direction, she responds quickly and without hesitation. Sometimes the best defense is a good nuzzle, and within moments she's purring loudly in his ear. Ah, but there's work to be done in the daylight, so Sean promises her another time, and grabs the hammer and crowbar from his collection of tools.

The paint is peeling and the porch steps creak loudly, yet the floorboards feel sturdy and welcome his weight. He smiles at the aluminum screen door, nostalgic for teenage summers with so much life ahead. Shaking his head, Sean sets to task, while the cat simply watches his sweat trickle. Her only distraction seems to be the glimmer of light that keeps reflecting off their telescopic lens.

Elijah has fans he never realized, and in all walks of life, and he was quickly identified through airport security.

"A WORLD MORE IN COMMON"

Liz looks up from a pile of expense reports to see Mirabella entering from the elevators. Welcoming the break, Liz greets her with a smile. She likes Mirabella, and admires the effect that she's having on Grant. He's definitely happier since meeting her, and a few of his raw edges appear to have softened.

"Hey, Liz! How's your world today?" Bella asks with a smile.

"Excellent. And you?"

"Growing brighter by the minute, if the truth be told."

"Really? What's your secret?"

"Live in the moment, consider possibilities and walk with intention," Bella answers, succinctly.

Liz leans back in her chair, taken with her precise and unexpected response. So seldom do we actually engage one another beyond polite conversation, that encountering genuine thought can be startling. Lately, Liz has been experiencing this same honesty in all areas of her life, and is finding the results both intriguing and enlightening.

"You know, Bella, you're absolutely right," she concedes, allowing the spirit of the insight to fully absorb.

"Works for me," Bella grins. "Oh, can you let Grant know I'm here? I have a surprise for him."

"He's meeting with the new CFO, and he asked that I not interrupt them. They're scheduled for another half hour," she confirms from his online calendar. "You can leave it for him, or you're welcome to wait here with me if you'd like."

Bella looks down at her watch and then mulls her own schedule before eventually deciding to leave the present with Liz. She removes a tissue-wrapped item from an elegant tote, and slips a delicate finger beneath the sealing tape. Disassembling the faux origami, she uncovers a handsome frame that will certainly complement Grant's office décor.

Disposing of the crumpled paper, Bella blows away dust specks from the matte-finished glass, and admires the image for a moment before handing it over. Lizzie's well-applied blush turns a ghastly shade the moment she lays eyes on the photograph.

"Liz, are you okay? Can I get you some water or something?"

Shaking her head, Liz carefully positions the frame on the desktop, and stares down at the image for several long minutes.

"How do you know this woman?" she asks, careful to avoid interrogating her boss's new girlfriend.

"She's Grant's grandmother," Bella answers, though puzzled with her reaction.

About then, Liz starts laughing, in that hysterical sort of way that can sometimes accompany a severe mental break.

"I'm sorry," she stammers, swiping a finger beneath her lower lid with little regard for the paint or the polish. "I just can't believe I found her like that, or that she found me, I really don't know," she rambles, rather incoherently.

"What are you talking about?" Bella demands, now lost in her disjointed story.

"This woman, Grant's grandmother, came to my rescue one day. She appeared out of nowhere, gave me a present, then simply vanished right into thin air. I really have to thank her. You have no idea," Lizzie insists.

"Perhaps I do," Bella confides, as the two women discover that they have a whole world more in common than Grant.

"CARTWHEELS"

Jonas doesn't like getting up at the crack of friggin' dawn. Instead, he prefers to linger for as long as he possibly can in a lame attempt to shorten up the day. Lizzie tiptoed around for the whole first week trying not to wake him while she got ready for work. He slipped up though, or simply tested the envelope. Lizzie came home early one afternoon and caught him still in his bathrobe, and since then she has laid down the law.

First, she made him responsible for coffee. Although it did require an engineering degree, he soon mastered the programmable feature to favor him loitering in bed. So now, to add insult to injury, she expects him up for breakfast. He's not sure how much longer he can take this. While he hates to let her down, none of this was his idea, and he'd just as soon be lonely in his own house, falling down or not.

Forbidden from smoking inside, he stumbles out into the pre-dawn air for his first precious fix of nicotine. He's not the only one in exile though, and they exchange mutual grunts while shuffling for warmth.

Meanwhile, Lizzie retrieves her magnificent stone and begins rinsing it gently beneath a flow of cool water, as she has every morning since arriving back home. Supporting it with her fingers, she allows the water to splash over its surfaces, and for that brief moment, she can just be Lizzie. And when she's just being Lizzie, both she and the crystal are shining together, and it's become her favorite time of day.

Drawing a good, deep breath, Lizzie inhales every ounce of goodness and light, pats the stone dry, and returns it to the driftwood stand she's fashioned in the living room. Renewed and refreshed, she queues up some blues for their breakfast, clears off the central collection unit *(also known as her kitchen table)* and slides four slices of wheat bread into the toaster.

Jonas shoves his key into the lock *(another thing he hates about living here!)* and pushes his way into the apartment.

"Ready for breakfast, Dad? I fixed oatmeal just the way you like it!" she calls out, hoping to entice him.

Back in his bedroom, Jonas quietly debates crawling back under the covers. She's just so damn happy all the time. In the end, he's not sure what compels him, yet he shuffles back down the hallway, grumbling every step of the way.

He yanks out his chair *(assigned seating around here!)* and settles down begrudgingly to a steamy bowl of banana nut oatmeal, prepared with just a touch of vanilla. In addition to the cereal, his daughter has included toast triangles, orange juice and coffee. So, while he was hoping for something to gripe about, Jonas may actually be feeling just the *slightest* bit better. The food is as good as it looks, but all too soon they're finished and Lizzie is off to work.

After washing up the dishes - *another rule* - he heads outside to grab himself a butt. This lady he's been eyeballing usually leaves about now, and Jonas has taken to being out there to wish her good morning. In fact, she's become the highpoint of his home-alone day. She's got a walk that can only be described as a female John Wayne, and something about it makes him picture her with six-guns. *Ain't takin' nothin' off-a nobody. My kinda gal.*

Cupping his cigarette behind his back, he averts his eyes and bows his head, and opens the door in grand style. She allows him just the hint of a smile, which only serves to tempt him further. So far they haven't gone past *Good Morning*, yet anticipation's growing every day. He watches her walk down the sidewalk then disappear around the corner toward her car, and for the first time in a very long while, Jonas actually smiles.

With one final drag, he grinds out the cigarette and watches her drive out of the lot. And now for the boredom. Back in the apartment, he searches around for some reading material, certain he will at least find a copy of the subscription he purchased for her birthday. He finds them stacked neatly in the cupboard, by month and by year, and chooses the latest edition for his daily constitutional.

145

Just as the process is getting underway, the telephone rings, and he can hear Peggy's voice on the answering machine. Straining in both directions, he gives up listening when the refrigerator kicks on and reduces her message to mere mumbles. She can wait until later; his bowels may not.

It's terrible, but something about that girl's voice just irritates the crap out of him, no pun intended. There's a timid-ness to it that always seems to come off a bit whiny. Of course her skittish, field mouse reactions have little to do with the screaming or breaking of furniture that occurred all around his children on a regular basis. Jonas himself was an only child, and on more than one occasion has wished he'd done the same.

Finishing up the article, he takes care of his business then quickly adjourns to the living room to catch up on Peggy's news. There's a fortitude to her voice that hasn't been there before, and it really knocks him on his cushions when she drops the bomb. His house has been rented.

Jonas is furious! Snatching up his jacket and stomps out the door, slamming it loudly behind him. *The <u>NERVE</u> of them! Renting it out from under me! Who do they think they are?! I bet that Warren is behind this! Or Vincent! Peggy sure doesn't have the gonads for this one!* The mental rant continues as he chain smokes, inhaling several cigarettes before his breathing finally slows or perhaps is impaired.

Just as he is about to go back inside and find someone to suffer his wrath, he notices "The Duchess" (feminine for "The Duke") is pulling into the parking lot. He'd always assumed that she left for the day, and the surprise of seeing her shifts him abruptly. She's juggling an armload of groceries, so he quickly steps to her rescue before her eggs get scrambled.

Ultimately, she agrees under protest, and allows him to carry several bags to her apartment. Jonas is searching for witty conversation, yet in lieu of something truly clever, he goes with his best version of charming. She invites him in for coffee, as it's still before noon, and he flips a mental cartwheel on his way through the door. He can't remember the last time he looked more than twice at anybody, much less had anyone look back.

Somehow conversation takes them well through lunch, and by the time Lizzie gets home, Jonas has all but forgotten his earlier tirade. Of course, he musters a fair dose of indignation when relaying the details, yet is nowhere near as invested as he was this morning. The thrill of meeting Beverly has him wholly consumed, and Lizzie sees right through his attempts to be casual. Smiling at her favorite curmudgeon, she spies an unmistakable glow from the far end of the room.

"INTERFERENCE"

"Roy! Wake up! Something's happening!" shouts Dan.

"What's goin' on?" Roy snaps to attention, bolting upright in his chair.

"Look! They're all running out of the house! Even the dog! What the hell is going on over there?" Dan demands.

"The barn cam's useless in that direction! Let's see if we can catch it from the tree," Roy suggests, struggling to readjust the camera angle. "Damn! I told 'em we should've installed full sweep!" he complains. "There's not enough swing! I can't get it around!"

"Adjust the audio! What's with all the interference?" he barks.

"Sorry sir, nothing's happening. Even the friggin' birds are freaking out!" exclaims Roy, pointing to the screen.

"That's it. It's full-on surveillance tonight," Dan commands, while Roy rolls his eyes at the thought of spending another night lying in that meadow.

"TALKING TO STRANGERS"

Roy never heard Joe holler to Aurora, who ran and woke Loretta from her afternoon nap. Joe was changing the oil in Henry's old pickup when he first saw the bright colors appear through the trees. It's not a sight one sees every day, and considering their recent invasion, he will be taking no chances. Gold Dog is first by his side, and they're soon joined by the women, who are not far behind.

The ladies arrive seconds before the canopy collapses, and Aurora is immediately intrigued. Recent events aside, that's a whole lot of color for a covert operation, so she advances with minimal fear. Joe, however, intends to take nothing for granted, and approaches square-shouldered with steel in his eyes.

The stranger appears to be looking for something, and is getting more frantic by the moment. Desperately searching, he barely registers their presence until they're nearly on top of him. He looks up to find a small group of people and one very concerned dog quickly closing the gap. *Where the hell is it? I saw it fall. It's gotta be around here somewhere,* he reasons, hoping to locate it before he's forced to explain.

Of course, that's not how things were meant to unfold. Instead, Joe storms toward him with the ominous threat of a grizzly, and he realizes that now is the perfect time to pour on some charm.

"You are one lucky man, my friend, waking up to this kind of beauty every morning!" he offers, extending with his hand along with an enormous smile. "I hope you'll forgive me for dropping in like this. Life's full of surprises, you know?"

"Yes, I do," Joe agrees, and grasps the hand firmly despite his uncertainty.

Gold Dog keeps his hackles up, but feels no need for growling or barking. Sniffing at the airborne stranger, he detects a new yet now familiar smell that puts him instantly at ease. Joe observes the dog's response, and chooses to more or less join him, at least for the time being. Loretta invites him for a glass of sweet tea, and Sean knows all too well that it's only good manners to accept. So he gathers his chute in a bundle, and reluctantly abandons his search.

It was clear to everyone that he was hunting for something, and they can sense his discomfort at leaving the meadow. Yet suspicion is high, and with recent experiences still fresh in their minds, no stranger will be left unattended.

Depositing his parachute on the front porch, he sheds the harness and other equipment while fielding their questions on gliding and flight. With one final glance toward the tall grass, Sean draws a deep breath and steps over the threshold.

Tea and introductions are a winning combination, and with all her sweet demeanor, Loretta is first to address the elephant cluttering up her kitchen.

"So, what exactly were you looking for out there?"

"It's pretty silly, really. And my chances of finding it are probably slim to none," he resigns with a sigh. "But it was a gift from my sister, and it means a lot to me."

"Well perhaps we can help," Aurora volunteers. "We still have plenty of daylight. What are we looking for?"

"It's a stone," he begins, yet before he has a chance to describe it, Loretta interrupts.

"Tell me about your sister."

Bewildered, Sean proceeds as instructed, describing his sister as best he can. Joe has his eye on Loretta, and is perplexed by the emotions unfolding in her eyes. At first it appeared like a warm recognition before slowly progressing toward trepidation, then fear.

"Loretta?" Joe inquires, voicing his concern. The room falls silent as all faces turn toward hers.

"Is your sister's name Carlie?" Loretta inquires.

"How did you know that?" he asks, completely dumbstruck.

Shifting her sights toward Aurora and Joe, Loretta states clearly and in the calmest voice possible, "We have us a stone that needs to come home, and I suggest we all get busy and find it."

"BRIDGES AND TUNNELS"

It's late in the day by the time Levi arrives into town, sporting a shiny, new pickup. Cadence insisted on replacing the death mobile. She's an amazing lady, and they really got close in the weeks that it took him to finish her barns. By the time he left yesterday, they were talking and laughing like the lifelong friends they had truly become. Neither could have imagined how much a farm boy and an heiress would find in common, yet he said goodnight with a lump in his throat and she turned away hiding her tears.

Adventure, however, has a way of salving young wounds, and Levi is soon swept up with the thrill of the ride. He loves the bridges and the tunnels, the valleys and the peaks. The city traffic makes his heart race before he discovers the rush of white-knuckled driving. Before long he's weaving through traffic like a NASCAR driver enjoying the time of his life. All the while the stone is riding shotgun on the dashboard, glowing fluorescent for all the world to see.

Cruising past the pizza parlor, he scopes the parking lot for Jillian's car, and grins when he spots it over by the dumpster. A few miles up the road is the motel where he camped out the last time, and he checks in with the hope of staying there until he finds an apartment. Of course the owners, Mr.

Danielson and his wife Linda, remember him well, and he is treated to their very best room.

Tossing his duffle bags onto the bed, he strikes out for ChinaMart to pick up some supplies. Jillian will be working for the next several hours, and she has no idea he's back in town. To be honest, they haven't spoken since he left, yet there's barely been a moment she's been out of his thoughts. Something about her just sucked him in, and since crossing the state line, he's been helpless to wipe off the grin.

The Greeter at the storefront offers him a cart, which he gladly accepts upon entering. Touring aisle after aisle can be mind-numbing, and Levi is practically in a trance by the time he finds the shampoo. His demeanor shifts completely, however, when he spots her standing in the aisle by the pain relievers.

He practically leaps the span between them and manages to startle a shriek out of her before she finally finds her smile. Her eyes are warm and welcoming as he throws his arms around her and lifts her nearly off her feet. With a heartfelt grin, she pulls him close, and time simply falls away.

"You're all coming home now, aren't you?" Loretta croons into his chest.

"POWER AND MOMENTUM"

While Elijah was first to be identified, Cadence Merriweather was not far behind. However, surveillance on old money rich can be easier said than done. Acres of private property separate her from the road, and it appears her small staff is both closed-mouthed and loyal. Ted's attempts to goad the handyman into some gossip were met only with silence and a cold, flat stare. And when Jeannine tried to pump Maggie at the supermarket, she too was promptly rebuffed.

Unfortunately, the season has ended for lawn care, so they move on to meter reading as their best bet for gaining access. While now handled remotely, the devices are still limited by distance and do require a clear view of the meter. The plan will provide for vehicular access and a possible drop-off, if the situation allows.

Within hours, they've obtained the uniforms, equipment and the clearances necessary to execute their assignment. It's amazing how fast things get accomplished when you have enough power and momentum. By mid-morning the following day, they begin the operation. With Jeannine in the driver's seat, Ted is lying in the truck bed, covertly tucked beneath a tarp.

After treating him a few potholes, she enters through the huge iron gate, that's stood open to guests for over a hundred years. The wide, paved lane is lined with enormous old trees, and stretches nearly half a mile before the house finally comes into view. Satellite images have determined that Jeannine will need to exit the vehicle to access the meter, which provides a convenient distraction for potential onlookers.

Guiding the pickup toward the right of the circular drive, she intentionally parks beside some convenient shrubbery. Ted slithers over the bed rail and into the brush, then scrambles across the front of the house to the side door. Jeannine has a view straight into the kitchen and nods that the coast is clear. Within seconds he disengages the simple knob lock and breaches Merriweather Hall for the first time in history.

"REVERENCE"

Rosalie looks over at Justin mapping crayon schematics on the living room floor, and wonders exactly what happened while her son was away. The difference is indescribable and all-encompassing. He hasn't cried once since the accident, and he seems to understand things on a whole different level. It's like her above average boy just leapt into an intellectual stratosphere she can barely conceive.

And his eyes have changed. Not really the color, but the depth, and his entire perspective is just broader. The doctors checked for all sorts of things before he left the hospital, yet she suspects there may be no diagnosis for his particular condition. They explained that brain trauma can cause a shift in personality, although that hardly seems an accurate description for such a complete transformation.

The *sensation* around Justin keeps drawing a crowd, and now Rosalie hesitates to even take him out for groceries. His newfound wisdom seems to inspire true reverence, yet there's a danger in being chosen, and as his mother, she will protect him with her life.

"FETCHING CADY"

With the arrival of Levi, Loretta calls a meeting with Aurora and Joe to discuss what to do about the stones. Although they went to great lengths to separate them, it appears they're all finding their way home, thanks, among other things, to the scent of cosmic dust.

To the surveillance team, Sean is still a complete John Doe, unless and until they make a connection with Carlie. Their resemblance is more in spirit than feature, so the airport footage won't prove much of a lead. He certainly has their curiosity piqued, as they all work feverishly to pinpoint the stones. Sources speak of an incredible power, and of those who'd pay dearly for gaining control. A few know a little, and far fewer know more, yet their resources are infinite as a means to their end.

Inside Loretta's house, the bedroom détente is wrestling issues of their own. While their initial effort may have been misdirected, born as it was out of fear, the question remains of what to do now. Safety is clearly a factor and Aurora is also curious about what the others have been experiencing. With little debate, they decide on full disclosure, and agree that sooner will be better than later.

Wandering around outside, Levi and Sean discover a camera mounted up in a tree that's pointing directly toward the kitchen. They're in the process of searching for others when Aurora and Joe come to find them. Joe immediately halts the conversation, and silently motions them back to the house. He suspects they've come equipped with audio, so phone taps must now be a foregone conclusion.

"I say we take a bat to it," Levi pipes up, "and any others we come across!"

"Well, I guess we know they're serious," Joe reasons. "Whoever 'They' are."

"Those are some expensive toys they're playing with," observes Sean. "Not your typical Japan-City markdown."

"So, we're talking serious initiative and serious money," Aurora summarizes, turning toward Levi. "And a bat is a bat, and war is war, and I think we're better off playing our own game than challenging them at theirs."

"What do you mean?" Loretta asks, speaking for everyone.

"Well, we're the ones with the stones," she reminds them. "Granted, they arrived without instructions, but there were no extra parts either. I think we've got everything we need to figure this thing out."

"Unless we need the other stones," Loretta speculates.

That rolls into an entirely new conversation that quickly reveals Levi's connection with Cadence. Concern begins to show on Loretta's face as he describes Cady's circumstance and situation. Her safety is a serious issue, particularly in light of her condition. She is vulnerable and in danger, and first thing tomorrow, Levi and Joe will be heading back north.

"Knowns and Unknowns"

"Okay, let's begin with a recap of what we have, and then take it from there," directs Commander Reardon to the table of onlookers. "Nine stones were identified following the official investigation. Surveillance of the primary subject revealed what appeared to be a transfer to at least seven random strangers. We now have a potential lock on three, and possibly four of the recipients, that leaves a minimum of five stones unaccounted for. What've you got for me, Lou?"

"Well, Sir, we've come up with two other names, a Mrs. Carlie West and a Mrs. Lorna Sinclair. Mrs. West was recently married and manages a corner coffee shop, while Mrs. Sinclair is the widow of retired Colonel Eric Sinclair of the United States Marines."

"Very good. Now that we have their identities, have we begun surveillance?" Reardon asks, turning to the next member of his team. "Mitch?"

"We've been collecting data on Mrs. West from both her home and business, yet have found absolutely no indication that she's in possession of a stone," he relays somewhat nervously.

"What?! How can that be? She was clearly identified from the airport footage!" rants Reardon. "Okay. Let's keep looking. Riley, you start checking into her background. Let's look at her

161

friends, relatives, staff, anyone she may have been in contact with over the last several months, particularly since the sighting. Alright, Zach, tell me about Mrs. Sinclair."

"Well, aside from being the widow of a decorated veteran, she's basically a homemaker, mother and grandmother. From the airport, she was en route to visit her daughter and grandson, who were recently involved in a head-on collision. While the boy remained in a coma for several weeks, both have now been released from the hospital, and Lorna, Mrs. Sinclair, is presently in residence, presumably to assist with their recovery," Zachary states, closing his notebook.

"Excellent. Keep a respectful distance, but keep an eye on them and let me know what develops. And Mitchell," he says, directing his attention back to Mitch, *"That* was a report. I'll expect full details from you at our next session," he instructs before returning to the group. "Now, let's move on to our *knowns.* Jeannine, Ted, what can you tell me about Cadence Merriweather?"

"Well, we'll need to keep this from the tabloids, but Miss Merriweather appears to be pregnant. And while listening devices were installed immediately, it appears we just missed a visitor who had been enjoying an extended stay at Merriweather Hall. Sources reveal that the young man was hired to paint her barns, yet witnesses state they were seen off-road the other day in what some may regard as a compromising position. He was seen driving south out of town just days ago in a brand new pickup, paid for by Miss Merriweather," Jeannine informs the table before shifting the attention toward her partner. Ted proceeds to outline the array of technical devices that have now been installed throughout the residence of America's wealthiest heiresses.

"Let me make this perfectly clear," Reardon states, standing for further emphasis. "All matters concerning Miss Merriweather <u>must</u> be handled with the utmost discretion. If I find that one word has been leaked to the press, you won't need to find another line of work," he informs them, looking from one face to the next before settling again on Jeannine. "I'll be following your reports very closely. I want to be notified *in advance* before *any* further initiatives. Let's just keep an ear to the conversation and make sure we stay well below the radar. Alright then."

Finally, the Commander focuses on the last two individuals seated at the table. "Lloyd, Stanley, what can you tell me?"

"COMPADRES"

Hot water may well be man's best invention, Elijah reasons as it spills over his body and washes off two full days of sweat and grime. A phone call ensured that the power was on when he got here so he could at least take a shower ... that was until the well pump up and took a $500 dirt nap on the very first day! Parker's showed up today to install the replacement only seconds before Juvie was driven off by his smell.

Human again, he sprawls out on the couch with a sandwich, chips and a cold one, clicks on the television and settles back for an all-American TV dinner. A loud knock sounds at the door just as he's reaching for his pickle, and with a groan, he gets up to answer the door.

He can scarcely believe who's standing on the other side. Squinting in the glow of the porch light stands his teenage compadre, and he's quite possibly wearing the same black t-shirt. Lloyd was always a dangerous blend, and just a hair wilder than Elijah ever dared.

"You're still alive!" Elijah exclaims, riding the line between joking and not. Pushing open the screen door, he invites him inside.

"Yeah, I thought I saw a light on over here the other night, and figured I'd stop by an' take a look," Lloyd shares. "Been a long time! I heard about you, all famous and everything!"

164

"Yeah, well, it's been a wild ride so far. How 'bout you? What're you up to?"

"Ah well, I went into machinin' after high school, but I been outta work for a while now. Ol' lady's got a good job at the factory, though, second shift. So, it ain't great, but it's all right, ya know? Hell, I didn't come over here to bitch! How's about a beer and a little backroad tour for ol' times sake? What d'ya say?"

"Great! Jus' let me grab a clean shirt. I'll be right back," Elijah tells him, in lieu of the absolute truth. To be honest, this isn't exactly his scene anymore, yet with a few graphic words, Lloyd has painted a fairly vivid picture of his reality. Looks like he's gained a few scars along the way, and picked up a forearm tattoo, yet the twinkle remains exactly the same, and Elijah can clearly see yesterday alive in his eyes.

Danger always hung in the air when Lloyd came around. He likes tipping the scale between adventure and death, which makes Elijah decide to leave the stone in his dresser. Tromping down the staircase, he can hear the old boards complaining under pressure, howling like his head come tomorrow. He never has been much of a drinker. His west coast friends used to tease him that he had a three beer limit: drink one, spill one and give one away. But it's a whole different world back here, and a person can only go forward.

165

Lloyd's already waiting in the driver's seat, caressing the steering wheel of his tricked-out 440. Hosting no illusions, Elijah climbs into the cab and straps himself in. Lloyd just laughs and hands him a beer. Within minutes they're weaving through a mountainous maze of back roads, tipping back brewskis and talking glory days.

The beer seems to be going straight to Lloyd's right foot, and Elijah can hardly take his eyes off the speedometer as it climbs straight on up to scary. He's relieved when police lights appear in the rearview, yet makes a point of cursing them as he corrals the empties and gets ready for the bust.

His stomach pays a visit to his throat when old Lloyd just laughs and presses the accelerator. There's no question Elijah stopped breathing for a moment, until his beer-addled brain finally sent out the signal. Of course adrenaline has a sobering effect, and he's feeling every bit of his fear when Lloyd corners up on two wheels. The undercover car with the flashing blue bubble chases them through several intersections, yet it's the airborne maneuver that really leaves them in the dust. They nearly take out some poor electrical worker before dodging into a cornfield off the side of the road. Lloyd is hooting and hollering as he shuts down the Hemi and cracks open a couple of fresh ones.

"Here's to kickin' ass! Whatever it takes, man! Whatever it takes!"

Elijah is enormously grateful, mostly for being alive, and offers a salute from the passenger seat by upending one bright green glass bottle.

"ONE HECK OF A SALES TACTIC"

They approach with their backs to the sun just as Harry, Grant's doorman, is hailing down a taxi for Mrs. Leifkowicz. Something about them screams *"security,"* yet a little too clipped, a little too pressed, and a little to creepy for comfort. Studying their reflection through the window of the cab, Harry could swear he noticed a camera flash as they passed the lobby entrance. Yet by the time Mrs. L. is tucked neatly away, both men have blended into the late-morning foot traffic.

Nancy arrives at the lunch counter by 11:05 to ensure that she's back by noon on the dot. She's hoping for a full-time position, and promptness as a receptionist can only move that along. Chad and Neil merge fairly well with the corporate crowd, at least to the untrained eye, and Nancy barely notices them as she jockeys for position at the counter. Chad, however, is bent on manipulating the young woman, and uses a bit of male posturing to gain her attention.

He's clean and he's confident and he's looking right at *her,* and Nancy so craves validation, that she requires little else. Within minutes, she's squirming like a worm under a magnifying glass, and all for the price of a smile. *This will be easy,* he gloats smugly, and the wink only heightens her blush to a rosier shade.

168

Flustered by the attention, Nancy requests her food *To Go,* and retreats to the safety of her automobile.

Chad nudges Neil beneath the table, and Neil nods his agreement as the door closes behind her. The two consume a leisurely lunch, confident they found their mark, and pleased they nailed the setup. Nancy, on the other hand, spends the next forty minutes consternating every aspect of her behavior, until digestion is clearly disrupted. The antacids are locked up back at her desk, so she's only too happy to return a little early.

As receptionist, she assumes all the phones through the lunch hour, in addition to screening the visitors, and her rotating stand-ins are always grateful to escape before the mid-day rush. Plugging in the headset, she listens through the voicemails, jotting down messages accordingly, then rolls across to check out her email. The door alarm sounds at twenty after announcing the arrival of a visitor, and Nancy is decidedly taken aback when they enter. Her heart stutters for a second when Neil and Chad come strolling across the lobby headed straight for her station.

Despite her over-zealous greeting, the smooth-talking gentlemen never miss an opportunity to flatter. Their company is premiering the cutting-edge in payroll software, and Chad wants to leave some promotional material for Mr. Fontaine. As a personal favor, Nancy offers to see if

Grant's assistant is available, which could provide them a definitive edge.

Liz is playing noon hour catch-up when the phone rings in on her personal line. With an exasperated sigh, she realizes that Nancy has put her on the spot for a couple of salesman, and they're not even on the vendor list. Yet professional is as professional does, so she'll deal with the receptionist later. For now, she'll see them, as long as they're brief.

That's one heck of a sales tactic, stealing a person's lunch hour, she grumbles waiting for the elevator. What Nancy saw as charming appears nothing short of smarmy to Liz, so she accepts the pen set with a lukewarm smile and a promise to pass it along. When they go so far as demonstrating the pen, she herds them back into the elevator, and sends them on their way. Liz questions their career choice as the two exchange a satisfied grin, exceedingly pleased with their lackluster performance. *Grant will love hearing about these jamokes,* she chuckles to herself.

He went home at noon today to fix lunch for Mirabella, and had an interesting encounter with Harry the Doorman along with a disturbing message from Joe.

"Chivalry"

After reassuring her grandson, Loretta hands the phone back to Joe, who provides him with an update on events at the farm. Since Grant's departure, Sean dropped in from the afternoon sky, Levi found Loretta at ChinaMart and they rescued an heiress from an uncertain fate. Of course, all of this was completed under the watchful eye of cameras, black-op intruders and the vehicular surveillance that followed them home.

Grant grows silent on the other end, and then informs Joe he'll be down there tomorrow. Ending the conversation, Loretta hangs the receiver back up on the wall, feeling more than a little distraught over how thing are unfolding. Aurora places an arm around her shoulder as the Rock of Gibraltar sways just a bit, and tears well up in her eyes.

"I'm so sorry… How could I have gotten all of you into this?" spills out from her heart to her lips.

Aurora begins laughing right out loud. Shocked at her callousness, the others grow instantly defensive, and the air in the room becomes charged.

"Loretta, dear Loretta," says Rori, taking ahold of her hand, "First you gifted us with the most incredible stones to ever enter this world, and now you've opened your home to a houseful of

171

strangers.   For all we know, this is divine intervention, and you know what? It's the most exciting thing that's ever happened to me. We're all a part of something. I don't know what it is, but I know we're all in it together. Don't you feel it?" she asks, looking around the room. "And you, dear lady, have absolutely nothing to apologize for," she informs Loretta, who is standing there with tears still in her eyes.

As she continues to talk, hearts around the room begin to join forces, forge bonds, and connect from a place rarely exposed to the light. The shift is deep and palpable, and is felt by everyone. The glow is now clearly visible around the edges of the window shades, and Roy curses the black dog for foiling his earlier efforts. He'd have taken the stones that first night, if not for the interruption. Now he's armed with doggie tranqs and blessings from the powers that be, and if the opportunity presents itself again, you can bet he won't hesitate.

Commander Reardon himself will be visiting tomorrow to update their instructions and observe the operation firsthand. Dan worries they may be replaced for not breaching the farmhouse. Roy, on the other hand, is clearly resenting the fact that he's stuck tracking the whereabouts of five people, while the other teams are two to one in the other direction. For some reason, Dan doesn't see Roy advancing, and for the same reason, Roy sleeps far better than Dan.

Levi is bored and picks up Henry's newspaper, which still arrives every day. Loretta and Sean are finishing up the lunch dishes while Levi reads the comic strips aloud, describing each panel between chuckles and yucks. His silence comes too soon for his audience, until his sudden exclamation gives them all a start.

"Hey! I've heard of this guy!" Levi exclaims.

"Oh yeah? Who's that?" Sean inquires from the kitchen.

"He was playing back home not long ago. Sax player. Had him all over the radio. Name's Elijah," is all he gets out before the glass slips from Loretta's hand and smashes against the sink.

"Who's Elijah?" Joe asks, with a knowing smile as he calmly sweeps up the broken glass.

Loretta, of course, confirms his suspicion, and begins describing the circumstance around Elijah and his stone. Though drawn by his saxophone, she was completely hooked by Elijah's playful spirit. He smiled a lot and spoke to lots of people, and that made them smile too. It was as simple as that.

"He'll make a great house guest," Loretta grins, as Aurora and Cady head off with clean sheets.

"MISCHIEVOUS SPARKS"

"Oh, hey Grant, Bella," Lizzie calls out from her desk as they step from the elevator. "You should have seen these clowns," she begins, yet stops cold once she eyes his expression. "Grant? Is everything alright?"

"Liz, I need to speak with you. Will you step into my office, please?" he asks, while Bella stands pensively aside.

"Certainly," tumbles from her lips, and she clutches the promotional pen just a little bit tighter.

Closing the office door, he invites both women to sit, then positions his chair opposite Liz. Just about the time she's fixin' to get fired, Grant finally dishes up the dirt - or rocks as the case may be. Beyond keeping her job, the rest of the story borders on surreal, yet the exhilaration is undeniable as her mind jumps into hyper-drive. She and Bella are in perfect alignment, and quickly develop a plan, while Grant drafts the paperwork for two emergency leaves and prepares for the fallout from Marsbeck.

Liz sets about clearing their calendars and addressing whatever priorities she can before going home to pack. She makes a point of printing out Grant's entire address book, and slips it into her purse, along with a secret listening device that is masquerading as one sexy new pen.

Having eavesdropped on the planning session, Neil and Chad are ecstatic, and immediately report back to Reardon that, in essence, they'll breach the farmhouse by morning.

Liz stops by to tell Nancy that she's forwarded their phones, and that neither of them will be in the office for days. That should put the old rumor mill into full gear. As an afterthought, she decides to gift Nancy with that sexy promo pen, in hopes of influencing her later conversations.

Jonas and Beverly are playing cards in the kitchen when Lizzie startles them by arriving home early. He's still on his best behavior, so the subtle breath of sarcasm is barely discernable, yet disappears completely when he glimpses her expression.

"What's up, Number One?"

"Not sure, Dad, but I know there's a whole lot more going on than any of us realized," Lizzie confides. "How are you with cloak and dagger?" she asks, focusing her attention on Beverly.

The Duchess seals their alliance with a wry smile and a mischievous spark that dances like lightening in the depths of her eyes. Lizzie does her best to explain the situation, and that nothing whatsoever is business as usual. For their own protection, they will stay at Grant's apartment until she can contact them with news. He has a doorman and security, yet they are ultimately convinced by the big screen and hot tub.

175

On the way over to her boss's apartment, they stop by a Quick Chick to share their last meal. James Bond aside, Jonas is worried about his baby, and pulls her aside for some fatherly advice. He clears his throat to disguise the slight tremor, and then draws her in close to look straight in her eyes.

"Lizzie, you're a Breslen. I can't speak for your mother's side, but we Breslens are thinkers. We've been thinking our way out of things, around things and through things since the beginning of time. And you, my daughter, are a Breslen," he tells her, this time coughing to conceal his emotion. Lizzie lays her head on his chest, and he holds her tight and kisses her hair before finally returning to Beverly and their three steaming plates.

They arrive at Grant's by six thirty on the dot, as agreed, and he shows them the highpoints and lays out his rules. After introducing them to security, he eventually turns over the keys. Seems Jonas has a few concerns of his own regarding the care of his daughter, and despite the adrenaline crackling around them, both men acknowledge the danger and that they're on the same page. So, with parting hugs and handshakes, they pile into Grant's car and are heading down the road by six forty-seven.

Jonas sniffs a little in the evening air and remains just a half-step ahead, and Beverly raises a hand to his back in an effort to ease the goodbye. They enter the building under a cloud of uncertainty, with Jonas especially, feeling fairly grave. However, on reaching the apartment, both Jonas and the Duchess share an illicit grin, and head straight for the hot tub and a taste of posh living.

"MIRACLE" AT STUFFOLKS MALL

by Brogan Cantrell

An unexplained power surge on Wednesday triggered the alarm system at Stuffolks Mall, causing frightened infants burst into tears from one end of the complex to the other. Witnesses report that the entire mall fell silent, however, at the prompting of one small boy.

Linda Wiley of Buttons & Bibs described her experience. "I was checking out customers as fast as I could when the alarms finally shut down, and all you could hear were babies screaming to high heaven!"

"He was standing right over there," said Joyce Rogers, pointing to the second floor railing adjacent to her *Shadows* art gallery. "Couldn't have been more than four or five years old. Just opened his little mouth and filled this place with the most incredible sound," Rogers recalled wistfully.

Both patrons and business owners confirmed that with just a few notes, the boy managed to silence the entire building and literally "tranquilized" all within earshot.

Stuffolks Mall management has agreed to provide us with security footage, as a curious community seeks to locate our very own "Miracle Boy." We will keep you advised with exclusive details.

PART III

"POWER IS AS POWER DOES"

PART III
"POWER IS AS POWER DOES"

"THE TRIAD"

The exquisitely carved balcony overlooks a sweeping valley, nestled along the far edge of the bay. Madeleine inhales the fresh scent of dawn, yet her thoughts remain shrouded beneath a layer of fog. Allowing the heavy drapes to fall back across the window, she contemplates the summit that is now just an hour away.

A rap sounds at the door with her breakfast, and a crisply uniformed woman enters with an elegant cart that's been stunningly arranged. With permission, she pulls open the elaborate draperies, one layer at a time until finally arriving at the innermost stratum, a highly intricate lace of an unusual pattern. Hand-made, for pennies on the dollar, Madeleine suspects.

Wilhelm is presently enjoying the bite of morning grapefruit, along with the discipline of Earl Grey, no sugar, no cream. He once fired a servant for mucking up his tea, and they've since had no difficulty maintaining his standards. At best he's deemed fair, sometimes bordering on generous, yet none of his subordinates would dare mistake him for a friend.

Upon finishing the meal, he dons his running gear and descends the western staircase toward the music room. At one time the great hall had hosted lively ensembles, yet with dwindling lineage, it's been years between guests. Thrusting his bones

181

into the morning chill, Wilhelm steels himself for the challenge that awaits him post-run.

Emanuel is first to arrive in the *Golden Room*, so named for the gold leaf accents that adorn so much of the trim work. A crown molding of graceful leaves and tendrils is mahogany carved in relief, and brought further to life with a generous application of the coveted mineral. The overall effect is both stunning and decadent, although less so to those most accustomed to opulence. Through a series of nods, Emanuel guides the server in preparing his fruit plate, while enjoying the taste of Blue Mountain coffee, grown half way around the world.

Several blessings later, he sinks his teeth into an enormous strawberry that is so succulent, the sweet juices spill down his chin and emblazon his white cotton with a crimson stain. He chastises the smirk with a menacing glare, and claps his hands loudly while demanding assistance. Servants quickly appear from every direction to clean and redress him before the others arrive. He can hear Madeleine and Wilhelm in the main hall just as he's being reseated, and quickly shoos all the urchins back into their corners.

Wilhelm strolls in with Madeleine at his elbow, always the gentleman, unless and until. Beyond the poise, her eyes are calculating, and she walks in full awareness of her position at the table. Emanuel rises to greet her, as tactically planned, and draws her in close for a buss on both cheeks. As they assume their places, they're immediately embraced by a squadron of servants, who are intent on providing every bit of graciousness that grandeur will allow. Once seated and settled, pampered and plumped, all that remains is their pointed conversation.

Speaking on behalf of the World Trade Organization, Madeleine was selected both for her integrity and her ability to negotiate, as well as her feminine perspective. Wilhelm was carefully chosen as well, to represent the interests of world government. Retired from the Swiss Federal Council, in the days of staunch neutrality, he is known for his clarity along with his decisiveness. Emanuel is here representing the Church, of course, as keepers of the sacred prophecy.

"I'd like to begin at the beginning," states Emanuel, anxious to get things underway. "An ancient, yet ill-regarded prophet recorded the following prediction:

>*'Hailing in a ball of fire,*
>*It will rain down in the*
>*spirit of man,*
>*And all of humanity will*
>*Divinely realign.'*

Madeleine and Wilhelm exchange a questioning glance, to which Emanuel offers the most disturbing response.

"Prophecies the world over all reference destruction of biblical proportions, and we have reason to believe that the countdown has begun. On 17 August, astronomers notified us of the sighting, and a team was immediately dispatched. While a meteor had indeed landed, it appeared to have disintegrated completely on impact. The search team scoured the debris field for days, only to return suspiciously empty-handed."

At this point, both Madeleine and Wilhelm are maintaining a safe layer of skepticism. Neither is leaping to any conclusions, and Wilhelm, in particular, is already questioning.

"All due respect, Emanuel, but why should we be concerned with this – how did you put it? – ill-regarded prophecy? It sounds like little more than coincidence to me," he declares, with growing agitation. "May I ask why we've been summoned?"

"Please make no mistake," Emanuel counters firmly, "we had reason to believe that evidence was being withheld. A second, more covert inspection, revealed the existence of nine strange crystals that appear to be demonstrating some rather unearthly properties. So while a certain level of faith is required here, it would be criminal to dismiss this event as coincidence, only to discover we were grievously wrong."

"I think the least we can do is recover the stones," suggests Madeleine, glancing from one to the other.

Unconvinced, it is the least and most he is willing to do, so Wilhelm nods his head, and agrees to take care of the necessary arrangements.

"ONTARIO"

Despite years of quiet dusting, Loretta's formal dining room quickly springs back to life as *Information Central* for her growing entourage. Aurora appears to have been anointed their de-facto leader, chosen as she was by the crows, yet the house population has shifted significantly, and a variety of perspectives are now rising to the surface.

Assuming head position opposite Loretta, Rori places her stone on the table and waits as the others follow suit. With four new arrivals, there's plenty to discuss, and she's excited to hear all about their observations. Grant shifts uncomfortably in the middle chair, annoyed over the usurped authority to his grandfather's seat. Loretta casts a sharp glance that keeps him quiet, yet the tension is palpable as resentment clutches at the back of his neck.

"Grant? Are you okay?" Aurora asks.

"That was my grandfather's chair," he practically snarls.

"Oh, I'm sorry," Rori concedes. "I've just been so caught up in the moment. Please, let's change seats. I won't feel right," she declares, collecting her belongings as Gold Dog clambers out from under the table.

"If you insist," he replies from behind moistening eyes.

While the exchange is somewhat awkward, the entire room can feel the shift. Just about the time their shoulders relax and Lizzie's stomach unclenches, several of the stones begin fluttering to life.

"Well, I'm glad we got that out of the way," Rori laughs, as two more begin to flicker.

Bella is first to offer up her story, as much to keep things moving as to get it out of the way. As a Licensed Massage Therapist, energy work is a standard part of her practice, and the stone has amplified the work for amazing results. She recounts how in just a few sessions, one client managed to avoid a permanent wheelchair. Numerous mouths are standing agape and the tissue box is circling the room by the time she finishes her account. Mirabella's stone glows so much of the time, her clients just assume it has batteries.

"Mine glows when I wash it," Lizzie throws out there, scanning the room.

"I've found that too," seconds Aurora, as both of their stones glow a shade or two brighter. The remainder of the group admits that they hadn't thought to wash them.

Cadence shares the story of her continuing transformation, and of her commitment to raising a healthier generation. Levi shares a few tales about the fair lady Merriweather that would tarnish her dear mother's brass, and seems to carry the chiding one titter too far. Recovering the true essence of Cadence, he paints an eloquent portrait of a great woman and her barns. Well, by then it's hard to

187

know which is shining brighter, the guy, the girl or the stones that brought them together.

"I think they've got it exactly right," agrees Loretta, from behind a knowing grin. "It glows when your heart feels good!"

Heads are nodding around the table when all eyes come to rest on Sean. Last to report his findings, he begins, of course, with Carlie, who had it glowing all the time. His less frequent encounters have revolved around creating, and they seem to resonate most when he's working on something. Waxing on about seduction and the moment of truth, he catches himself, yet not before certain members of the household have been swept up as well.

Soon the ladies are swooning with his seductive descriptions, yet only one reaction is of particular concern. Witnessing the exchange, Grant's insecurities begin to ferment, and soon he's seething in the differences between him and Sean. His emotions finally escalate into an angry attack, and one by one the stones grow dark and then the air gets deathly still.

All at once, the house goes black, and a web of terror straps them to their seats. High above the darkened room, where tempers continue to flare, menacing clouds vie dangerously … and a freak tornado kills six in Ontario.

"GOOSEFLESH"

"What the hell is going on over there?" Dan barks into the mouthpiece.

"The power went out," is Chad's obvious answer.

"I caught that," Dan counters sarcastically. "What caused it? They're the only ones out on the line."

"Holy crap!" blurts Neil, rolling from his belly to his back.

As newbies on the crew, the two have been assigned level one field surveillance, which translates into lying on their bellies throughout the night and observing the farmhouse from the trees. They're thrilled with the opportunity to be on the front lines, and Roy is tickled pink to be manning the receivers, out of the muck and away from that damn dog.

"What, already?!" Dan demands.

"The sky, Sir! The sky over the house is swirling! I've never seen anything like it! It's like an inverted funnel cloud! A tornado in reverse! Sir, you gotta see this thing!" Neil shouts, as he captures the image and transmits.

Within seconds, the pixels take shape before Dan's eyes and the gooseflesh rises up on his skin. He speaks clearly, yet in monotone, and avoids showing Roy the fear in his eyes.

"Get a hold of Reardon. NOW."

"DO YOURSELF PROUD"

Gold Dog begins barking the moment the lights go out, and all ears are trained on him as he swiftly crosses the room and stops just shy of the bolted front door. Joe leaps to his feet, having witnessed this before, and attempts to capture the culprit before he disappears again. Much to his surprise, there is no intruder, no mud on the porch, and despite the dog's reaction, even the crows are remaining silent in the trees.

It's hard to say which is more unsettling, their silence or the atmosphere, which seems to hang eerily over them like a heavy shroud. Desperate to get their attention, Gold Dog dashes out into the front yard and just stands there, barking for all he's worth. Joe steps cautiously into the night with Aurora following close on his heels.

Rori opens her mouth to warn the others, yet all she can muster is a silent scream. Joe feels torn apart, like gravity is gripping his feet to the earth while his spirit explodes into a brooding sky. Unbeknownst to either, the group has assembled all around them, each witnessing the phenomenon from their own unique perspective.

Lizzie and her innards are in turmoil, frothing like the clouds overhead, while she struggles with her demons of perfection. Mirabella is clearly incensed with Grant's behavior, and is battling a vacuum of energy that threatens to drain her completely. Levi is screaming at Zeke, while their ultimate conflict rages within his chest. Cady succumbs after just a few moments, and bolts from the crowd to vomit her last meal.

And Sean, Sean is debating whether he belongs here at all. *Loretta gave the stone to Carlie. She's the one who should be here. Maybe I should be on my way, and just leave them the stone.* While each stands absorbed in their dimension of fear, innocence is being devoured across the globe with the savage hunger of ravenous winds.

Loretta's heart does not feel good. Grant's behavior will no more be resolved with a look than her pain can be cured with a smile. Henry was the closest thing he had to a father, and now that he's gone, Grant's ship is adrift. It's in his eyes. While she longs for Henry daily, she can feel him with her, and Loretta set her own course many years ago. And with that, she smiles, and remembers what to do.

"Love will not be forged or forced. Do yourself proud, son, and walk beyond the fear," she whispers into his ear.

Grant suddenly begins choking, retching on his fears and his doubts, and stares in disbelief at Loretta as he struggles to regain his breath.

"Do yourself proud, Grant. You've always been good at that," she offers tenderly, brushing his cheek with the back of her fingers.

As awareness creeps into his crevices, Grant's anger toward Sean begins to evaporate, along with all the differences that had held such importance. As the truth spills over him and through him, he undergoes a realignment so profound that it alters his entire perspective, and the world begins shifting right before his eyes.

First a halo of light appears around Sean, and Grant blinks several times, rubbing at his eyes, before finally accepting the vision. Sean senses the attention and turns to face Grant, just as the last of their differences melt into the light. The sincerity of his apology resonates from core to core, and the power of that resolution, their faith in possibility, dismantles the cyclone whirling overhead and opens the sky to reveal a brilliance of stars.

The house lights have returned, yet none of them actually notices above the blinding white light now radiating out from the stones.

"OPERATION STARLIGHT"

"In light of recent events, it appears the prophecy may well be unfolding," Wilhelm states gravely, studying the expressions on each of their faces. "Whatever form of mishandling took place, the consequences were clearly of epic proportion."

"Clearly," agrees Madeleine. "Beyond the cost in human suffering, current estimates are placing global damages into the trillions. The impact of further devastation could have a serious impact on our worldwide economy."

"Any news from surveillance?" Wilhelm asks Emanuel.

While he appears to have shed a pound or two of pretense, Emanuel's pallor appears less than robust. The presence of dark circles is but a shadow of the fear now reflecting in his eyes.

"According to your Commander Reardon, the tornados indeed coincided with relocation of the stones," Emanuel shares gravely.

"We're gathering scientists from around the planet," Wilhelm informs them. "An extensive underground laboratory will be solely dedicated to our *Operation Starlight*. Independent researchers are already flocking to investigate the vortexes, and media speculation is well underway."

"With so much at stake, our experts have unanimously concluded that a little patience will go a long way. Any disturbance with collection could pose disastrous results. It's too much of an unknown to chance multiple reactions. Experts say leave them alone until they're all reunited."

"What about the mathematicians? The statisticians? Have they been consulted as well?" demands Madeleine, as desperation seeps from the corner of one eye. "I have grandchildren," she pleads, now anxious to gain custody and control of the stones.

"The numbers are too close to call," Wilhelm discloses, patting her forearm. While the gesture may be foreign, so is the circumstance.

"Faith is all we have, my friends," Emanuel offers, yet his words seem to offer little consolation.

"WHATEVER IT TAKES"

Reardon has convened an emergency briefing to assess their overall status. The powers that be are getting nervous, and demanding they be brought up to date. Knuckles braced on the table, the commander looms ominously, and foreboding hangs thick in the air.

"Thanks to Lieutenant Dan," he motions with a nod, "we now know that seven of the nine crystals are at the farmhouse. And while this is certainly convenient, recent events indicate a strengthening in their force field. To be honest, ladies and gentlemen, there's nothing in the rulebooks on this one. We're breaking new ground here, and the stakes could not be higher. Communication is key, all the way around, so let's stay connected. Okay, now that we've all got the picture, Zach, Jeannine, what've you got on grandma?"

"This one's getting complicated, Sir. The grandson has *"abilities,"* Jeannine explains with finger quotations, "and the media is interested. Surveillance reveals that mom is beginning to show signs of wear, and seems terrified about what the attention is doing to her boy."

"And the grandmother appears to be lingering," adds Zachary. "As long as she's with them, she's insulated."

"Be the paparazzi," Reardon orders to Zack. "And Jeannine, you go in and plug the story. Put the mother at ease and you'll have the grandmother. Okay, let's keep this thing moving. Lloyd, Stanley, fill us in on our musician."

"Well, Lloyd nearly scared the piss out of him on their joy ride, and now he's convinced that his old compadre is a fairly dangerous man. It allows us to keep an eye on him and drop in whenever we please," Stanley explains before turning it over to Lloyd.

"The rock is typically in his shirt pocket, or occasionally hidden upstairs. I've seen it glow from a distance, you know, but it never seems to happen when I'm around," he reports, with just a twinge of remorse.

"Touching," Reardon comments sarcastically. "Your instructions are to get as close as possible, and to protect that stone with your life. I need you to stay glued to this guy. Move in if you have to."

"Now," the Commander declares, pausing for everyone's attention, "I have something important to show you."

The image on the left depicts a malevolent cloud formation that completely dwarfs the farmhouse, and on the right, devastated storm victims cradling limp and lifeless bodies.

"It is my job to make sure you understand the gravity of our situation. This is what happens when amateurs dabble. Whatever it takes, ladies and gentlemen, we need those stones. As of now, he world is in your hands."

Hotel to Host Holy Men
by Brogan Cantrell

"The *Hotel Stuffolks* located on Route 7A, will be providing accommodations for a unique assembly of religious leaders representing every denomination throughout the world," announced General Manager, Barry Nyack.

Event coordinators are extending an open invitation to sanctioned officials from any and every church to attend this landmark conference. The *Stuffolks Symposium*, as it has been deemed, will focus on the series of meteorological abnormalities that have taken place across the globe. Literally thousands of families from all seven continents were affected by the freak tornados that terrorized the planet just three nights ago.

Stuffolks was chosen because of the mysterious vortex that appeared overhead, and that may have a direct correlation to the catastrophic storms. The widespread disaster has inspired religion leaders the world over to make unprecedented strides for the good of humanity.

In addition to attracting spiritual leaders, key members of the scientific and meteorological communities have been arriving daily to participate in the groundbreaking study. It has been reported that ours was just one of three similar weather events that occurred that fateful night. Sources state that while investigations are underway at each of the locations,

Stuffolks was selected as best able to accommodate the influx of world travelers.

As a community, our sympathies remain with all those brave families who are continuing to struggle in the aftermath. Every business in town is collecting donations for the injured and the homeless. Speaking on behalf of this publication, we are proud to serve such a noble cause, and we will be sharing details on the conference as they become available.

"WONDER WORLD"

Through the beauty of satellite imaging, a number of organizations have already located the neighborhood, yet Brogan is first to correctly identify the exact house centered below the vortex. It's mid-morning when Rosalie peers through the peephole at the official-looking stranger out on her stoop. Recent events have left her more than a little paranoid, so as far as she's concerned, he can talk through the storm door.

Despite his dismay on recognizing her from the mall footage, he somehow manages to form sentences while his mind grinds between gears. At Rosalie's insistence, Brogan slides his press pass up against the glass, and she squints to read it through double panes. After verifying his face with the photograph, she's reasonably certain that he is who he says, yet entertains no intention of letting him inside.

Snippets of his articles are coursing through her memory, while her heart nearly pounds through her chest, as if that would somehow prove more effective. Arguing for their safety, he protests through the glass, yet his words only heighten her anxiety until she hastily turns him away. Brogan issues her a warning as she closes the door, that while he may be the first, he will not be the last. Tucking his card into the doorjamb, he heads back down the sidewalk, quietly pondering the little boy's fate.

On engaging the final deadbolt, Rosalie leans back against the steel door and draws a deep breath in hopes of slowing down the blood that's pulsing in her ears. Peeking around the corner, Lorna checks to make sure the coast is clear before leaving their Justin unattended. His interest in puzzles seems to have subsided, and now he's taken to creating an entirely new world.

Using plenty of color and creativity, they've managed to transform flat surfaces into an incredible panorama, the likes of which she could only dream. What began as simple crayon drawings has evolved into a masterpiece, and Lorna is taking delight in each new addition to their world. Although she had never considered herself particularly talented, she's been amazed with the creativity flowing from her hand. Once the room was awash in a vibrant blue, the birds were drafted on the ceiling in formation – the crow, the eagle, the heron and the swan.

The ceiling, of course, was the toughest, yet completing each wall in succession has brought her peace beyond any she'd known. They began with the north wall where the pale pinks and yellows of dawn are stretched behind a myriad of dazzling tropical leaves. Hummingbirds sip nectar from red hibiscus flowers as green frogs lick their eyeballs down by the water. Otters are playing tag amid the tall grass while a bemused mountain lion observes them from the trees.

The east wall emerges into a bright, sunny sky, high above a salmon-dancing stream. The bear and her cub are too busy watching butterflies commune with the daisies to spy the speckled salamanders sunning on the log.

The horizon then sweeps upward toward the southern wall before giving way to a craggy, windswept cliff overlooking a magnificent valley. A noble wolf sits howling at the sunset, while an industrious beaver builds a spectacular marshland that bursts with all the colors of fall. The spiny porcupine is barely noticeable, hidden as he is among the grass, yet nothing escapes the stately jaguar that lies casually stretched along one low-hanging branch.

The darkening forest soon silhouettes against the western wall as three shadowy figures stand tall on the horizon – the lion, the buffalo and the bear. Smooth lines coupled with unadorned trees suggest the solitude and thoughtfulness of winter. High above the tree line, emerging from the depths of a deep purple sky, nine simple stars illuminate the heavens.

Lorna opens the door to find Justin seated at his tiny desk with a crayon clenched busily in hand. Squatting beside him, she tickles his hair with her fingertips and admires his brilliance at work. His abilities are boundless, and Lorna has been carefully dating and storing each creation, for the proper eyes at the proper time. The telephone startles a shriek out of Rosalie, who quickly shuts down the vacuum to answer the call.

The woman on the other end asks to speak with Lorna, so she walks the cordless down the hallway to *Wonder World*. Whenever Rosalie enters her son's room, she finds it nearly impossible to leave, so the three have been spending a great deal of time in here lately. Lorna appears to be doing the bulk of the listening on this mysterious phone call. When Rosalie notices a shift in her color, she settles in beside her on the bed.

Justin simply continues to work on his drawings as a tiny smile dances on his lips. *It's almost time.*

"WINTER GRASSES"

Daily adventure to the mailbox, planted deep at the far end of the lane, has somehow become the highpoint of Elijah's day. Juvie the cat wanders out with him, often chasing the occasional field mouse. The walks allow them a brief yet cherished intermission from the chronically unfortunate Lloyd.

What began as a social call has somehow evolved into a semi-permanent arrangement. Seems Lloyd's ol' lady finally gave him the boot, and to Elijah's disappointment, he landed right here, slammed against his front door, as even the sky was spinning out of control. He arrived on the doorstep in a drunken rage, ranting on the failings of his four-letter wife. Through a series of manipulations and intimidations, he finagled a night on the sofa into an unlimited stay two doors down the hall.

Since the night of his encampment, challenge after challenge has arisen on the farm. Lightning struck the well cap, which fried the brand new pump, and set the winter grasses all ablaze. Thanks to a quick response from the local volunteers, they were able to save both the barn and the house. And if that weren't enough, appliances seem to be dropping like flies, as if they too want to escape from the presence of Lloyd.

Today, in addition to junk mail and flyers from the grocery, the rusted box reveals an envelope from Elijah's agent. His favorite flat rock affords the perfect sitting space, with room for him and Juvie plus a little bit to spare. Sifting through the superfluous, he tears open the seal and withdraws a well-written letter in an unfamiliar hand. While fan mail is always a hoot, this appears to be correspondence of a completely different nature.

The first paragraph establishes she is closer than a fan, and what follows makes him glad he sat down. The gypsy is inviting him home. While Loretta's note is decidedly cryptic, the invitation is clear – he and his stone are requested to join them.

For some reason, Elijah has a sneaking suspicion she may just hold the secret to his looming black cloud.

"MEANWHILE, BACK AT THE FARM..."

Thank goodness for Loretta's six bedrooms, and a table that always has room for one more, or four as the case may be. Shortly after posting her letter to Elijah, another arrives from an unknown location. The contents provide a host of winning smiles, as each member of the household celebrates the news.

Seems one stranded little boy has found his way home, and arrived with all his magnificence. Having heard the story of Lorna and Justin, they've all been interested, if not a bit anxious, for word on the little boy's condition. The news comes as no surprise to Cadence, however, who has been dreaming of a boy just his age for several weeks now. She's startled, however, to discover a similar awareness in Joe. The nod and the twinkled appear to offer confirmation to facts he had no way of knowing.

Gold Dog is smiling as well, as Joe reaches down with a scritch for his head. Some are able to glimpse far beyond the conventional to experience the wisdom of Gold Dogs and crows. After enjoying a bit of attention, our favorite canine trots off after Rori as she quietly disappears up the staircase.

She's feeling really lost today, and has been finding it harder and harder to sleep at night sans the company of Ryan. In the wee hours she listens for Lizzie's rhythmic breathing before allowing herself the solace of her tears. Today, of all days, is proving particularly daunting, and she once again catches herself spinning the ring on her finger.

It's his birthday, and for the first time in decades, he's celebrating without her. She assumes that he's staying with his brother, yet they've exchanged not so much as a word since he left. The ache inside is truly overwhelming, and the emptiness is threatening to swallow her alive.

Mirabella is first to notice when the stones begin to pulse, and quickly begins searching for the source of the disturbance. Loretta spots them as well, and quickly crosses the room to stand by her side.

"Where's Rori?" Bella asks Loretta, or whoever else is listening.

"She's upstairs with Gold Dog," offers Joe. "Is everything alright?" he asks, as his eyes follow hers toward the dining room.

By unanimous decision, they keep the stones together by day, yet separate them at night for protection. The three begin moving calmly toward the staircase, gathering up housemates along the way. Loretta cajoles her into opening up the door, and Rori greets her new family tear-stained and rather embarrassed.

"We're only as strong as our frailest heart," offers Grant, who understands the consequence of remaining injured and alone.

The correlation between his anger and the ensuing tornados has not been lost on any of them. There in the darkness, in the absence of all light, Grant saw to the core of his truth. He saw his fear of being left again, of not being good enough or strong enough, and then it occurred to him. Once the awareness overtook him that the decision had always been his, he swore off his fear and accepted his magnificence. Maime was right all along. It's mathematically correct.

So now he's become their foremost crusader for wounded hearts, and tonight that happens to be Rori. Together they slowly and gently weave the frayed bits of her spirit, until she's fully reconnected with all the strength she'll ever need.

"ESPIONAGE 101"

Justin has no interest in the crowd forming out front, yet he does admire the shiny black crows that have taken up residence out back. Rosalie, on the other hand, is keenly aware of the horde of newscasters and the vein that's now pulsing from her forehead as she peeks through the living room blinds. She keeps imagining the gate they had planned for the sidewalk, and wishing she'd gotten around to installing the fence.

Zach and Jeannine pull their mock television van alongside the curb, and are pleased to see how well they blend in. The front lawn is crawling with reporters and camera people scrambling for a glimpse or a quote or anything else they can put out over the airwaves. *The Mystery House*, as it's being called, is now drawing worldwide attention, and Brogan's warning keeps replaying in Rosalie's ears.

Clutching his card in her hand, she debates the merits of contacting the devil she knows. Hovering on the brink of an emotional collapse, she slips down the hallway and steps into *Wonder World*. A calm washes over her as Justin looks up with a smile – that beautiful, wonderful smile – and she can feel her anxiety slipping away, like an ill-fitting garment happily shed.

"He'll help us, Mommy, you and me and Grammy," Justin volunteers out of nowhere.

"You think so, do ya? How will he help us?" she asks, half humoring, half not.

"Ask him."

Something about his expression, and the surety in his little voice, actually moves her to contemplate the advice of a four-year-old. Inside she realizes he's advanced far beyond his years, but what if he's wrong? Considering the lack of groceries in the house, they certainly can't hide here forever. Being local, Cantrell knows more about her son than the others, which could work for her or against her, she surmises. Just then, Lorna comes strolling out of the bathroom, toweling dry her freshly showered hair.

"How 'bout Chinese food?" Rosalie asks them, temporarily fortified with a new sense of resolve.

Lorna looks surprised, while Rosalie is sporting a Cheshire grin, and dials up take-out for four. Fishing his card from her pocket, she presses the digits and wades through the series of automated instructions before getting a live voice on the line.

"Brogan Cantrell."

"If you'll deliver the Chinese food, I'm ready to talk," she states rather cryptically.

Glancing down at the Caller-ID, the scowl that's been deeply embedded transforms itself slowly to a grin.

"I'm already there," he answers, making his way toward the door.

With so much focus on the front of the house, no one really noticed his van entering the alleyway. Lorna is positively thrilled with *Espionage 101, and* steals across the back lawn to disengage the gate. One twist of the lock and she's ushering him in with bags of fragrant Chinese food in tow.

Rosalie adeptly guides him through the patio door, and straight toward a whole new perspective.

"SOMEWHERE UNDERGROUND"

"Hey Kevin, have you met Alex?" asks Richard from Human Resources.

"Can't say I've had the pleasure," he answers, extending his right hand.

"Alexandra is an Astrophysicist joining us from the Atacama Desert," Richard continues. "Her work with the ALMA project has drawn critical acclaim, and we're thrilled to have her insights toward Operation Starlight. Do you think you can show her around? Scientists are arriving by the van load, and I could really use some help."

"Consider it done," confirms Kevin to the back of Richard's head as he disappears down the hallway to greet the next wave. "So Alex, shall we start you with some coffee or would you prefer something cold?"

A dozen laboratory clusters encircle the main conference center, that's equipped with every piece of wizardry electronics can provide, along with several still under development. From mass spectrometers to neutrino detectors, the complex has been equipped to accommodate a full range of experiments. Additionally, each accompanying office has access to a supercomputer that links them to research centers across the globe.

Beyond the labs, the periphery of the compound feeds and houses well over two hundred people. The amenities resemble that of an airport:

211

restaurants to satisfy a diversity of palates; lounges for music and entertainment; gyms for working out; sundries shops; theaters; and a myriad of other services to appease a truly captive audience.

In addition to its visible features, the infrastructure has been designed to withstand virtually any surface disaster. All things considered, it's the best-equipped facility on the planet, and will soon be housing the finest minds of our age. Mathematicians, statisticians, physicists and brilliant thinkers from every corner of the world are being gathered for their insights, their perspectives and their recommendations. It is intellectualism stripped of all ethnicity. Ideas are king in this subterranean world, and no single nation holds the crown.

Aika hails from the University of Groningen, and landed with the very first drop. Having arrived several days ago now, he's anxious to begin the discussions, and frankly, he's far too social to remain quiet for long. The waitress just retreated to the backroom and stocking, when Aik hones in on voices from the corridor. Bounding to his feet, he accidentally bumps a table and nearly knocks over a chair in his rush to exit the restaurant. Regaining his balance and composure, he is casually positioned at the entrance when Alex and Kevin appear around the bend.

"Let there be life," he interjects during a pause in conversation.

"More prophetic words have not been spoken," Alex replies.

"Always an optimist," he offers, along with his hand. "I am Aika of Groningen."

"Groningen. Are you with familiar with LOFAR?" she asks.

"Quite. Our lengthy courtship still amazes and intrigues," he croons of the radio telescopes installed throughout Europe. "Do you have an ear to the sky as well?"

"ALMA," she counters, referring to the Atacama Large Millimeter Array, which for a long time was the largest single scope in the world. "Oh, and I'm Alex, by the way, and this is Kevin."

"Another desert rat," quips Kevin. "Sonoran. U of A, Tucson, Meteoritical Society, Minerology. We rock," he slips in dryly.

"What's your Lab assignment?" inquires Aika.

"We're both Eleven, I believe," Kevin answers, deferring to Alex as she nods her confirmation.

"I'm Six." After a slight pause, he adds, "Anybody hungry?" and motions over his shoulder toward the restaurant.

"In every way possible," chuckles Alex.

"Big Brass Ones"

"What the hell did you get yourself into now?" demands the voice on the other end of the phone line.

"Brandi?" Levi wonders into the receiver.

"Who else was put on this earth to cover your ass?"

"Only you, darlin'," rolls off his tongue while a huge grin spreads over his face.

"Yeah, bite me. There were suits down at the Hog, and it looks like they been followin' your brother. Geez, Levi, for a guy who's never been in any trouble, you sure seem to be making a habit of it lately!"

"If you only knew."

"That's why I'm calling! What in hell is going on?!"

He does his best to explain without divulging too much, as they're certain all the phone lines are tapped. Little does he realize, the listeners know almost as much, and in some cases more.

"Well, I guess you really *can* find anything at ChinaMart!" Brandi chuckles, referring to Loretta. "What about Jillian? Have you seen her?"

"No. I was all set to sweep her off her feet, ya know, and then everything happened, and here I am."

"So who all is there with you?"

Describing his housemates is challenging at best, yet he manages to find a few words about each, with perhaps a few more about Joe, having bonded over late night conversations. He tells her about rescuing Cady, and she grins at his description of the pregnancy. While he's accustomed to regurgitating cows, regurgitating women is a whole different ballgame.

All too soon, their conversation succumbs to her schedule and his heart sinks with the reality of the impending disconnect. Hearing the lump in his throat, Brandi briefly draws him back home with a bit of raw humor.

"Yeah, well, your suits ask me anything, 'n I'll tell 'em to stick it where the sun don't shine!"

"I know you got brass ones bigger 'n mine, darlin', but you be careful. They're armed, and it's anybody's guess who hired 'em."

"Yeah, yeah."

"Really, Bran, take care of yourself. Just keep me posted, okay?"

"Always. Hey, I'm late. Gotta roll."

"Later, Babe."

As Levi hangs up the phone, a slow burn ignites in his belly. *How dare they follow my brother! Who they hell are they anyway?* Sean walks into the kitchen at just the right moment to catch the angry expression on his face.

"What's up, Levi?"

215

"They're after my family," he states in a low and dangerous growl that raises the hairs on the back of Sean's neck. "Something's got to give. We can't stay here forever," Levi concludes, as his frustration ripples out just two rooms away.

"PUSHES AND PULLS"

"Come on, people! What've we got to do here?! Send a limo?" Reardon bellows at the speaker phone. "You were supposed to have them moving by now. What's the hold up?"

"They're locked in there tighter than a drum," Jeannine informs him. "Satellite imaging reveals that they snuck someone in through the back gate, with what appeared to be Chinese food, and the subject has yet to exit the home. Word in the yard identifies him as one Brogan Cantrell, a local newspaper man."

"How did *he* make contact?"

"He was invited. It appears they have some previous relationship, so when it all broke loose, she called the one she knew," Jeannine replies.

"Well, I gather from the news reports that you're knee deep in witnesses, so at this point any type of force is clearly out of the question. Just hang close and wait them out. With any luck, the stress will drive them south. Keep me posted. Okay people, let's keep the pressure on. We need to use every bit of influence to get these stragglers moving. Lloyd, what's the status on Elijah?"

"I found an envelope in the trash with the right zip code, so I believe the farm has contacted him. He's obviously planning a trip, yet has remained fairly closed-mouthed on details. Been slowing down on the beer in hopes of getting a little closer.

217

He's a far cry from the naïve kid I knew back then. Intimidation may have brought us together, but it sure hasn't done much for the friendship."

"Maybe you need to turn over a new leaf," Reardon suggests. "Try attending an AA meeting. Invite him along for support. Take up cooking, hell I don't know! Just get yourself in there so you know what's going on."

"Yes, sir."

"Ted and Mitch have been dispatched to farm country to make their presence known. There are no real plans for questioning, but hanging around and following people tends to make them nervous, and nervous is what we're after. The more disturbed we can keep their families, the quicker they'll rein in the others. All right everybody, show me some action," he states firmly, and then disconnects the call.

Alone in the room, Reardon hangs his head in frustration. It's a race for time, and he fears he may be losing.

"CHARLOTTE CALLING"

Dan is on the phone with Reardon as the Towne Car signals it's final turn into the driveway. They've been tracking them since her departure, and have been on high alert pending her arrival. No one is quite sure what her presence will mean on the farm, yet with all eyes trained, the well-dressed woman climbs the porch steps and raps soundly on the door.

"Charlotte Merriweather calling … for my daughter," she informs Loretta through the screen.

"Cady? She's lying down. Please, come in and make yourself comfortable while I let her know you're here," Loretta says, and welcomes the woman into her humble home.

Despite her judgments, Charlotte accepts the invitation and signals her driver to remain with the car. Loretta offers her a seat on the sofa and disappears up the staircase to get Cady. Emerging from the basement with laundry on her hip, Lizzie is startled to see a stranger left alone in the house. Dropping the basket, she quickly crosses the room and engages the official-looking woman.

"Hi, I'm Lizzie," she offers on approach.

"Charlotte Merriweather."

"Oh, you must be Cady's mom," Lizzie smiles, extending her hand.

"Indeed," she responds in clipped fashion, making no movement to reciprocate the gesture.

219

Shrugging off the social slap, Liz rebounds with tea and conversation. Having failed at dismissing her, Charlotte quietly relinquishes and accepts the warm drink. The others may be tending to errands, yet Lizzie has no intention of leaving this woman alone with the stones just a few feet away.

"So, how was your trip down?" she asks, lighting on the edge of Loretta's favorite wingback.

Before either is forced to acknowledge Charlotte's right to ignore the conversation completely, Loretta appears at the foot of the staircase with Cadence directly behind. She squeezes Cady's hand for reassurance before stepping respectfully off to the side. Resting her teacup on the coffee table, Charlotte turns to face her daughter.

"My God, Cadence, what you done?!" Charlotte exclaims, in betrayal of all etiquette and training.

"I've produced you an heir, Mother, and spared you the nuisance of pruning the family tree," Cadence replies, in a voice that is somehow less familiar now. Even the tone is unsettling, and she swallows hard to fend off the ensuing wave of nausea.

As the energy in the room escalates, the stones begin to flicker, and Lizzie and Loretta quickly disappear into the dining room. From either side of the table, they join hands around the stones.

Neither is exactly sure how to fan this fire, yet both know instinctively, there is no time to waste.

"Love something," Loretta whispers, "Love it with all your heart." Bella simply nods, and the two women set to wholeheartedly to task.

Meanwhile, several steps and an entire world away, Cady cradles her well-rounded belly and steels herself for battle. The air in the room is so thick, she's finding it hard to breath, yet presses forward despite her resistance. Every cell in her body, including her baby, is fighting hard to keep hold of her newfound perspective. Several deep breaths later, she begins anew – this time from a place of true compassion.

"Mother, between where you stand and where I stand, between the words and the obligations, rests the truth of who we really are." Bending down on one knee, Cady looks into her mother's eyes and takes her by the hand. "Do you remember how it felt when you found out your were pregnant? Or while your were watching your babies sleep? That's where we need to talk from, Mom, from that open place that still holds possibility. We've no time for anything else now. The world has reached its tipping point, and each of us must choose love for the sake of love and nothing else."

Uncharacteristically dumbstruck, Charlotte's instincts are pressing her to reassert control, yet other forces are clearly at work. Something in Cadence's eyes is imploring – not begging, not

221

pleading, but *imploring* – a designation which demands, by its very tenacity, an intellectual, rather than emotional response. Always the negotiator, Charlotte's questions are succinct and to the point.

"To what tipping point are you referring?" she asks, incredulously.

"The tornados, for a start. Have you read about the vortexes?" With a nod from her mother, she continues, "One of the three was positioned directly over top of this house."

While she would have preferred to dismiss the statement as high drama, a documented vortex is hard to negate. As the mother and now grandmother, begins to absorb that reality, every drop of moisture disappears from Charlotte's mouth. She can feel the color draining away from her face, and reaches for her daughter and what remains of her composure.

"What does all this mean?" she asks, minus all of her earlier arrogance.

"It means we have to change, Mother. We all have to change," shares Cady, glancing over her shoulder toward Loretta and the stones.

"Salt of the Earth"

"Dan, I think you're gonna wanna see this," Roy relays, while his eyes remain fixated on the screen.

The permanent furrow that separates Dan's eyebrows gets more firmly entrenched as he peers into the monitor. They've all grown accustomed to the otherworldly glow that seeps around the edges of Loretta's window shades. This, however, is something entirely new. Policy dictates immediate contact with any deviation to the stones, and the pulsing they're witnessing now certainly qualifies.

Fingering the digits on his speed dial, Dan waits breathlessly as the signal seeks the headset affixed to Reardon's ear. With each countless second, images of devastation are flashing through his brain. The Commander's voice comes on the line just an instant before the stomach acid reaches Dan's esophagus.

"Reardon."

"Sir, we have a situation," Dan informs him.

"What's happening?" questions Reardon, swallowing hard in an effort to keep his innards from going AWOL.

"The crystals are flickering, Sir, and as you're aware, we're accustomed to a fairly steady glow. This is the most rapid pulse we've seen since the vortex. Please advise."

With one hand stretched wide across his forehead, the Commander hesitates, momentarily lost in debate. He knows he's wasting precious seconds, yet one does not want to react too quickly nor too slowly when the fate of the world is at stake. On the other end, Dan simply waits, barely breathing for fear he might miss the instruction.

"Sir!" Dan exclaims into his mouthpiece. "Crisis averted, Sir! Output has returned to normal levels," spills from his lips like rain following a drought, sweeter than candy and more welcome than dawn.

Despite miles of separation, both men retreat to their respective restrooms, and return a little salt to the earth.

"INTERNAL EARTHQUAKES"

Having finished his dinner, Kevin excuses himself from the now crowded dining room and adjourns to the solitude of Laboratory Eleven. His head is swimming with so many new faces and names that he can barely remember his own. Closing the door behind him, he welcomes the cold familiarity of the gages and instruments.

Kevin makes it a point to remove himself from social situations as hastily as humanly possible. The anxiety of group interaction is practically crippling. His energy recoils so far inward, at times he's afraid he'll disappear altogether.

Settling into his executive chair, *"Doctor"* Kevin draws a deep breath, lets it slowly escape, and waits for his heart to resume a normal pace. As the internal clamor begins to subside, Kevin notices some activity on the seismometers and rolls across the aisle to investigate. All peculiarities are to be reported to the Shift Supervisor, who this evening is none other than Dr. Walter Fröenenberg.

Familiar with Dr. Fröenenberg's work, Kevin finds the thought of meeting him in person simultaneously thrilling and equally unnerving. Never in his wildest dreams had he imagined they'd be working together. Now, just days into the project, he's directly initiating contact. Flipping through the directory, he locates the number and voices the digits aloud into his mouthpiece. Seconds later, Walter's voice is on the line.

"This is Dr. Fröenenberg. How may I be of assistance?"

"Doctor, we have abnormal seismic activity recording in Lab Eleven. It appears we're experiencing earthquakes in at least eleven separate locations across the globe. Looks like one on each tectonic plate," Kevin reports.

"I'll be right there," instructs Fröenenberg, careful to keep the panic from his voice.

"THE STUFFOLKS SYMPOSIUM"

"Where are my live centerpieces?!" Jennifer barks at the floral delivery person. "They'd better be on that truck or so help me," she trails off, leaving the unspoken threat to hang idle in the air. Returning to the truck, Sam rolls his eyes at the thought of driving back across town in the middle of morning rush hour.

"I'm sorry, Ma'am, we set them aside for safekeeping, and apparently they never made it on the truck," Sam explains, preparing himself for the verbal assault.

Veins are popping in every direction, and it appears Jennifer may just hyperventilate right here on the spot. Sam pulls a chair from the one of the tables and quickly slips it behind her as she crumbles. Expectations dropping, she chokes out a ragged sigh and cradles her head in her hands.

Just about the time she has resigned herself to failure, one of the attendees wanders into the room. From her position in the doorway, Jennifer and Sam look like two frightened animals. Their eyes are wide and furtive, and she can practically hear their hearts racing from across the room. While her first reaction is to simply close the door, it is a compassionate heart that urges her forward.

"What a lovely room you have prepared for us," she states, admiring the pressed linens and sparkling fixtures.

"If only there were centerpieces," Jennifer laments, immediately wishing she could pluck the words right out of the air before they ever reached the ears of a paying guest. Her eyes are brimming now, and threaten to spill over, as the bell sounds round two of her brutal inner beating.

"I can't promise to get them here by nine, but I'll get them here as soon as I can," Sam offers, all but certain his proposal will be ruled out of the question.

"Centerpieces," the woman ponders aloud, "Pieces for the center…pieces to center on…. Do you have any glass bowls?"

The question catches Jennifer off balance, and she responds quite naturally without really thinking. "Why yes we do. How large do you need?"

She indicates with her hands what appears to be a medium-sized serving dish, and Jennifer nods. Glancing around the room, the woman counts the tables and asks Jennifer to collect just that many and to meet them back here. She then turns to Sam and enlists his services, as well. Jen is halfway to the hotel kitchen before realizing she's no longer in a panic, yet decides to keep moving so it doesn't catch up.

As General Manager of the Hotel Stuffolks, Mr. Barry Nyack is anxious to make their first international symposium a gleaming success. Upper management has been calling daily to ensure that every detail is being properly attended. Now, on the morning of the event, he arrives early to review the arrangements and go over final details with Jennifer, his Food and Beverage Manager.

"The centerpieces?" Barry wonders aloud, now a shade paler than moments ago.

"Aren't they lovely?" the woman suggests with a smile, as she locks her arm into his and escorts him from table to table. All the glass bowls have been filled with water, and at the bottom of each they have placed a single stone.

"You'll notice that every stone is different," she informs him, patting his hand, as they glide from table to table. "Much like the attendees of this conference, each is safe and secure within its own little pond. That is where we must begin, Mr. Nyack. That is where we all begin."

Walking the room with this delightful woman, Barry can feel his stress just evaporating, like water from the bowls, and he can truly sense the peace they were meant to invoke. Returning to the serving area, he rejoins the others with a much clearer and calmer perspective. He even greets Jennifer with a very real smile, as the two set about finalizing the many details, now certain that all will go well.

"NOTHING COMFORTABLE"

"I have an urgent call for you, Ma'am," Sophia whispers into Madeleine's ear, and then discreetly slips antacids into her palm.

Excusing herself from the meeting, Madeleine devours the chalky tablets en route to her office, where she then closes and locks the door. Settling back in her chair, she glances down at the secured line and realizes, there will be nothing comfortable about *this* conversation. With a fortifying breath, she secures her headset and connects with the call.

"Good afternoon, gentlemen."

"Perhaps," replies Wilhelm. "We have reports of earthquakes on each tectonic plate," he relays, as evenly as he is able. "All registered as moderate on the Richter Scale, with the largest coming in at 5.7."

"Praise God, there have been no casualties," Emanuel adds. "It appears they all took place in uninhabited areas."

"What did Reardon have to say?" she asks to whomever will answer.

"We'll be raising him directly, as it seems this information was received through scientific channels rather than surveillance. There appears to have been a breach in protocol which requires our immediate attention," Wilhelm relays with a solemn conviction.

"Without a doubt," she asserts, affirming his position.

With a few brief clicks and pauses, the connection is established and a fourth voice joins the line.

"Reardon."

"Yes, Commander. We understand there has been a seismic disruption of the substructure. Is there unusual activity we should know about?" Wilhelm asks him outright.

"I'll be happy to address that for you, sir, if you'll allow me a moment to secure my surroundings," Reardon suggests, maneuvering toward his office. Closing the door behind him, he shuts his eyes and prepares for the worst. "Yes, sir, we did observe a recent anomaly. It was brief in duration and quickly resolved, and was believed to have avoided any consequence."

"That was outside of your parameters, Commander," Wilhelm admonishes.

"Commander Reardon," Madeleine interjects, "With our experts and resources and the fate of the world at stake, this is not a decision to be shouldered alone. Have we made ourselves perfectly clear?"

"Yes, Ma'am," replies Reardon, who in truth is feeling more than a little relieved. "In the spirit of full disclosure, this is the third such episode we've witnessed." There's an audible gasp over the phone lines as he flips through his notebook, relaying the facts, as he knows them. "The previous incidents involved a slow pulsing, yet this latest disturbance

231

produced quick bursts of light, and created a rather strobe-like effect."

"Thank you, Commander," Wilhelm resumes. "Excellent information. We'll be sharing your observations with our research team. It's time we hasten our progress, and start making preparations for the final maneuver. From this point on, Commander, we'll require daily conversations. Alright then, tomorrow it is," Wilhelm states before abruptly disconnecting and leaving each to their own private thoughts.

Alone in his office, Emanuel prays to his God with a tear in his eye, while a spectacular sunset waits just beyond the window.

"Bridled and Unbridled"

Carlie and Patrick return from their honeymoon feeling as playful and jovial as a couple of newlyweds. Tossing her over one shoulder, he carries her across the threshold and then into the foyer of their shiny new home. Patrick's heart swells at the mere sight of his bride, and he can no longer imagine a morning without her.

Had they stopped by the Post Office on their way home from the airport, Carlie would have noticed a letter from Sean. Yet under the blissful spell of ignorance, Pat chases her up the staircase two steps at a time until he traps her against the railing in a captive embrace. Just as he's about to plant a passionate kiss on her lips, Carlie drops into a squat and ducks beneath his arm. Before he's even had a chance to open his eyes, she's squealing down the hallway amidst a trail of laughter.

Life with this woman will never be dull, he surmises from the backside of a grin. Already she has disappeared behind the door to their spacious boudoir, and Patrick decides not to rush whatever she may have in mind.

"I'm getting champagne," he calls out. "Promise you'll let me in?"

"Only if you swear your undying love!"

"I swear," he hollers out over his shoulder, and then bounds down the back stairs toward the kitchen.

233

His mother had agreed to stock the refrigerator with a few necessities pending their arrival, yet to his surprise, front and center waits a gorgeous platter that is truly befitting of royalty. A domed glass lid displays a soft mango goat cheese, along with several selections of nut breads and fruits. Grateful for her thoughtfulness, as well as her penchant for romance, he scoops up the platter, along with bottle and glasses, and hurries back up to his bride.

Carlie left the double doors slightly ajar to be easily parted for a truly grand entrance. Pushing into the room, Patrick is presented with his fantasy come true. The afternoon sunlight spilling through the windows highlights the golden shimmer of her skin against the sheets. She is truly a vision sprawled across their bed, and he barely remembers to set down the platter.

Eyes drawn toward the curves of her body, Patrick traces her gently arching back toward the cleft of her buttocks. Her delicate toes seem to be bobbing like cat toys, taunting and teasing as they lure him to play. The impish seductress stares back through a tumble of lashes, and the man can contain himself no longer. Within seconds he is totally naked, stripped down to a wrinkle-free suit. Drawing a moist tongue over her warm, soft lips, Carlie is suddenly starving to taste his mouth against hers.

"Kiss me," she breathes from deep at her core.

Champagne be damned, neither can wait another second to feel skin upon skin, flesh upon flesh. In an instant, he's down there beside her, pulling her naked body to his as they press their lips together for a fevered kiss. Lacing his fingers through her hair, the two dive headlong into passion with unbridle abandon. Trailing her fingertips against his afternoon stubble, she grasps his face with both hands and then draws his mouth firmly to hers.

Withdrawing coyly, she smiles a mischievous smile, and then plants her wet mouth against the warmth of his neck. Wriggling with pleasure, he can do little to stop her as she alternates kisses all over his body with tender, little love bites that are driving him wild. Every one of his nerve endings is alive with anticipation, and the electricity between them is radiating far beyond their wooden walls. Suspending her hand just over his belly, she laughs as each tiny hair stands at attention, before positioning her hand lower with similar results.

Unwilling to relinquish control just yet, Patrick rises to a sitting position and abruptly turns the table on his bride. Taking her firmly into his arms, he rests her head gently against the pillows and sketches invisible lines across her skin. Carefully outlining her most delicate parts, he teases until she's writhing and begging for more. Once the warmth of his mouth is hovering just an instant from her waiting breast, they are rudely interrupted with

235

the sound of a doorbell. They hesitate for one short moment on the edge of decorum, before agreeing to ignore the uninvited guest.

As our newlyweds return to their lovemaking and the neighborhood welcome wagon retreats to their homes, Lou and Riley just smile and enjoy the surveillance.

"A Venomous Stare"

Elijah is busy loading up the trunk for his journey, while Lloyd anxiously queues up Reardon on the speed-dial.

"Lloyd here. Sorry, sir, no luck. He could be heading for the farm, or he could be headed to Timbuktu, for all I know. Not enough time to win him over. Stanley is still invisible though, so he'll stay on his tail and report back. Yes, sir. Right, sir. We'll keep you posted, sir."

One last trip inside for Genevieve and Elijah will be ready to hit the road. This is one trip that could not have come at a better time. While not above helping out a friend, he had no intention of taking on a roommate, particularly a hard drinking rough rider with whom he has nothing in common. Ah, serendipity can be such a beautiful thing, and his spirits have brightened significantly since receiving the note from Loretta.

Juvie, however, is looking rather forlorn, and he wonders if she'll stay around 'til he gets back. She's become such a good friend, and he'll miss her companionship. Swooping her up in his arms, he nuzzles and she snuggles and both enjoy a good purr while the moment allows.

"When do you think you'll be back?" Lloyd asks him, per his instructions from Reardon. He doesn't really expect an answer, yet it would seem strange for him not to inquire.

"That's still up in the air, I guess. Don't worry about the bills; the accountant will take care of them. I would appreciate you feeding Juvie, though," he says, stroking the head of one smiling feline. "There's plenty of food for her in the pantry," Elijah relays over the ridiculous lump in his throat. With a wink for the cat and a pat on Lloyd's shoulder, he collects Genevieve and heads out the door.

Before his car disappears from the driveway, Lloyd is on the phone with Stanley, who begins tailing him in the first of many nondescript vehicles. Next, he contacts Reardon, who passes the information upstream to Wilhelm and the Triad. Although delighted with the news that movement is underway, there is an air of trepidation as all hold their breath for the transfer. Regardless of any philosophical differences, each finds themselves praying for a peaceful dawn.

Stan's a little confused when Elijah ventures north instead of west-southwest, and immediately contacts the Commander with an update. Following a number of exquisite superlatives, Reardon instructs Stanley to keep him apprised and debates a second call to the honchos. Perhaps by tonight, they'll have a better idea where he's headed, so he decides to hold off until he can pass on some facts.

As usual, Elijah is enjoying his journey, singing with the radio and serenading fellow travelers at rest stops along the way. Genevieve makes friends quite easily and is always happy to introduce him as well. Music is truly a universal language, and he enjoys the real connection with his fans. Stanley simply smiles and shakes his head, certain he will never understand.

As the sun hangs low in the western sky, a solitary finger of light points directly toward the Castaway Motor Lodge. In obeyance of the sign, Elijah signals his intention and exits the freeway directly. A murder of crows already adorns the roofline of the two-story motel, quietly awaiting his arrival. Stanley watches from a distance as Elijah enters the office and returns moments later twirling a key. Once secured safely inside, Stan is lucky enough to book the adjoining room.

In truth, it wouldn't have been an issue either way, thanks to the electronic advantage stored in Stanley's trunk. A bionic ear can do wonders in lieu of a wiretap, although he's usually privy to just one side of the conversation. From the touchtone, he is able to decipher the phone number, which he promptly records in his notebook. That's enough information to get started, so he programs the device to continue recording while he enters a reverse search on the number.

Within seconds, the data springs up on the screen, which he immediately forwards to Reardon along with a phone call. From what he just overheard, the Commander has less than twelve hours to set a plan in motion. Comfortable with completing his part, Stan kicks off his shoes, switches on the television and begins thumbing through the restaurant guide.

Elijah, on the other hand, decides to take himself out for dinner, and strolls across the tarmac for a taste of the local cuisine. Stan watches from behind stale draperies, and takes note of the bounce in his step. He's the kind of man Stan knew he'd never be, particularly given his career choice of blending with the background. It's comfortable here behind the scenes, yet every now and then, he still finds himself admiring a patch or two of greener grass.

Stanley is up well before dawn, monitoring each and every one of his subject's morning rituals. When Elijah places the prearranged call, it becomes obvious that Reardon accomplished his objective. Bridgette picks up after only two rings. Her voice is warm, although there's a distinct edge to it as she spoon-feeds Elijah with an extra-large serving of misinformation.

"They both just started vomiting around two in the morning, and neither can keep anything down. We're so sorry, Elijah. Hannah's been looking so forward to your visit. She's really enjoyed talking with you on the telephone. Yes, we'll make some fresh plans once everyone's feeling better. Okay then. Bye, bye now," she closes, placing the handset back into its cradle.

"Excellent. Highly believable," Mitch assures her, as Bridgette rebuffs him with a venomous stare.

Disappointed, Elijah sets down the receiver, and a long sigh escapes from his heart. Six months ago, he would never have believed something could change him so much. Now, he can't even pass a child without thinking of her, and he takes joy in the simple fact of her existence. Just knowing she's here, walking the planet, brings a smile to his lips and a lightness of being he can barely express.

Not one to dwell on the negative, he enjoys sipping on some delicious flavored coffee and maps a new route to the farm.

"THE DOOR TO TOMORROW"

The Moderator stands quietly at the podium while the participants find their spots at the tables. No assignments were made, and she is interested to observe their methods for choosing. Next, she sets her sights on the water bowls, and once the rippling subsides, she calls the room to order.

"Welcome to the Stuffolks Symposium! We have come thousands of miles and thousands of years to take up our place at this table. As we pass through this door to tomorrow, I wish to thank each and every one of you for joining this landmark conversation. Our assembly here is unprecedented, so let us take it upon ourselves to make this just the first in a series of such gatherings. While it may have taken disaster to bring us together, it is important that we take this opportunity to explore every possibility. For our children and our children's children, it's time that we remember our humanity."

Heads are nodding throughout the room as the message is translated electronically into nearly as many languages as are there are faces in the room.

"Today we will examine the heart of *all* spiritual teaching, as we seek to identify the unifying force that binds us as one. It is in this spirit of harmony that we will set aside our differences. Success will come when we can arrive at a singular perspective, a common ground, and all can move forward together.

"So please, begin with your table. As certain themes arise, share them with the group. Abandon whatever separates. By tomorrow evening we hope to have found a universal message that we can share with the world.

"Each individual in this room is a respected community leader. You have the ability to move people, and each human heart has the capacity for change. It is our duty, and indeed our obligation, to walk this path together. And it is together, in this very room, that we will take our first step."

"DUE SOUTH"

Poised off a side street with a pair of night goggles, Zach is observing the alleyway out behind the house. There have been no real developments since Cantrell's initial visit, and many of the news people have moved on to the Symposium. Jeannine is asleep in the back of the van, having covered the day shift for all it was worth. She attempted to gain access, as she has every day, yet was once again rebuffed by an exasperated mom.

"When are you people going to give up?" Rosalie barked in frustration.

"When you give us your story, Ma'am. And not a moment sooner," she added, as the door was closed abruptly in her face.

So far this has been an exercise in futility, and both she and Zach are beginning to feel a bit frayed around the edges. Just about the time the snoring starts, Zach whacks her with a fly swatter to bring her around.

"Jeannine, wake up! The van's back, and he's rolling up to the gate right now!"

They're on the far range for their listening device, so Jeannine adjusts it up to the maximum frequency before slipping on her headset. Now fully conscious, she dials up Reardon, as per his instructions.

"Reardon here," he grumbles, still heavy with sleep. "What's going on?"

"Jeannine, Sir. We have movement in Stuffolks, Commander, and they may be trying to make a break for it. Cantrell's van was left running at the back gate. Please advise."

"Okay, right now, I need Zach to slip down the alley and affix a GPS to the van. Then I need both of you to return to the hotel and collect your things. Leave the news van. There will be two rental cars waiting for you. I want you to follow them, and I want Zach heading north for the dairy farm. We'll need him there by evening to meet Lloyd. Any questions?"

"Do you have an address for Zach?"

"Sending it via email as we speak. Are we good?"

"Yes, Sir. Thank you, Sir."

Meanwhile, inside the house, Justin is carefully setting the tone for their adventure. His excitement is contagious as he packs his tiny suitcase with lots of drawings to share with his new friends. Lorna tells him how Loretta prayed for him while he was in the hospital, and Justin smiles that smile that always leaves her wondering how much he really knows.

In truth, few people on the planet can even understand him now, yet for him that's of little concern. Now is about toothbrushes, underpants and socks. And now is about smiling and remaining lighthearted. Having completed their assignments, he and Brogan simply watch as

Mommy and Grandma scoot from room to room gathering up items that cannot be done without.

"Tell me about your bedroom," Cantrell suggests, as much from curiosity as simply biding time. "Do you mind if I take a few pictures? I've never seen anything like this."

A huge grin spreads over Justin's face as he welcomes Brogan into his Wonder World. Within minutes the newsman is completely enchanted. The sheer volume of symbolism nearly sends him into overload as his mind reels to categorize the images. Eventually he stops, though, and simply absorbs. He can't remember such a sense of contentment, and soon relaxes to just breathe in the pure joy.

He was pleased enough with the story he received from Rosalie, yet was ill-prepared for the reality of Justin. Although moments ago, he had planned on dropping them at the bus station, the thought of abandoning them to mass transit now seems morally reprehensible. This boy, this child, has been sent like a gift – and not only to him, but to the very world itself. Brogan excuses himself to the hallway, where he leaves a few clipped words for his supervisor, and in the wee hours of the morning, they set their course due south.

"A REAL TROOPER"

Levi, Joe and Gold Dog are watching from the porch when the two-door sedan begins crawling up the driveway. There's no barking, just waiting and wondering. Elijah approaches tentatively, not altogether certain if he's lost or if he's found.

"I'm looking for Loretta," he calls out the window. "Have I come to the right place?"

"I do believe you have," answers Joe, resting a hand on the back of Gold Dog's neck.

Switching off the ignition, he reaches around for Genevieve, his familiar companion and friend. Levi lights up when he spies the case, and immediately jumps to his feet.

"You must be Elijah!" he greets him excitedly. "Welcome, man! Really. Welcome! I've been waiting to meet you for the longest time," he gushes, thrusting out his hand as Elijah mounts the stairs.

The invitation could not have been warmer, and whatever doubts they may have harbored soon vanish like starlight. Gold Dog gives him the once over sniff test and promptly wags his approval, despite the lingering aroma of cat. Loretta is attending to stray buttons in the kitchen when the lively foursome comes trouncing inside.

"Loretta!" Levi hollers. "There's someone here to see you!"

The exuberance in his voice is infectious, and she's smiling before she ever reaches the door. Somewhere inside just knows it's Elijah, and she couldn't be happier that he's made it here safely. Her arms open wide, and he steps into the embrace like the lost child who's found his way home.

"Thank you for inviting me," Elijah whispers, with the wee bit of air that she's left him.

Lizzie and Sean hear the laughter, and quickly join them in the kitchen for their long-awaited introductions. Sean suggests he and Elijah bunk together, and the two return to the car to collect his belongings.

No sooner had they gotten him settled than Grant, Bella and Rori arrive with a carload of groceries. Mirabella has volunteered to work some kitchen magic, so the whole house is in for a treat. Hellos intermingled with the flurry of unpacking has managed to roust Cady from her afternoon nap. She appears around the corner rubbing sleep from her eyes. Loretta just leans back against the wall, happily sharing the moment with Henry, who could never really leave her alone.

Unbeknownst to the housemates, the additional stone has really amplified the light. Dan notices though. That, and a whole lot more. He envies them the laughter, the companionship, and most of all – he envies them the food! He and the boys have been living off convenience store sandwiches for far too long, and the wonderful smells emanating from that farmhouse tonight are almost more than he can bear.

Reardon can hear the frustration in Dan's voice when he calls in to report on the latest arrival. Unfortunately, the news he is about to deliver may only bring him further irritation, so he does his best to serve it up with a spoonful of sugar.

"Stanley will be yours for the duration, Dan, and I understand Jeannine is on her way, as well," Reardon offers before delivering the unappealing news. "I need you to send Chad and Neil back up to the city. Have them in place by tomorrow evening."

"But Sir," Dan objects, before Reardon interrupts him.

"I know, Dan. You've been a real trooper. I assure you, it's been noticed. Just keep your wits about you and this will all be over before you know it."

That's exactly what I'm afraid of, Dan thinks to himself, as he silently releases the call.

"ARE WE READY?"

Brogan had given little thought to his van in terms of family transportation, and the interior leaves a bit to be desired. The windowless compartment contains one small mattress along with an assortment of fast food containers that are strewn across the floor.

Bagging up the trash and random debris, he tosses it into a dumpster out in the alley, and takes a moment to contemplate their options. He could borrow a vehicle, yet it's the middle of the night and he's made no arrangements. Mass transit would limit his ability to protect them, now that their faces have been plastered the world over. To his mind, a rental car will be their best bet, so he returns to the house through the back gate to share his idea with the Moms.

Both Lorna and Rosalie are in agreement with his logic, and Justin is just happy to be going on a trip! So with duffles and grocery bags and one tiny suitcase, the escaping quartet shuffles out to the alley. Brogan opens the gate and checks in both directions before assisting them into the van. While the ladies are somewhat startled by such a true glimpse of bachelorhood, it looks an awful lot like camping to one adventure-craving boy.

Scrambling in through the side door, he quickly bolts for the tail section and starts building a fort. After determining that the rear doors are actually locked, Rosalie settles onto the mattress beside her son while Lorna agrees to ride shotgun. Brogan offers Rose a sheepish grin in the rearview, then rallies his troops with a resounding cry.

"Aaare weee readyyyy?!" he asks in his best carnival voice, to which Justin just squeals with delight!

They're well on their way long before Jeannine tracks the van to the rental agency. Tired and frustrated, she rings up the Commander, all the while preparing for the tongue-lashing.

"Jeannine, Sir. They ditched the van for a rental and I missed them," she confesses. "What would you like me to do?"

"Hmmmm," he ponders momentarily. "Okay. I want to you map the route to the farm from the rental place. Chances are, that's exactly what they did." Hearing her exhaustion, he offers her some words of support. "It's alright, Jeannine. You'll catch 'em, and then you can get a good night's sleep. Hang in there, kiddo. We're almost there," he assures her before signing off.

Brogan and Lorna are feeling rather bewildered as sunrise slowly creeps onto the interstate. What they had been mistaking for roadkill in the early morning light are actual living creatures perched beside the highway. Deer and raccoon stand poised at the shoulder, and if Brogan's not mistaken, they're seem to be observing their passage. Squirrels and rabbits are scrambling

251

for position as a beaver wanders up from the marshlands below. Just beyond the wood line a mother bear quiets her cubs, all the while watching for the coming of the boy.

Jeannine too is noticing the abundance of wildlife, and is getting rather irritated with the slow moving traffic. Weaving into the passing lane, she draws up beside the offending vehicle and can't resist a glimpse of the slothful driver. As she peers into the other vehicle, Jeannine is startled to discover that Justin is smiling back at her through the rear window.

He presses his tiny hand against the glass, and something inside her just shifts. A veil has been lifted, and the sensation overtaking her body can only be described as *grace*. It's beauty; it's forgiveness; it's peace. Looking into the faces of the animals, she now recognizes the source of their reverence and watches their eyes as they wait and then follow his every movement.

Faced with the miraculous, Jeannine is now struggling to drive through the tears. Her heart is overflowing with the knowledge, and with the truth of what this mission entails.

"AND THEN THERE WERE NINE"

It's late afternoon when the entourage arrives. Regardless of any misgivings, they had a wonderful adventure, full of bridges and hotel rooms and lots of new experiences for an impressionable four-year-old. The tollbooths were a particular favorite, as all the cars jockeyed for position and then raced headlong from the starting gate as if there were a prize.

Even Rosalie has regained her smile, and let go of the serious crinkles that had been distorting her perspective. Their welcome is as warm as sunlight itself with each member of the household awaiting the grand event. Loretta instantly spots a shift within Lorna – her eyes, and in fact her whole demeanor, are different than the woman she had met in the airport. Studying her amidst the commotion, she suspects that they all have been changed.

However, her thoughts are soon disrupted by a perceptive black dog who begins barking excitedly at the dancing of crows. The trees are just full of them today. Rori can't seem to shake the tickle at the back of her brain, which is as good a reason as any to keep the old hands moving. With a bit of reshuffling, they quickly open the last room for Rosalie, Lorna and Justin, and with a house full of people, Brogan's grateful for the couch.

Grant and Bella are whipping up a mountain of her very own *Cornbread Fried Chicken* and the enticing aroma has mouths watering as far as the scent will travel. Lizzie is busy snapping the ends off fresh green beans when Justin wanders out into the kitchen, and she gives him one to sample as he continues on his way. He's never seen a house with more than one floor, and she chuckles as he surveys the back staircase like he's preparing to tackle Mount Everest.

Before long, dinner is ready and the entire crowd, including one pint-sized explorer, find a seat along Loretta's dining table. Once everyone is seated, a smiling Justin stands up on his chair and places his stone with the others at the center of the table.

With the addition of the ninth and completion of the set, the bowl emits a halo of light that reaches far beyond the walls that surround them. Recognizing the now familiar sight, Dan contacts the Commander with confirmation of the ninth.

There's lots of laughter and conversation around the table as fourteen people and one black dog celebrate a reunion more sacred than most of them know. It's a feast fit for a king with fresh corn on the cob, creamy mashed potatoes, green bean casserole and enough chicken to feed a small army. This evening, at least, all is well in the world.

With full bellies and plenty to discuss, the adults linger over coffee and dessert while Justin suggests a walk outside with Joe. Rosalie is having difficulty letting him go, yet the longing in his eyes is undeniable. Her instincts have been on overdrive since the accident, not to mention the mall and the reporters. Gazing down at his pale complexion, she knows that what he really needs is some sunshine and a dose of fresh air. So Mom swallows hard and offers up her blessing, as six happy, little feet, along with two larger ones, tromp off for adventure in the great outdoors.

"Can you keep a secret?" Justin asks, with a twinkle.

"That depends on the secret," Joe answers him honestly.

Moments later, the screen door slams, and the man, the boy and the dog start out down the old dirt lane. Gold Dog is practically prancing in the company of his newfound friend, and the three go marching off together to capture what's left of the day. Boyhood comes calling in the form of crickets and grasshoppers, which quickly disappear between the tall meadow grasses. With a heart-full of smiles, Joe watches over them as they explore the great world with their very new eyes.

Upon reaching the edge of the paved road, Justin reaches up to take hold of Joe's hand. It's been a long while since Joe's felt a hand so small in his, and he cherishes this moment with his newest, youngest friend. The last stretch is brief with just a few hundred feet to their final destination, a rusted, old bread truck, tucked discreetly away under low-hanging branches. Despite Joe's hesitation and Gold Dog's raised hackles *(the scent of malevolence is strong here)*, the three strangers boldly approach the rear of the truck. With a boost from Joe, Justin raps soundly on the metal door.

Dumbfounded, Roy turns to Dan and offers a gesture to match his expression. Dan simply shrugs and shakes his head, then reaches down and tugs open the latch.

"And what can I do for you gentlemen," Dan asks, with a bit of a smirk.

"I know you're hungry, and this tastes *really* good," states Justin quite matter-of-factly, handing him the bag.

Dan hesitates a moment before accepting, yet hasn't the heart to disappoint the boy…or maybe he's been smelling it all afternoon. Either way, he thanks them politely and exchanges a nod before closing the door. Bewildered and amazed, he sets down the sack and immediately dials up Reardon.

Although, despite better judgment, Roy is chompin' that chicken before Dan even hangs up the call.

"SPECULATION"

After hours of conversation and a mountain of food, the entire house is fast asleep when the Commander arrives on the scene. Stanley has been appointed to the night shift, and greets him on arrival at their now-revealed outpost. The others are resting at a nearby motel, although both Dan and Jeannine are both battling nightmares from opposite sides of their adjoining wall. Each arrives independently at a similar conclusion, that first thing in the morning, they'll be talking to Reardon.

Perhaps he sensed their discomfort, or maybe his own, but the Commander will not be involving either of them in the extraction. By 4:30am, he's established his command center and is initiating contact with each separate faction. Lou and Riley are in position outside the home of our newlyweds, Carlie and Patrick. Work is already underway at the family farm, so Zach and Lloyd put the focus on Levi's mom.

Mitch and Ted have remained in the company of Eleanor, Bridgette and Hannah for the past several days, under the guise of national security. While Mitch has practice his diplomacy, Ted has clear instructions not to engage. To say the least, it's not been comfortable for anyone involved, and even Eleanor, the pacifist, has at times considered violence.

257

Last to confirm will be Neil and Chad, who breached Grant's secure complex posing as elevator maintenance. They plan to be inside the apartment well before daybreak, to secure the hostages with minimal disturbance.

With all peripheral elements in place, Reardon has exactly one hour to coordinate the primary offensive. The team is already en route, and scheduled to arrive within minutes. These are the order-takers. They're not paid to think or to reason, just to get the job done. The Commander has always respected that in a person, yet in this particular instance, he is finding it rather disturbing.

The further he's gotten into this project, the more at odds he's felt. He's not a questioner. Once he accepts the mission, he accepts the charge, and all it entails. Conscience has no business in the end zone, he reasons. Granted, the stakes have never been higher, yet the Commander has never been prone to speculation. So he sends Stanley out for coffee, dons his black flak jacket and stares out intently at the pre-dawn sky.

"THE EXTRACTION"

Loretta rises promptly at six, just as she has for most of her life. She quietly makes her way to the kitchen, careful to avoid the squeaky spots she has come to know well. The aroma of coffee soon sweeps up the back staircase, then drifts along the corridor until it touches every room.

Grant awakens with images of destruction. Bella is still sleeping, so he slips down the stairs, grateful for the comfort of Maimie and her old percolator. Next up is Justin, whose tiny feet sound like magic scampering over their heads. At the foot of the stairs, he disappears into Loretta's arms as she greets him with a big, morning hug. His smile holds all the promise of a sunrise, and penetrates her straight to the core.

Levi and Joe are at the front of the herd, followed by Rori and Lizzie, who leave Cady behind to sleep. Sean and Elijah are stumbling close behind, scratching and yawning as they shoulder each other down the hallway. Lorna can no longer stand the suspense and soon creeps from her room to join the parade.

Perhaps Brogan felt their eyes on him as he lay sprawled on the sofa, or maybe his own snoring finally brought him around. Either way, he bolts wide-awake as nine sets of eyes peek around the corner. Donning his best comedic grin, he disappears like a flash into the first floor

259

restroom, as the kitchen explodes into laughter. It appears all the hoopla is enough to rally the others, and by 6:45, they're all seated at the breakfast table, and gathered 'round their centerpiece of stones.

Outside the window glass, past the porch and past the yard, the room appears positively radiant with an extraordinary light. No doubt the image will be etched into dozens of memories, for crouched along the tree line and out beyond the barn, throughout the meadow and behind the stonewalls, soldiers are preparing to advance.

Men dressed all in black sporting helmets and shields, tear gas and flash grenades, AK's and Mac-10's, are watching from the mud and listening for the call. All across Loretta's farm, perched on every branch on every tree, the crows are observing silently through coal black eyes.

On Reardon's signal, helicopters swarm overhead, dangling men like spiders high above the rooftop. SWAT teams storm the farmhouse from both the ground and the air, penetrating windows and doorways from every possible direction. Within seconds, the entire house is inundated, and weapons of all description are expertly trained on Loretta's breakfast table. By the time the stone keepers grasp what is happening, they're completely surrounded with nowhere to go.

Gold Dog may never forgive himself for being distracted by the bacon while malevolence crept up and took him by surprise. Leaping to his feet, he begins growling from a place deep down in his chest. He has never felt more fierce in his life. Circling his people, he snaps and lunges and staves off the intruders as best he can. Suddenly, he feels a sharp pinch behind his left shoulder, and all at once the brave dog slumps lifeless to the floor.

Joe and Aurora drop instantly to their knees, and Rori is crying as she stares up in bewilderment at the unremorseful shooter. Cady feels nauseous, yet refuses to succumb. Her maternal instincts are torn between the stones and her baby, as she is not at all certain one will survive without the other. Loretta is beside herself as fat tears roll down her cheeks, and begins praying wholeheartedly for all that she's worth. The other men are posturing defensively, while somewhere in the background, Justin begins to speak.

When the voice of reason rises above the chaos, Bella looks to Lizzie and together they lift Justin up onto the table. Opening his mouth, he issues a single note that pierces the confusion and silences the room. Dumbfounded, all eyes are trained on the boy, as Lizzie takes Bella's hand, who takes Loretta's, who takes Sean's, and so forth, until all of the housemates are joined together around Justin and the stones.

Just as the boy is getting ready to speak, the kitchen phone rings, and Reardon snatches it quickly to his ear. With all eyes on him now, he listens intently for countless seconds before uttering two words that send a chill down their spines.

"Collateral damage," he states flatly without so much as a blink, then promptly hangs the receiver back up on the wall. His eyes are flat, yet not quite merciless, as he redirects their attention back onto the boy and secretly disables the ringer. Stunned and silenced, both invaders and housemates stand before Justin until even the Commander is holding his breath.

"The stones will be taken, yet all is not lost. We can lay down with our fear or we can find the courage to become something more. Have faith in what is possible, and all will be well in the world," speaks the wise prophet with a child-sized tongue.

Part IV

"CHOOSING WISELY"

PART IV
"CHOOSING WISELY"

"COLLATERAL DAMAGE"

"Well, well, I guess you two are more disposable than we realized," scoffs Jonas to his captives.

"Collateral damage," he indicates with finger quotes. "That's what your precious Reardon called you – *collateral damage*. How's that for ya? We'll show him some damage," he snarls, as Beverly threatens Chad's testicles with a meat tenderizer.

Duct taped to a kitchen chair, he's hoping for a miracle, but even a cheap trick will do about now. He can feel her breath, hot and sour by morning, taunting him with whispers that still linger in his ear.

"Pretty boy like you, I bet yer momma is jus' *prayin'* for grandkids," she spews, leaving traces of spittle to cool against his cheek. Circling their regret-filled intruders, she slaps the cold mallet repeatedly into her palm with all the calculation of a street-trained survivor.

"Who's behind this, and what have they done with my daughter?!" Jonas demands, with but a thin layer of carbon dioxide between his face and Neil's.

Exchanging frightened glances, the two bound men look pleadingly from Jonas to Beverly and back again.

And so the interrogation begins.

"DELIVERANCE"

The helicopter hovering just out of earshot drops into Loretta's front yard mere inches from the site of dear Henry's demise. Lifetimes have passed in no time at all, and as the extraction team relays their precious cargo, the Triad is in transit as well.

On separate planes from separate locations, each is being quietly held hostage by their own brand of fear. Madeleine's thoughts are of course with her children and grandchildren. Her grandson is a junior in high school, and has an exceptional talent for music. In fact, she's listening to his latest composition right now.

And from the moment Bethany was born, the air just smelled a little sweeter. It was as if she arrived on a sunbeam to spread light to spread light throughout the world. So filled as they are with potential, Madeleine can barely imagine a reality without them. Her heart begins to spill over, and she reaches for a tissue to dab at her eyes. *There are a world full of reasons to keep trying,* she assures herself, gazing out the window at a brooding sky.

On a distant plane and from a far different perspective, Emanuel is busy weighing the odds of mankind's survival. He, on the other hand, is focused on our shortcomings. *Has God, in his infinite wisdom, grown tired of our cruelty?* he speculates, rolling through the myriad of atrocities committed each day. They can be witnessed any time, on any given channel and in nearly every language. From torture and genocide to slavery and sex abuse, the ethics of humanity have worn dangerously thin.

Corporations know that homogenized greed is more palatable to shareholders, so they disguise the truth in profit margins that allow a blind eye. Disease and starvation can be easily lost between balance sheets while hoping no one will notice that the babies are dying. The more he considers, the more he condemns, before finally relinquishing judgment. Frustrated, he asserts his power elsewhere, and summons up the flight attendant to bring him more wine.

On yet another aircraft, Wilhelm is entertaining more pragmatic concerns. *Will the world be intact when we finally touch ground? What forms of communication can be sustained? If the stones crash the transport plane, can they be retrieved from the ocean floor?* His mind is so consumed with scenarios, it's practically dizzying. Wilhelm takes a solid pull from his single malt, then releases a long and uneasy sigh. Whatever the outcome of this fateful day, he had better be prepared to hit the ground running.

Handing off the highball glass, he closes his eyes and settles back into the seat, determined to quiet his restless mind. No amount of fretting will prepare him, and exhaustive speculation is an indulgence he can ill afford. Focusing his energy, he regulates his breathing, slows his heart rate and eventually silences the whirlwind inside his head. It's a skill he's been practicing since college, shared as it was by his favorite professor. Few from the class took it seriously, yet those who did have long reaped the rewards.

Certainly, Reardon could benefit from a similar knowledge, flying thousands of miles with his heart in his throat. The stones have been pulsing since they stormed the farmhouse – not exactly a slow pulse, but not quite the strobe effect that Dan had described. The image of that little boy has stayed with him, and he's absolutely certain that Justin is all that saved them. The Commander no more than forces one fear into submission than another arrives in its place.

Thank goodness the rest of his extraction team are oblivious to the point of their mission. Looking from one clueless face to the next, Reardon finds a semblance of comfort in their naïve expressions. He is surrounded by a sea of young faces, each brimming with ignorance and so much potential. It's an enviable position, especially today. As far as they're concerned, the sun will rise tomorrow on their parents and children, just as it has every day of their lives.

He resides with those innocent faces for the duration of the journey, barely breathing for fear they'll see through his disguise. When the pilot finally signals their descent, Reardon feels his abdominals tighten, followed by his shoulders and then the remainder of his body. He's fought wars, combated terrorism, lived through multiple marriages and even survived the death of his beloved son, yet he has never been more frightened than he is right now.

It's one thing to fight for freedom, for democracy, or to defend against oppression and tyranny, yet he has never before been asked to champion the planet. If what they've been telling him is true, there are just a handful of people standing between life as we know it and complete global extinction.

He doubts sleep will come any easier once he's finished this assignment. In fact, releasing the stones to strangers may prove far more difficult than he ever imagined.

"A GOOD DASH OF PROTOCOL"

As managing director of the laboratory complex, Julian reports to whichever client currently signing his paycheck. Today he is awaiting the Triad from within the back of a stretch limousine. Each on private planes, they are scheduled to arrive within minutes of one another, with Wilhelm the last to touch down. Therefore, Julian will be handling his own introductions, and nods to the driver as the first plane taxis to a stop.

Emanuel emerges quickly, disembarking amid a flurry of support staff, which speaks volumes of his need for indulgence. Taking note, Julian phones Richard with instructions to have plenty of servants on hand for their arrival, and then steps from the limo with a broad smile and a welcoming handshake. Despite feeling brusque and more than a little haggard from the trip, Emanuel grasps Julian's hand between both of his own and offers a heartfelt greeting.

In Emanuel's mind, Julian holds the key to all that lies ahead, and plans to afford him all due respect. The baggage is quickly deposited as both men take their places in the limo. Next they find Madeleine, tipping her Skycap, who swiftly stacks her luggage alongside the others in the trunk.

She's sizing up Julian as he crosses the tarmac, and approves of his posture, mannerisms and gait. A lot can be gleaned from how a person carries himself, and her assessment reveals confidence with a good dash of protocol. *Wilhelm has chosen wisely*, she concludes, matching the grip of Julian's handshake. Returning to the car, Emanuel greets her with a kiss on both cheeks as they depart to collect their final member.

The expression on Wilhelm's face can best be described as matter-of-fact. Of the three, he is most devoid of emotion, although Madeleine does a fine job of concealing. Wilhelm is nearly to the car by the time Julian steps out, and quickly dismisses all attempts at cordiality. A brisk handshake, a couple of nods and Wilhelm will accept no further delay.

His main concern is to brief the staff before Reardon arrives, so he foregoes any socializing in exchange for barking at his colleagues. Ignoring a hard stare from Madeleine, Wilhelm continues to deliver his list of instructions. The words are heard and messages received, yet he's done little to cultivate good will among his counterparts. It's a cool ride over to the complex, despite ample attention to climate control.

The supervisors are all assembled in the auditorium as Richard anticipates the arrival of big wigs. He's played host to Presidents and many corporate executives, yet these three people have earned respect the world over, from statesmen and commoners alike. There is something to be said for being chosen, so without hesitation, he's pulled all the stops. Iceberg water from Newfoundland, the

271

finest beef flown in from Japan, and only the freshest, locally grown produce has been procured for their guests.

Richard, Fatima and Lenore are waiting in the lobby, and they can literally feel the friction when the elevator doors finally part. One look at Julian confirms their suspicions. It's regrettable to know that even the most powerful and well-respected people in the world can find conflict within minutes. Concealing his disappointment, he welcomes the Triad with the epitome of grace. After a few minutes of freshening, they are escorted to a small side room to await their introductions. Madeleine is first to address the unspoken, determined as she is to set the proper tone.

"We're in this together, you know," she states, plainly directing her comments toward Wilhelm. "Each of us has a role here, none more important than the next, and I believe we can agree that the world is best served by our unity."

"Of course," agrees Emanuel. "These men and women hold our future in their hands, and they are looking to us for guidance and direction."

Wilhelm garners his comeuppance, which he follows with a splash of water to wash down his pride. Drawing fresh filtered air deep into his lungs, he straightens his spine, relaxes his jaw and proceeds to address his comrades with absolute deference. Action plan in place, the three make their entrance through a private door concealed at the back of the room.

Following Julian's introduction, Emanuel steps to the podium with his usual flourish, robes swaying for maximum effect. He taps the microphone several times before speaking to ensure that each ear in the room is focused on his words.

"On 17 August, a meteor entered our atmosphere, under the watchful eye of Church astronomers. Despite our quick response, nine stones were secretly recovered and then quickly dispatched into the random hands of strangers. Following an exhaustive search, all nine have finally been recovered, and within the hour, the prophesized crystals will be safely in our hands," Emanuel states to a round of applause.

"*Operation Starlight*," he continues, "was created to determine the mechanics, if you will, of these powerful stones. Mastery holds the key to immense possibility, the likes of which we've never known," he shares, smiling down at the sea of hopeful faces.

"Failure," he announces firmly, seeking eyes throughout the room, "will mean the end of our world. Complete devastation. A series of natural disasters will leave no corner of the planet unscathed, and according to the prophecy, it will render all of mankind virtually extinct. If our calculations are correct, as of today, we have less than four months."

The room falls silent with a sickening hush as the greatest minds of our time attempt to digest the unimaginable. Glances are exchanged, but few can find words to break the dread-filled silence.

"Faith!" booms Emanuel in a strong, clear voice, "Can move mountains. And we are putting our faith in your hands, your hearts, your minds. You are the best; you are the brightest; and we have every reason to believe you will succeed. It is your destiny. Bless you, and bless the work you are about to begin," he concludes, relinquishing the podium to Wilhelm.

"I want to thank you for setting aside your projects, your families and your lives to participate in *Operation Starlight*. This project is, and will continue to be conducted under the utmost secrecy. I cannot begin to stress the importance that the world remains insulated from the dangers at hand. We've seen the result of mass panic, and let me assure you, whatever challenges we have faced in the past pale in comparison to the one we're facing right now. Your knowledge, your expertise and your unique abilities have brought you to this room. The fate of the world now rests in your hands, and I want you to know that we are doing everything in *our* power to support you. And with that, please welcome my dear friend, Madeleine."

Allowing a moment for the chatter to subside, Madeleine clears her throat and begins. "We need you to suspend all forms of disbelief, and to open your minds to new modes of thinking. You have what it takes. You *are The Right Stuff.* Governments from across the globe have come together as never before," she reveals with a nod to Wilhelm. "Religions have convened in unprecedented fashion," she states, with a matching nod toward Emanuel. "Corporations the world over have declared bottomless pockets. You have the resources. You have the ability. All we're short on is time, so I will take no more of yours. The crystals are slated to arrive within minutes, so I wish you Godspeed on your mission, and I encourage each of you to do what you do best – *Succeed.*"

"THE AFTERMATH"

Following the extraction, Dan watches as the SWAT team emerge from the farmhouse like a swarm of angry bees. Turning away from the monitor, he catches Jeannine swiping away tears with the back of her hand. This has been a tough one. Probably the toughest.

In all the years they've been with Reardon, there's never been cause to question. The jobs have always been exciting, the crusades fairly ethical and the money – well let's just say they've always been well compensated for their efforts. Over the years, each has sacrificed a lot to remain with the unit, and about now both of them are questioning any number of those choices.

After two divorces, Dan gave up the illusion that marriage could ever survive 2:00am call-outs that leave him half way around the world, yet there was something about that chicken…. When Roy didn't fall over dead, he just couldn't help himself, and hungrily devoured several pieces, lickity-split, shall we say. He admires how complete strangers have become such a family. Glancing down, he sees the empty plate, and wonders if he'll ever return it.

Jeannine steps outside, and the roar of the chopper absorbs a frustrated scream. *What am I doing here? What if we're wrong? What if this boy could change the world and we just blew it?* Once the tears start, it's like she's tapped an artery with no way to stop the bleeding. Dan simply watches her climb into her car and drive away, while he himself stands frozen, just seconds from retching up breakfast.

And as the helicopter vanishes over the treetops, Loretta can practically taste the emptiness creeping up from the pit of her stomach. Swallowing hard, she sniffs back the tears, missing her Henry now more than ever. Within seconds, she's surrounded, first by Grant and Mirabella, then Justin, Sean and Levi. Soon the entire group is huddled around her, consoling one another in the wake of the invasion.

A beautiful noise rises out of the stillness, and though it's barely discernable, Aurora turns her head. Soon there is no mistaking the sound, as Gold Dog struggles to awaken from his anesthetic nap. Clambering to his feet, he is embraced by the loved ones he so bravely defended, and within moments begins sniffing for any leftover bacon.

"Will someone please tell me what the hell just happened?" Brogan finally asks incredulously.

Everyone laughs, including Justin, regardless of the "swear word." Language aside, the reporter's confusion is well warranted; so they all sit down to fill him in on the details. For two days they talk, comfort and plan, and on the third day, Brogan sets out for home, equipped with the story of a lifetime.

"THIRD DOWN"

By their third time touching down to earth, the stones appear to be maintaining a slow pulse status, which Reardon interprets as *Code Yellow – Be Alert*. He finds himself wishing Dan was along, or even Roy for that matter, both of them having witnessed different phases, if only from a distance.

His heart, not to mention his stomach, is jockeying for position in his esophagus, so he swallows hard and concentrates on breathing for the remainder of the flight. Once on the ground, he firmly grips the handle of the carrying case and swiftly disembarks. His steps are sure and certain, despite the beads of perspiration that have formed along his hairline and across his brow.

Had his attention been a little less focused, he may have noticed the crows pecking around the edges of the tarmac. They, however, are fully aware of his presence, or more specifically, that of the cargo he carries.

Julian, the Triad, and everyone else who can possibly fit, are packed into the lobby for a glimpse of the stones. The excitement is nearly electric as the Commander makes his debut. Crossing the foyer, he is escorted into a glass room that has been specifically designed for housing the crystals.

Cracking open the case, Reardon is relieved to find the stones glowing brilliantly as observers shield their eyes. Madeleine is first to place one hand against the other until the hallways are echoing with waves of applause. It's hard to feel the hero when you know you nearly wet yourself on more than one occasion. Although the banquet is delicious and the cocktails even better, the Commander is grateful when he can finally retire to his room. He may never admit it, and might just deny it under oath, but even the old man broke down that night.

Come morning begins the debriefing, and interviews with scientists on a myriad of subjects. For some he has answers, for others, more questions, yet all Reardon can think of is getting back home to his fish. Yeah, they're just fish, but the *tiger oscar* waits for him and always wags his tail. He smiles for a second, imagining those big, bulbous eyes rolling around to greet him.

He's ready now – for simpler things.

"AND A CHILD SHALL LEAD THEM"

by Brogan Cantrell

Researchers are investigating possible connections between the recent tornados and the vortex that recently appeared over Stuffolks. Further studies now reveal that a total of three similar events were witnessed across the continent, thousands of miles apart.

While satellite imaging was able to determine the location of each vortex, specifics are being withheld for reasons of personal privacy. In pinpointing the local sighting, we were astonished to discover the residence of none other than our "Miracle Boy " from Stuffolks Mall! After days of media hounding from around the globe, the boy's mother decided to contact this reporter with exclusive rights to their story.

At first meeting, there seems nothing particularly remarkable about the boy, yet within minutes it becomes clearly evident that there is no one else like him in the world. Readers may recall a terrible accident earlier this year that involved a mother, a child and a brakeless18-wheeler. All were severely injured, and the child lapsed into a lengthy coma.

In route to the hospital, the boy's grandmother encountered a traveler who presented her with a seemingly innocuous stone as a gift for her injured grandson. So she placed the stone beside the boy's pillow as she and her daughter endured weeks watching over the comatose child. From the moment he regained consciousness, the child was clearly different. The boy had awakened with knowledge and insights far beyond his years.

What began as a friendly update on his condition, turned into a welcome invitation, so, late last Thursday, amid a hail of reporters, they asked me to help them escape. After securing a proper vehicle, we gathered our belongings and proceeded straight toward the location of the largest vortex.

The trip was, without a doubt, the most extraordinary experience of my lifetime. Traveling down the road with dawn in the distance, shadows began to appear along the edges of our headlamps. Close inspection soon revealed a truth more amazing than fiction. All manner of wildlife – deer, eagles, rabbits, bear, you name it – were all there at the sides of the road, paying silent tribute as we rolled on past. Regardless of faith or denomination, the experience was nothing short of divine.

On arrival. we were greeted by a variety of others, all of whom had also been keepers of the stones. They welcomed us with such warmth and hospitality that it felt like going home – except for the bowl of glowing crystals at the center of the dining room table. Seems we brought the final stone, and with the addition of the ninth, a brilliant halo of light formed around the bowl that must have been visible for miles.

Each discussed changes they had undergone since receiving their stone, and their experiences ranged from feeling more peaceful to the actual healing of lifelong afflictions. Their stories were all quite compelling, yet this reporter still fell asleep on the skeptical side. Come morning, however, all doubts were clearly shattered.

At 6:48am, a SWAT team invaded the home and confiscated the crystals under threat of extreme force. No identification was presented, and for the sake of fourteen people, none was requested. It was the child's voice that was ultimately heard above the din, as he shared the following message:

"We can lay down with our fear, or we can find the courage to become something more. Have faith in what is possible, and all will be well in the world."

An undeniable calm overtook the room, while this amazing young man convinced a group of total strangers to quietly release their most prized possessions.

Clearly powerful, the stones were confiscated and have now been taken into custody. As citizens, we can only trust that these officials will act in our best interest. In the meantime, this reporter will be following our Miracle Boy, and promptly reporting any new wisdom from this pint-sized prophet.

"THE EXODUS"

Brogan's departure marks the beginning of the exodus, though he is quickly followed by an apologetic Grant. Marsbeck issued his final decree: return by next Monday or find a new job. Although it seemed perfectly logical on the telephone, Grant is already starting to wonder if he is willing, or able, to resume the corporate perspective. It's like he's in a dream that hasn't ended, so what's the dream and what's reality?

Kinship notwithstanding, the post-raid let-down has left them tired and disoriented, and for many it's just time to go home. Lizzie was offered the same ultimatum, and it's with a heavy heart that she's bidding farewell to her housemates. She and Aurora found more in common than either expected, and the experience of sharing Cady's pregnancy will remain with her for life. Every relationship holds it's own unique moments, and promises are exchanged along with best intentions.

A tearful Bella hugs Loretta goodbye, having bonded far more than words will ever know. Within each of their hearts, the stones are still glowing – forever and ever. Amen. Following a list of assurances used to prolong the conversation, Loretta finally turns her loose with a kiss on both cheeks. Grant, on the other hand, is looking more and more like his Grandfather with each passing second.   *That's not who he is,* Loretta reminds herself.

Packing the final items into the car, Grant notices someone walking up the driveway. As he draws closer, it's clear he's carrying something, and as soon as he gets within earshot, the man calls out to them.

"I just wanted to thank you!" he exclaims, waving the plastic sack in his hand. When they make no move to escape, he picks up the pace and arrives slightly winded in front of Grant's dusty car. Catching his breath, Dan returns the plate to Loretta, along with a response to her baffled expression.

"The boy brought me some chicken," he explains. A tiny curl tugs at the corner of Loretta's mouth as she nods her acceptance. "Best I've ever eaten. Thank you." After a brief pause that hovers along the edges of awkward, Dan finally finds some words. "I'm truly sorry for how things went down. I had no idea they would play it that way."

"Who's 'they?'" poses Grant, in a tone less accusatory than either would have guessed.

"Couldn't tell you. Not that high on the food chain," he admits, shaking his head. "I just want to tell you that what you did here was special. I'm not sure what happened, but I know it was good." Regulations aside, Dan hands Loretta his card. "My job here is over. Mission complete. But, if you ever find yourself needing somebody like me, you just a call, okay? Anytime," he assures her, quickly turning away before a tear brims the lid.

He waves a quick goodbye as he walks back down the dirt lane, leaving them silently staring until he disappears completely into the shimmering distance.

"HEAR HIM ROAR"

Gretchen actually winces when she places the newspaper at the center of Wilhelm's desk. He's still out on his morning run, and she'd just as soon be absent for the headline if she can think up and errand before he returns. Working as Wilhelm's assistant for nearly seven years now, she knows better than anyone how he hates an oversight, particularly when it's his own.

Fortunately, the slap of the storm door alerts her that's he's home, and she quickly retreats to the rear of the house. Just about the time the roar reaches up around the rafters, she realizes this will be a perfect day for archiving. Having left him with his usual morning tea, Gretchen has no intention of being seen unless summoned. He's a good man, and a fair man, yet can be entirely inconsolable in the face of his mistakes.

Fuming, Wilhelm swirls a mouthful of tea in an effort to douse the fire now raging inside. *How could I have been so careless? What was I thinking?! Clearly not thinking at all!* he chastises, glaring down at the headline: *"And A Child Shall Lead Them."* Disgusted, he tosses the newspaper aside and stares out across the dense valley. *So much for secrecy,* he concludes, and begins mentally preparing for the inevitable fallout.

"IN UNISON"

Elijah and Sean choose to exit in unison. Be it chivalry, chemistry, perspective or humor, the bond between them is unmistakable. Yesterday, for instance, they handed out rock candy anointed as "surrogates," and with a grin and a twinkle, warned Lizzie not to wash hers.

Loretta will miss their antics, like tossing pumpkins in the house until her hair became just a shade whiter, or serenading the sunset from up on the rooftop. In her heart, they're all her children now, and it pains her to see them getting ready to leave. The beds are stripped and the sheets are in the wash, and all too soon, it's time for goodbye. She waves them down the driveway through teardrops, until Levi sneaks up behind her and covers her eyes with his hands.

"Hey, G-2, whatcha doin' lookin' backwards?" he asks her.

"G-2? What in the world are you talking about?" Loretta squalls, all at once happy for the distraction.

"Well…" Cady begins, "it seems this baby is short one grandmother. Think you'd be up for the job?"

Loretta covers her heart with both hands to keep it from leaping right out of her chest. The smile on her face could swallow the whole south in one sweet mouthful. Clearly her hands will be first to speak, as they draw Cadence close for a legendary hug. Between the waterworks and rocking, it's practically a carnival ride, and one that Cady's been waiting a lifetime to enjoy.

Levi leaves them alone to go finish packing and to coordinate a secret mission with Rori. Justin likes watching the adults sneak around, and follows them upstairs to find out what they're doing. Already, he thinks the world of Levi, and has decided to enlist him as his older brother. Levi and Rori make him promise to keep the secret, so he crosses his heart and runs off down the hallway with a small but mischievous grin.

By the time Rori makes it back to the kitchen, Justin's already whispering into Rosalie's ear, and with a nod she and Lorna disappear up the stairs. A wonderful secret can be simply delicious, and one little boy looks ready to burst!

"Way to go, buddy," Rori proclaims, giving him a big thumbs up.

The surprise has been underway for some time now, and when Cady and Loretta come back inside, Levi and the others are all gathered in the living room. Remaining at Loretta's side, Cady smiles and squeezes her hand.

"We all just wanted to say thank you, you know, for everything you've done," stammers a rather nervous Levi as he presents their gracious hostess with an exquisitely carved box.

288

Her expression is stunned as she looks repeatedly from his face to the box and back again.

"Sean made the box, Grant did the carving and Elijah, he did the beautiful painting. That's real gold, you know," he can't help but tell her, despite a careful look from Cady. "Open it."

Loretta slowly raises the hinged lid, and then gasps on glimpsing its contents. Inside the rich, velvet lining rests a hand-tooled book covered with genuine leather.

"Joe made the book and Lizzie made the paper. Isn't that amazing? Who knew you could make paper? Huh? Well, she knew just what she was doing, let me tell ya," Levi rambles.

"And who did this beautiful tool work?" Loretta asks him, running her palm across the surface of the book.

The blush probably started somewhere below his neckline, but we're absolutely certain it traveled all the way up before finally turning back. He nudges Aurora to move things along before the crimson gets into his eyes. With a chuckle, she obliges, and offers Loretta another beautifully wrapped gift.

"You were chosen, and then you chose us, and there's no way we can ever quite thank you enough," smiles Aurora.

Finding a seat in the wingback, Loretta rests the small package in her lap. Her eyes are traveling around the room, moving from face to face as she works at untying the ribbons.

On opening the first box, she is presented with another – this one of the velvet variety. She slips it into her hand, and with one last look around the room, Loretta pries open the fancy, hinged case. There, on a bed of satin, rests a gorgeous heart pendant made entirely of gold. It's a nice size, nothing garish, and well rounded with a softly brushed finish. In the center is a brilliant heart-shaped diamond, surrounded by nine gleaming rays etched deeply into the surface. Loretta is simply beside herself.

"Mirabella is responsible for the lovely design," explains Aurora. "She said it came to her in a dream, and as soon as she sketched it, we knew. Cady found that fabulous stone and had it specially cut for the centerpiece. And well, you know me and Gold Dog have a knack for the shiny stuff," she grins.

Once the chain is clasped around her neck, Loretta stands proudly before the mirror admiring the gift. It's questionable if she'll move beyond speechless, yet with a good deal of courage, she swallows the lump and finally takes charge of her words.

"Each of you mean the world to me," she beams at them through the tears. "You arrived just about the time I thought my life was over. Leave it to Henry to never leave me alone!" she chuckles, dabbing at her eyes. "When I picked you, I thought it was just for a moment, for a reason. Now I just know, you'll be in my heart forever. I love you all so very much. Thank you!"

"And we love you back," replies Cady, squeezing Loretta's hand, "Yet I can almost hear Charlotte calling from here, and we all know what *that* means," she teases, offering up a reprieve from the overwhelm.

The pickup truck is loaded, and Levi helps Cady climb into the cab. Returning to Loretta, he swoops her up in a huge bear hug that literally lifts her off of her feet. She's giggling like a schoolgirl with a secret, and she hugs him right back in good measure.

"I'll never go to ChinaMart without you," he promises, piling himself into the truck.

Spinning a few rocks, he waves an arm out the window, and quickly disappears in a dust cloud that forces them all inside. Lorna has fixed a pitcher of tea, laced with lemon and mint and enough sugar to lure a small child. So imagine her surprise at not finding him anywhere, though he was standing right here just a moment ago.

"Has anyone seen Justin?" she asks, although mostly to Rosalie.

About then, he comes trouncing down the staircase waving a very special drawing that he hands straight to Loretta. She thanks him warmly with a kiss and a hug before he abruptly runs off in search of the dog.   Smiling, she looks down at the picture, and in that moment, her whole world begins to shift.

Reaching instinctively for something to steady herself, she clutches the edge of the table as Joe moves in quickly to steady her.   Settling Loretta onto a dining room chair, Joe hot-foots it to the kitchen for a glass of that tea. He returns with the drink, along with a bevy of women, each of them exchanging worried glances.

"Please everyone, just sit down," she urges, motioning toward the empty chairs.

Once they're all seated, Loretta reveals the piece of paper that has been waiting face down on the table.   There's an audible gasp as recognition spreads throughout the room. Centered on the page is a crayon drawing, which bears a striking resemblance to the pendant now draped around Loretta's neck. Yet thanks to Lorna, this drawing has been carefully dated – the day Justin came home from the hospital. A series of glances are exchanged, while each attempts to digest the information.

"May I invite you to stay on a while longer?" Loretta asks, glancing from Rosalie to Lorna. Both heads are nodding in unison, with relief is clearly evident in their eyes.

"SENIOR AVENGERS"

The curbside welcome proves warmer than expected, with handshakes and hugs all around. Perhaps it's Harry who is most surprised when his gesture is so wholeheartedly returned. Something in Grant's eyes seems warmer now, as if Harry is seeing him for the very first time.

As the two men remove Grant's bags from the trunk, Bella grabs one of her own. Tomorrow will be soon enough to see her own apartment. Lizzie leaves hers in the car for now, as at this particular moment, they are the least of her concern. The old fear in her belly has been replaced with excitement, and she is practically dancing with anticipation as the elevator creeps between floors.

Hearts on either side of the apartment door have reached full crescendo, and Jonas can hardly wait to lay eyes on his beautiful daughter. There are no words as he sways and rocks his darling Lizzie – the child he was none too certain would return. There are unexpected tears in all of their eyes, as Beverly helps the others with their bags.

"Not to worry, we took care of everything," Beverly whispers conspiratorially to Bella, who assumes she's referring to the apartment.

The two set about rounding up some beverages while Grant hauls their luggage to his room. The father and daughter reunion is heartfelt and permeating, reconnecting from a place that neither has visited in years. For the first time in nearly forever, Jonas feels strong and comfortable in his skin. Tears and all, right here, right now, he's exactly the man he had once hoped to become.

"Well," Jonas grins, "So far no cops, so I guess we're in the clear," he laughs, wiping away teardrops with the back of his hand. When three perplexed faces turn in his direction, Jonas suggests they may want to sit down.

About the time Lizzie's hand gets stuck to the kitchen chair, Jonas and the *Duchess* exchange a furtive glance, and Beverly makes a quick exit for the bathroom. When Grant phoned two days ago to announce their return, Jonas finally cut through the duct tape and set the captives free.

"Ya see, Beverly was up to pee," Jonas reveals loudly, "when she heard someone out in the hallway, and then the door knob starts moving, ya know, and sure enough, they were picking the lock! So she wakes me up, real quiet like, and I'll be damned if they weren't tryin' to get in! So we grabbed your bat, Grant, and that metal lamp off your dresser, right, and we're standin' there, on either side of the bedroom door just waitin' for 'em." Beverly's nodding as she reenters the room, and you can practically watch their adrenaline rise.

"Sure enough, they come creepin' into the bedroom, and that's when we let 'em have it! We clobbered 'em somethin' good, let me tell ya. And, well, then we duct taped 'em to your chairs, Grant.

Sorry about the glue and all – I'm sure it'll come off. Anyway, so the next thing we did was call down to your Grandma's house, ya know, and told the fella that answered the phone that we were holdin' his men and that if he knew what was good for 'em, he'd better let you go," he recounts with just a glimmer of his former ferocity.

"'*Collateral damage,*' was all he said. Can you imagine? So we held 'em as hostages, 'cause you never know, right? What else could I do?"

By now his hands are trembling and there's a slight crack in his voice, and Lizzie moves quickly to her father's side. She hugs them both, and pulls them in close, grateful for their courage and that no one was harmed.

This new information only heightens Grant's suspicions, and he ponders the necessity of such an elaborate operation. He is mid-speculation when Bella raises her glass for a toast.

"I'd say we're in the company of some first class heroes! Here's to you Mr. Breslen, and to you Beverly! To our *Senior Avengers* and *Protectors of the Realm!*"

"FROTHING AT THE MOUTH"

While it was difficult to leave her at Merriweather Hall, Justin could hardly imagine Cady looking any happier. Her glow is positively priceless. Charlotte was on hand to greet them, and for the first time in years, Cadence actually saw her mother smile. Together, she and Maggie had assembled the nursery *(with Maggie in charge of assembly, no doubt)*, and Cady is simply overjoyed.

Levi stayed the night, then hit the road early that next morning, careful to avoid any tearful goodbyes. Maggie packed him a cooler chock full of goodies that could last him clear into next week. Leaving a note on the counter, he slips out the kitchen door, disappearing like a star into the bright face of dawn. There's half a smile on his face and half a tear in his eye as he watches the mansion grow distant in the rearview. *They'll be just fine,* he concludes, and redirects his attention toward the interstate.

Several rest stops and a few hundred miles later, he rolls into town just in time for dinner with Mom. She has no idea he's coming, yet that makes no mattermind – Mom's incapable of cooking for less than four people. He sneaks in the front door and creeps down the hallway hoping to surprise her in the kitchen.

"That you, Levi?" his mother calls out.

"How do you *do* that?!" he exclaims, both astonished and amazed.

"You're my boy," she answers, setting down the half-peeled potato and wiping her hands across a well-seasoned apron.

Arms wide, she draws him in close, as one hand travels north to grab a handful of hair. There are tears in her eyes when she looks into his, yet she will not allow her son to look away.

"Levi, you ever scare me like that again and I'll...I'll...," she stammers, before losing all control and sobbing openly into his chest.

"What are you talking about?" he bluffs, fully intending to spare her the details. This time her eyes are angry, yet Levi would rather endure her wrath than frighten her any more.

"Look," she addresses him sternly, slowly entwining her fingers with the front of his shirt. "Five days ago, men with guns came into my house." Levi's face goes a ghostly white as she continues to describe her terrifying ordeal. "Your father and brother were out in the barn, a' course, and I was right here fixin' breakfast. They walked right in, real quiet ya know, and I guess I didn't hear 'em over the bacon. You know *that* won't happen again!

"Anyway, they had handguns pointed right at me, an' told me to be quiet or someone might get hurt. Said they were only here to make sure you made the right decision. So we sat here at the table for nearly an hour until one got a phone call, and then they left. Your brother saw the car. Told him it was just some church people out on a mission. Haven't told your father yet either. Wanted to talk to you first. But that number you gave me just rings and rings...."

Levi's heart is breaking as he attempts to navigate the whirlpool of emotions now threatening to sink him. "I'm so sorry, Mom," he mouths through the tears, all at once breathless with the weight of so much guilt.

"Is it drugs, Levi? You can tell me if it is," she pleads courageously. "I just don't want to lose you," she chokes over of the thick lump wedged in her throat.

"No, Mom. It's not drugs," he assures her, shaking his head at the irony. "If you want the truth, I think it's some kind of miracle."

Taking him by the arm, she sits him down in a kitchen chair and settles in across the table to listen to her boy. Pausing for a moment, he carefully calculates exactly where to begin. He starts with meeting Loretta, skipping over Zeke and the saltier parts, and moves quickly to receiving the stone.

Watching his features, she listens as he talks, and it somewhere along the line it becomes painfully clear that her boy has truly grown into a man. The moment is cut short, however, when the kitchen door is practically yanked from its hinges.

"When the hell did you get back?" Brandi grills him threateningly. "I saw your truck on my way home, and just thought I'd stop by to find out *when the hell you planned on calling me!*" The sarcasm and hairy eyeball are accompanied with a solid punch to his right bicep, followed by a quick, but painful bear hug. With one glimpse at his Mom's face, Brandi turns back to Levi in astonishment.

"You told her, didn't you?" Not yet aware of more recent events, Brandi lets it all slide before Levi can even get a word in to stop her. "There's nothing he could have done, Ma. Zeke was dead within minutes."

Looking into her son's eyes, his mother can feel the fresh scars it has left on his soul. The inhalation is audible, as her hand moves instinctively to cover her mouth. She reaches for him, and Levi recoils, unworthy of forgiveness.

Refusing to take *no* for an answer, she pulls him to her and just rocks until each one finds some semblance of peace. Brandi has remained silent since the moment she realized her awful mistake. She thought of leaving once, yet one look from Levi's Mom glued her to the seat.

"I knew you two had a secret," she reveals. "Levi doesn't leave like that," she says to Brandi. Turning to face Levi, "And when you got back, you couldn't even look me in the eye."

"Forgive me for saying," Brandi prefaces gently.

"Why start now?" snorts Levi.

"Okay, whatever," she concedes. "I'm your friend and I love you, and I think you need to get the hell out of here and go find that girl!"

"What girl?!" demands Mom.

"Jillian! He's been frothing at the mouth since he met her," Brandi teases, expertly dodging the payback punch.

"ONE MORE PIECE OF THE PUZZLE"

As far as Hannah is concerned, a couple grumpy guys slept down the hall a few nights. Eleanor, however, recalls it all quite clearly, particularly the guns and the total invasion of their home and their privacy. Livid would best describe her reaction to Elijah when he phoned.

It took quite a few conversations to unravel the fear and the guilt, yet it always boils down to that same basic choice, whether to forgive and move on, or keep shouldering the weight of our anger and fear.

And after all, this is Elijah we're talking about – the man who charms cherubs from the rafters! So while he's busy making plans for their holiday feast, he is doubly delighted to host three very special guests.

Juvie saunters through the doorway sporting her full cattitude, only to be followed by Suzannah with a letter from Lloyd. In truth, it was more a relief than a shock to find that Lloyd wasn't really the man he portrayed. Prior to jetting up north to spend some quality time with Levi's mom, he had interviewed, checked references and hired Elijah a house sitter, and more specifically, he hired the lovely Suzannah.

Turns out Zannah, as her friends call her, happens to be a piccolo-playing cat lover

301

temporarily stranded between life destinations. Lloyd considered it destiny, and finding no wants or warrants against her, paid two full months in advance and left her with the keys to the farm. All in all, she took excellent care of things. Juvie adores her, the ladies from the market have already adopted her, and it really is nice to have more music in the house. She's in no more hurry to leave than he is to be alone, so she and Elijah are enjoying each other's company.

It appears Zannah is the embodiment of pure sensuality, at least according to Elijah's definition. It's effortless, without any specific intention, yet seems to blow across his skin like the warm breath of summer. Her mere presence inspires a subtle state of arousal, and she is equally swayed by his manly allure. In fact, one late afternoon in the parlor, they both placed their lips on his instrument, and somehow Elijah never missed a single note. With bliss taking place all over the house, who would have ever imagined they'd have Lloyd to thank?

Together, they dive into holiday preparations and soon the whole house feels warm and inviting. Guests begin showing days up before the feast, with Hannah and company arriving in the lead. Of course, Juvie the cat is a primary attraction, and thankfully she's up for the game. At any given moment, the two youngsters can be found chasing crickets or string, or stealthily stalking one another for attention. And in the face of a chilled cabernet, Bridgette and Eleanor soon surrender their reserve as well.

Next in is Sean, following a visit with the newlyweds, who now have stories for a lifetime of one high-caliber honeymoon. He can hardly wait to meet Hannah, having heard so much about her, and bows to her majesty, right down to the floor. Music soon accompanies the festivities, and Sean invites the young lady for a dance atop his shoes. While her tiny hands are dwarfed within his, her enormous smile is a but a small reflection of the joy in her father's heart. Seeing them all together, laughing and carrying on, Elijah feels the loose ends of his life are weaving together at last.

Soon Feast Day arrives, and as they're gathered 'round the table surrounded by friends, a firm knock echoes throughout the front hall. Elijah rises from the table to answer the door, and returns moments later with their last invited guest. Expressions are tolerant, if not slightly baffled, when he introduces them all to his good friend Lloyd. Zannah stands to greet him with a *"squunch"* and a peck, and then loops her arm through his as she turns to face the crowd.

"Everyone, I'd like to introduce you to the *new* Lloyd, as opposed to the *old* Lloyd you've heard so much about," she smiles, then looks to Elijah for details.

303

"It's an intriguing tale that will surely add more flavor to the evening! Lloyd, this is Sean," pointing to the head of the table, "and this is Bridgette, Hannah and Eleanor. I'm *so* glad you all could make it," he relays most sincerely, while offering Lloyd the empty seat next to Zannah.

As the meal gets underway, Lloyd begins the conversation with a "sanitized" version of the events from his perspective. Sean practically falls out of his chair when he realizes Lloyd was a primary player. For a few seconds, the tension is thick in the air, until Elijah asks them all to have a little faith.

As the truth of the stones begins to unfold, the atmosphere in the room warms accordingly. With acceptance comes forgiveness, and the truth that the danger was far greater than anyone knew. Despite reservations, Lloyd feels moved to lay down one more piece of the puzzle. Looking from person to person, eye to eye, heart to heart, he unearths their most coveted secret.

"You know, there's rumor of a prophecy tied to these stones…"

"A VOLATILE STATE"

"I don't know about you, but I'm starting to get nervous," admits Jacinda, resident geophysicist from Laboratory Eleven.

"Well, I think we should keep it to ourselves until we can gather more evidence," whispers Alexandra, glancing over her shoulder as the two women return from their meal break.

"How long should we wait? How long do we have?" Jacinda wonders desperately. "All I'm finding are more questions, Alex. Or answers no one will be comfortable hearing. I'd like to talk with the others and see how they feel," she asserts as they continue down the hallway, barely out of earshot of a now curious Dr. Fröenenberg.

After several weeks handling the stones, the complex is brimming with theoretical discussion. Polarities and electromagnetism, vibrational modes and quantum mechanics. Yet what started as a lively exchange of promising concepts, has degenerated over time into a heady brew of fear and desperation – a volatile state for such clever minds.

In his weekly presentation to the Triad, Julian will be reporting that the meteorite has been tentatively classified as a stony-iron mesosiderite, primarily silicate. Lars, the geochronologist, says, to the best of his knowledge, that the crystals may actually predate time. The remainder of the geoscientific team has determined that with the exception of gravity, they do not appear to react or interact with any known force, and the isotopic signature is dissimilar to all previous recordings. Simply put, they are unique and date back to the dawn of creation.

That said, we have arrived precisely at the point of frustration. Unknown territory commands a whole new set of possibilities, thereby complicating existing probabilities, to which we've grown truly accustomed. Their existence is realigning the synapses of science. Rules are breaking, laws are bending, and while they've identified as Majorana neutrinos of the Z Boson family, they have been unable to determine a causative force.

It works. We know it works. We just don't know how or why it works. Not a comforting thought for anyone involved. Fear bubbles up in frustration, which erupts into anger, that's now escalating throughout the complex at every possible level. Smug remarks are overheard in the distance; invitations are ignored. Royce snubs Guillermo at the Quick-Mart, and heated words are exchanged … and then all the lights go out.

"BACK TO YOU, BOB"

The late night news shared a few early rumblings, although no one was truly prepared for the enormity of the situation.

"Volcanic activity has been detected on all eleven tectonic plates," relays the stony-faced anchorman. "So far, we're only experiencing low level expulsions, yet the sheer number of volcanoes is positively staggering. Reports are coming in from around the globe: Russia, Kenya, Iceland, Chile, China, Antarctica, Oregon, Saudi Arabia, and that's just to name a few. Volcanologist, Harold Wexler, is currently on location in Yellowstone Park. Harold."

"Thank you, Bob. We are on site at the Yellowstone Caldera where you can witness steam eruptions occurring behind me as we speak. Teams are now on hand throughout the park to document potential lava flows. Park management is presently urging late season visitors to evacuate the park and to avoid isolation behind flow lines."

"Are there other hot spots we should be aware of, Harold?"

"We've also had reports from Mount St. Helens in Washington as well as Mount Tananga up in Alaska, which hasn't seen an eruption since 1914. The *Pacific Ring of Fire* is a string of active volcanoes, Bob, that roughly stretches from South America through Mexico, up the western U.S.

coast, and on up through Canada, Alaska, the Aleutian Islands, Russia, Japan and Indonesia. While we anticipate activity in this area, we are also receiving data on volcanoes that have been inactive for centuries and even thousands of years. The preponderance of movement is unprecedented, Bob. Speculation from our best geoscientists supposes we've not seen this level of activity in literally millions of years."

"What *exactly* do we need to watch out for, Dr. Wexler?"

"Due to the widespread nature of eruptions, the public should familiarize themselves with some basic information on volcanoes. For instance, there are three primary types of eruptions. The Hawaiian expels varying amounts of pyroclastic debris such as ash and small stones, and lava can expel through fissures located along the sides of the mountain. Strombolian blasts are known to spew fiery arcs of lava high into the air until rivulets of the molten material overflow the crater basin and spill down the sides of the mountain, as depicted in these photos. The largest, and potentially most dangerous, Bob, is the Vulcanian eruption. It is characterized by a loud explosion that violently launches gas clouds of ash and debris high into the atmosphere. The impact from these is often long-range."

"What about these so-called *super volcanoes?* What can you tell us about those?"

"Well, Bob, that is precisely why I am stationed at the Yellowstone Caldera. A *caldera* is basically a pool of lava that rises to the surface, filling volcanic craters. Some are ponds, some are lakes, and some are very large lakes with potential to become super volcanoes."

"Are there precautions our viewers could be taking?"

"According to our *Volcanic Warning System,* the majority of the planet is now in either an "Advisory" or "Watch" stage, which indicates an increasing level of unrest within the earth's crust. We are encouraging all citizens to have basic provisions on hand, such as food and water, to become familiar with local evacuation plans, and to stay tuned for emergency broadcasts in your area.

"We seem to be experiencing some increased activity," Wexler points out, as a plume of steam erupts just behind his left shoulder. "We'll be sure to keep you apprised. Back to you, Bob."

Brogan just shakes his head as he switches off the television set. *What in the world have they done?* Ignorance was definitely bliss, because now he has to walk around knowing that someone is *causing* all this disaster. It was so much simpler to attribute it to unknown forces, and relinquish all responsibility.

Setting his coffee cup in the sink, he gathers up his satchel and heads for the office. The morning crew is wide-eyed and several shades paler than usual. Apparently, they've all heard the news. His mood is dark, and far from social, so with a few cursory nods, he ducks into his cubicle. He barely has his second cup of coffee in hand when the telephone rings and nearly startles a spill. Resting the cup on its paper towel coaster, he settles back into his chair and picks up by the start of ring three.

"Brogan Cantrell," he answers, and is all at once intrigued with the story that unfolds.

"JUST A RUMOR"

"Fatima, please show in Dr. Fröenenberg," Julian speaks into his headset.

"Thank you for agreeing to see me, Sir. In light of recent developments, I may have some valuable information," Fröenenberg proposes.

"And what might that be?" he asks, motioning him to sit down. "And please, call me Julian."

"All right, Julian. I overheard an interesting conversation early in the evening on the night the lights went out."

"Do go on," he encourages, his interest now piqued.

"One comment, in particular, just seemed to stick with me," continues Walter. "Jacinda said she was finding answers that no one would be comfortable hearing."

"Hmmmm…."

"Yes. I have my theories. As do we all," he adds, chuckling at his scientific pun.

"Well?" Julian probes, with growing displeasure.

"Oh, yes. Well, in the fields of cosmology, mathematics, physics, and undoubtedly many others, there is somewhat of a grail-like quest underway to discover what is loosely referred to as a *Grand Theory of the Universe*. Einstein worked on a *Unified Theory*, as have others, and in many instances, they seem to lead us toward a source, or a *God-energy*, if you will.

"I've heard such speculation, and so far as I gather, that's all it's been – speculation," counters Julian. "Are you telling me that we've enlisted the world's most highly skilled scientists to solve a planetary crisis, and they're toying around with mythology?!"

"So far, it's just a rumor," Fröenenberg concedes.

"WHAT CAN WE DO?"

by Brogan Cantrell

With volcanoes erupting on every corner of the planet, tornadoes flinging houses into alternate zip codes, and what seems like a perpetual war throughout the Middle East, how can we just sit here wringing our hands?

What else can we do? Well, that's exactly how I felt sitting at my desk this morning – that is, until my telephone rang. The soft-spoken voice on the other end not only touched my heart, it served as an awakening, which is precisely what I hope to do for you.

The call was received from one of the coordinators of the recent Stuffolks Symposium, a groundbreaking conference that drew religious leaders from every corner of the world. For some, the need for unification has become crystal clear, particularly in the midst of such global disaster. To that end, the Symposium as a collective, discovered a singular message they've asked me to share.

We live every day with remnants of fear all around us. Fear causes war, causes doubt, causes addiction. Fear causes violence, it causes suffering, and it often leads to abuse and abandonment. Fear causes hate. And perhaps worst of all, fear breeds more fear. It's a strong sword, and highly effective, and while it may well be the dominant force on our planet, it is not the only one.

Faith has more power than fear. Have faith in what is possible. It is a driving force that connects us –

with ourselves, with each other and with the universe itself. It's moved mountains, won elections, and built cities, and it gets us out of bed every morning, yet is so wholly disregarded. So much so, that we have completely forgotten the enormity of its power.

So, what can you do? The Symposium suggests that we can actively weed fear from our lives, and put our faith in the world we have yet to create. Some may argue that's not enough. Perhaps. Yet this reporter prefers it to hand-wringing, and who really knows? We might just end up saving the world.

"SHE'S GOT CAKE!"

Jeannine tosses the newspaper back into the passenger seat, more certain now than ever of what she must do. In the weeks that have passed since she left the farm, she's had very little sleep – and never quite enough wine – to forget how she felt on that morning. So she keeps pointing her car where it needs to go, until there's just one right turn remaining, and she takes it.

The farmhouse looks a little different without the spectacular lighting, yet somehow she senses that not much has changed. Shifting the car into park, it occurs to her that this could quite possibly turn into the most hostile conversation she has ever endured. Smiling, Jeannine knows that won't stop her. Slipping her keys into her purse, she climbs from the car and ascends the front steps.

Rosalie greets her at the door, with suspicion nearly dripping from the screen. *Something about this woman is familiar... And she's not wearing enough color to look friendly,* Rose deduces. This being unofficial business, she'd best be remembering her smile and panache, so Jeannine offers a warm smile along with the recently-plated coffee cake she picked up in town.

"Hi. My name is Jeannine. I know you folks have been through an awful lot lately," she begins, "and I would be most grateful if you would allow me to come in and speak with you for a moment?"

Justin is standing to the left of the hall tree, and appears genuinely amused with her performance. He knows exactly who she is, yet aptly holds no bias. Likewise, he knows full well she was following them, although he sees no need to hold that against her either. Jeannine innately knows her chances are better with Justin than his mother, and silently pleads to the boy with her eyes.

"She's got cake!" he hollers excitedly, every bit the child when need be.

Loretta and the remainder of the housemates quickly respond to the call, and soon they're all seated in the living room, enjoying some coffee along with the cake.

"I know a little bit about what you've been through, and I know a little bit about your boy," Jeannine doles out sparingly, along with the requisite smile. "I've come down here to volunteer my services," she tells them, before focusing her attention on Justin. "And to let you know that I'd lay down my life to protect that child."

With that kind of introduction, it's hard not to listen, as Jeannine proceeds to fill them in on her resume and credentials. There's less shock here than elsewhere, with all the dreaming and crows and the like. Some things you just know, like when it's time to go home, and *Wonder World's* been calling for quite some time.

That next morning, the family of three, plus one bodyguard, begins the journey home, celebrating tollbooths like never before.

"A MOMENT OF BRILLIANCE"

Standing alone at some predawn hour, Julian hovers in the glow of organic light as he stares down at the crystals now encased behind glass.

There's barely a halo, and it's pulsing, neither of which is a positive sign. *They're running down,* he observes. *Wouldn't that be a treat. Buried alive for the end of the world.... So I guess it's my charge to keep them shining,* he presumes, in agreement with the Triad, who are due to arrive within hours.

From the brilliance they witnessed when the stones first arrived, the overall candlepower has consistently declined. It's as if they've experienced some kind of "brown out," and are now only operating at partial capacity. This does not bode well. The Triad will definitely be looking to the complex for an explanation on the volcanoes, and now just hours away, Julian has no idea what to tell them.

This time Richard is at the airstrip to collect them, while Julian stays behind to welcome them in the lobby. The less grill time, the better. They appear no less anxious than they did on their first visit, yet this time he doubts the happy ending. The only ending he can see from here is his. If this day closes with him both alive and employed, Julian will be truly amazed.

Richard escorts them into the conference room as Fatima graciously fulfills their standing orders.

Madeleine prefers lemon water – fresh lemons only, no packets; Wilhelm drinks Earl Grey, sans the garnishes, thank you very much; and Emanuel is a coffee man, who enjoys it with flavors, and fine cookies, if you please. All the fuss only makes for a welcome delay, as Julian attempts to engage them in light conversation.

"Yes, we have some fine chefs and wonderful bakers at our disposal. Perhaps you'd like to join us for a meal when we're through here. It would give you an opportunity to meet some of the staff, if you're so inclined."

"We'll see," hisses Wilhelm over the brim of his teacup, with an expression that suggests his patience is waning.

"Well, let's get straight to the point, then," Julian broaches, deciding to exert some control. "Our tests have succeeded in bringing us straight to the heart of science's greatest dilemma. Yet at the core of the issue, we are encountering the same obstacles as Einstein and Podolsky, and others, both before and since. The proverbial *Theory of Everything, M-Theory, Perturbative String Theory*, none have the evidentiary results to step beyond a theory. We have everything science has to offer at our disposal, yet certain truths remain elusive, out beyond the confines of theoretical physics as we know it," he concludes.

"So what you're actually telling us is that you don't know. Is that a fair assessment?" probes Wilhelm, staring him flatly in the eyes.

"Yes, that would be a fair assessment," admits Julian, casting his gaze to the floor. It's clear he'll not to be afforded the grace of sugar-coating. Then the thought occurs suddenly, like a moment of brilliance. "Emanuel, my colleagues suggest that at the crux of all this rests the *God-energy,* what do you think of that?" he asks, with a hair too much twinkle in his eye.

"My viewpoint must be clear. It's yours that is of interest," asserts Emanuel.

"I believe the time has come for us to explore both science and theology together," he retorts, spinning as fast as he can. "I propose contacting Symposium coordinators to recommend participants. Perhaps they, along with our cosmologists and theoretical physicists, can zero in on the source."

Julian is barely breathing as his eyes dash from one face to the next. Wilhelm is tapping his teacup while swirling the thought. He studies Julian for several uncomfortable minutes before turning back to the others for confirmation. Finally, after an exhaustively short meeting, Wilhelm sets his empty cup on the table and graciously stands up to leave.

"We shall leave no stone unturned," he declares. "Let us consider this done."

"ONCE IN A WHILE"

Months now since they've spoken, Levi has all but given up hope that Jillian will even want to see him again. By now he's envisioned a thousand scenarios, most with darkly alternative endings. Yet once in a while.... Once in a while he lets himself dream of that girl who makes his head spin, and she's completely thrilled to see him, and by then his heart is racing, his blood is pumping – and sometimes it's *really* hard to drive in that condition.

His motel is just ahead, yet he decides to keep driving. Night shift at the pizza parlor begins at 4:30, and he's looking for a spot next to the dumpster. Pulling into the dirt parking lot, he grins as he whips the truck around and slowly backs into her space. With shift change just minutes away, she should be arriving any time now, that is, if she's scheduled at all. Either way, she's worth the wait, so he bides his time striking poses in the rearview and working out a *hello* that's really cool. And it would have been *really cool* if she hadn't watched it three times before he noticed her.

Jillian is laughing when he sees her. Her smile is breathtaking, and for a moment, he simply forgets to swallow. Next thing he knows, he's choking on his own saliva, eyes tearing, nose running – truly a sight to behold. Slapping him on the back, Jillian offers him some water, which he gladly accepts, while she waits for his breath to return.

"I see that I've managed to charm you again," he smiles in a way that sends her insides reeling.

"Yeah, and I suppose you'd have called mouth-to-mouth a date, too!"

"Sorry, I didn't hear anything after the 'Yeah,'" he confides, before completely disappearing in her eyes. Her lips are moving, yet he can't seem to get past that incredible light that just dances in her eyes. Nothing else really matters right now, and without any notice, he reaches one strong hand around the back of her neck and pulls her lips to his for a kiss that sends shockwaves through history.

Jillian didn't make it in to work that night. In fact, she never made it in again.

"Right There At The Counter"

Sean high-tailed it from Elijah's to make it here in just two days, and arrived with just one speeding ticket. From the moment they announced the first volcanoes, to the instant he sees her face inside the Dew Drop, all he can think of is Daisy. *My God, her face is like an angel,* he thinks, catching her eye.

"Sean!" she calls out, gracefully sacheting through tables, with a full pot of decaf in hand.

He finds an empty space at the counter, one stools apart, as is socially proper. Although the menu is standing right there, wedged between the pepper and the salt, he makes no move to reach for it. There's no question what he wants.

After topping off a few customers, Daisy finally decides to wander back over to the counter. She was careful not to hurry, or to throw herself on him or anything, and neither task was especially easy. By the time they actually meet face-to-face, each has firmly harnessed whatever composure they can muster.

"So, what brings you back this way?" she asks him, blatantly fishing for whatever is biting.

"Ah, so she dives right in for the kill," he laughs. "I came back here because some clever enchantress swept down and captured my heart," Sean delivers gallantly, pausing to look her in the eyes. "You know, I'm not a regular guy, or on second thought maybe I am, and sometimes I can

323

be a real pain in the ass. At least that's what I've been told, but not really lately," he rambles, unable to shut down the stream of blather now spilling from his lips. And that's exactly when she kisses him square on the lips – right there at the counter – and suddenly a lifetime doesn't seem like very long.

"PERFECTLY ALIGNED"

The slam of those truck doors is music to her ears, and Loretta is relieved to see Levi finally arrive. Inside, she knew he was coming, though no words had been exchanged, and he's brought the long-awaited Jillian home to meet them.

His entrance is typically lively – a little loud, a little raucous, a little Levi. There's dancing with Gold Dog and a tango with Loretta, with perhaps a bit more animation in the presence of his lady. He's a force of nature you'd be blessed to experience. Rori suggests they get pizza, so the three pile into the pickup and head off into town.

"Levi, things are really happening, and we need to get ready," Aurora confides. "Can you stay with Loretta while Joe and I go home? With these volcanoes, we really need to check on the houses and boost up the savings, if you know what I mean."

"Of course. You got it," he answers, looking to his companion, who nods her approval. "I've got so much to tell you," is just the start of the much longer conversation.

Thankfully, they return to the farm with plenty of pizza, because the three that became five is now up to seven. Grant and Mirabella showed up unexpectedly with news that Grant resigned from his company. Try as he might, he just couldn't accept his life there anymore. His realigned priorities no longer focus on decimals, but rather on the disposition of nine immensely powerful stones.

He's been studying energy and working with Bella. She explained how to focus by imagining miniatures encircled in his hands. Envisioning his connection with both the source and the earth, he amplifies that energy into a whirlwind that flows through his body and exits his palms. It seemed a bit far-fetched at first, yet the more he practices, the more he can feel it coursing through his body like an electrical charge.

Aurora is fascinated, as is Loretta, so they ask Mirabella to show them as well. Jillian is watching from behind Levi's arm, so Rori invites her to join them, because they can use all the help they can get.

"It's really does work, you know," Loretta discloses. "Me and Lizzie had to do it when Charlotte came calling. Stones were goin' crazy when she started talkin' mean, flashin' all wild like they did. So Lizzie and I, we hooked our arms around that bowl and loved just as hard as we could, and we got 'em settled down. And Charlotte settled down, too, but I suspect Cady had quite a lot to do with that."

"That's exactly it," confirms Bella. "It's all the same energy. Once we know it's out there, we can learn how to work with it. We were hoping that Justin might still be here. He has such incredible insight."

Loretta looks at Rori, who promptly steps into the dining room. Mirabella is curious and waiting expectantly when Aurora returns a moment later with a single sheet of paper. Bella is smiling sweetly as she studies the Crayola rendition of Loretta's beautiful necklace, then notices the date on the corner of the page. As her jaw stands agape, they all share a good laugh and the knowledge that it's all intertwined. On the subject of connection, Grant walks over to the telephone, and swiftly reconnects the ringer.

"Thought you'd been out a lot lately," he grins. "At least the world was always at your fingertips."

There in the afternoon sun, Loretta finally sees her grandson, the one hidden beneath all that pain and fear, and he is every bit as magnificent as she always knew him to be. In fact, as she moves from one magnificent face to the next, she is absorbed with the abundance that surrounds her. *Can you see them, Henry? That's our family…*

Seeing her dear friend caught up in such rhapsody, Aurora grabs two slices of pizza and quietly disappears up the stairs. Her room is packed and all the beds made, so the only thing left is goodbye. *First in, last out,* loiters in her brain, until she remembers that there's no such thing. There were people here before her, and more people since, and Loretta will be just fine for a while.

Joe shows up at the door to fetch her bags, just as the lump in her throat reminds her that leaving may be harder than she imagined. With a quick hug for reassurance, they gather up her things and head back downstairs. A brief look of surprise crosses Loretta's face, yet is observed by the room, nonetheless. She quickly recovers with a genuine smile, and some social salve to ease the pain.

"I guess I never really thought of you as leaving, though I have no idea why," admits Loretta.

"You know that *Ring of Fire* they keep talking about on the news? Well, I guess Joe and I live somewhere along the *Ring of Embers,*" Aurora reveals. "Besides, I need to check in with my banker," she muses with a wink.

Loretta draws Aurora close and whispers into her hair, "With our paths interlocking and our hearts intertwined, should you happen on my doorstep, I will welcome you, for this is our destiny."

The words simply came to her from somewhere in time, at exactly the right moment, as if perfectly aligned.

"THE CAPACITY
OF ALL THAT IS KNOWN"

The Faithful, as deemed by Symposium leaders, managed to reignite the stones, and have kept them all glowing since their arrival. Volunteers are serving on a rotating basis, four at a time, based on schedules and commitments. Their reception was cordial, yet perhaps lacked the nuance typically afforded other colleagues. Conversation was light, and evasively brief, as the scientists held firmly, and defensively, to their piece of sacred ground.

Despite being treated like cult members, the Faithful continue to pray that all will be well, and the stones have continued to glow. It didn't take a genius to notice the change, yet it will require several dozen to understand the inspiration. The teams set to work, voraciously testing and retesting every element of their equations.

Yet when frustrations escalate and fear becomes once again dominant, the negativity soon overpowers the efforts of the Faithful. That evening as the crystals again begin to pulse, it becomes abundantly clear that this answer exceeds the capacity of all that is known.

"A SEA OF POSSIBILITY"

By the time she hangs up with Peggy, Lizzie has already formulated a game plan, and now it's time to put it into action. She has a three-day-weekend, which is the most she can expect for the next six months, having used up all her vacation time. Dad's tenants moved out several weeks ago, when the floor finally gave way beneath the toilet. It dropped clear down into the crawl space, and left poor Mr. Cabrone hanging on for dear life.

Lizzie has the list narrowed down to three contractors, all with great references. They will be interviewing tomorrow, with the intention of arriving at a decision by Sunday. It's a big job, so Lizzie's been doing her homework. Repairing the house is an investment that must be made, yet it's Jonas's retirement, so she's determined to be frugal. On the other hand, shoddy work does not an investment make, so she'll also be looking for a quality job.

With his engineering background, Jonas will be especially helpful with grilling them on specifics. Beverly, not quite surprisingly, knows a thing or two as well, having been partners with a contractor somewhat shy of a lifetime ago. So together, they make a fairly formidable team – as we know!

Tonight, however, they're having dinner with Peggy and Warren. Jonas is relieved to know that Vincent is not on the guest list, and thinks he may just have spotted him under a bridge outside of town… On the up side, Beverly is looking positively regal, as Jonas offers he his elbow and escorts her into the restaurant. Both Warren and Peggy are up on their feet by the time the Duchess and court reach the table.

"Jonas, you never told me how delightful she is," exclaims Beverly over cocktails.

Between her grace, her heart and her happy marriage, Peggy is everything Bev ever wished she could be. Instead, she had a lifetime of hard work and heartbreak, and long ago abandoned any thought of real happiness. Yet now so much is possible, and she is basking in the warmth of the evening, thrilled with the here and the now.

And for the first time in history, Peggy is enjoying being the center of attention for longer than a heartbeat. She and Beverly are happily discussing crafts and self-help, as they dive into their family style dinner. Roast turkey with all the trimmings is what they've served here for decades, and they'll bring you as much as you'll eat. It's Jonas's kind of place, and who can argue with delicious? All in all, it's been a wonderful evening when Peggy walks proudly, and dryly (eyes and undergarments) to the parking lot that night.

Strength of character has no uniform, and even Jonas is forced to admit the depth of his blindness. For an instant he recalls his expectation, and then it all shifts. The veil has been lifted. From here on out, he'll be seeing her more clearly, for all she is and is yet to become. That night Jonas lies in bed mourning the missed years with his daughter, his Peggy, yet goes to sleep dreaming of all the ways he can grow to know her better.

Lizzie awakens with the alarm clock, tickled to smell coffee as she rolls out of bed. Today's the big day, and she's excited to get their project started. After a quick shower, she appears in the kitchen dressed in blue jeans and flannel, fully looking the part. Jonas and Bev have bought breakfast, and the three of them strategize over bagels and eggs.

Their first appointment is scheduled for ten, which after a phone call becomes ten-thirty, and by the time it's eleven, he's out of a job. Contestant number two is slated for noon, so they entertain themselves with catalogs, and laying odds on what time he'll arrive. Holding to her optimism, Liz collects her winnings, when Thomas clocks in at eleven fifty-four.

He looks at her as if he knows her, which is unnerving, and feels far more like confidence than coincidence. Quickly assuming her role as project manager to Jonas's engineer and Beverly's consultant, Lizzie initiates the walk-through, bid sheets in hand. Discussing the project in stages, each one grilling him on varying specifics, Lizzie discovers he's been without an office manager for quite some time, which is definitely a noteworthy concern.

The last contractor arrives promptly at two, coming in with just seconds to spare. It's clear Ed has been doing this for years. His presentation sounds pre-recorded, like he wished it were over before it's begun. Jonas can easily relate, although in truth, he no longer subscribes to that perspective. With few questions, Ed is soon on his way, with their assurance of a decision by Sunday.

Estimates strewn across the counter, Lizzie suggests she continue the evaluation while Jonas and Beverly enjoy another dinner with Peggy and Warren. Jonas starts to give her the look, then smiles, and winks at her instead. Who knows what the night may hold?

Lizzie is going over their references along with her accompanying notes, when she spies *The Eatery* on Thomas's list of referrals. Of the two, he seemed most interested, and perhaps she can talk a little bit off his price. Well anyway, she's hungry, and it would be good to have a look at his work, so changing out of her jeans, she phones up a cab to take her down town.

The Eatery is dress casual, according to the phone book, so she enters wearing basics, a splash of color and some lipstick, yet draws the room's attention with a force that rivals gravity. Wherever she goes now, people turn around to look at her, as if they can feel her walk by. Jonas has been noticing something similar, as have the rest of the *alternative family*.

Lizzie is seated at a small table in the back, waiting to speak with the owner, when Thomas arrives to claim his take-out order. She laughs when their eyes connect across the room, certain she's been busted checking up on him. However, if the truth be told, thoughts of references might be last to cross his mind. He's delighted to see her, particularly at his favorite restaurant.

She invites him to join her, and he agrees, whereupon the server returns his order to the kitchen to be served along with Lizzie's meal. They share wine and conversation, and he shows her the renovations himself while the owners look on, appreciative for his assistance during the dinner rush. She is struck with his craftsmanship and quality of work, in addition to coordinating a job of this scale while maintaining such an obvious friendship.

Over dinner, she shares her expertise, of which he is equally impressed - perhaps more so than she realizes. With the business bases covered, they soon progress to delicately probing the highs and lows of their personal lives, all the while holding to decorum.

Although somewhere between the entree and dessert, Lizzie agrees to hire him for the job, so long as he agrees to hire her. She hasn't been happy with her job since returning from Loretta's, especially in the absence of Grant, and Thomas is offering a comparable salary.

By coffee, she's feeling awake and alive, and is mentally cavorting in a sea of possibility.

"WATERWAYS AND SMOKE"

Their trip home is decidedly less high-flying, sans the company of crows, and Aurora's thoughts are already at home. The nostalgia of November fields is almost more than her lonely heart can bear. Gold Dog nudges at her elbow in hopes of disturbing the thick layer of sadness that's settled over the truck like a pall.

Beyond feeling rather deflated in the wake of their gigantic adventure, she and Joe are also wondering about what remains of their homes. They rest in the shadow of several long-extinct volcanoes, yet all that's been changing of late. Neither left with arrangements or anyone to call, and that thought raises a lump in her throat that threatens to bring her to tears.

There's nothing like a wet tongue to bring you around, Gold Dog decides, lapping the full length of her unsuspecting cheek. Rori's laughter ripples through the air like a long-awaited breeze, and Joe's smile is both with her and for her.

"So, what's the next chapter? What's next for you, my friend?" invites Joe.

"Why Joe, I think you just struck gold!" she exclaims, all at once revived and renewed. "Yes, yes, that's it! We need to write this down, Joe. The world needs to know we can change things," she declares, as her minds flies down the path of all that is possible.

The duration of their trip is spent alive and empowered, and reveling in the strength of true alignment. In no particular hurry, they meander the waterways, soaking up immense, lazy rivers on their journey home to cacti and sand. More than ever, Joe is infused with the beauty that surrounds him. Since the night Justin arrived and all nine stones were reunited, Joe has become vastly aware of the infinite connections. Each changing vista now permeates his spirit with shifting versions of all that is, all that was and all that's yet to be.

It's late morning when they reach that last intersection and finally turn the trusty pickup toward home. Off in the distance, they notice a plume of smoke rising up against the mountains. If Aurora's not mistaken, their houses are situated right about there, and one glimpse at Joe confirms her suspicion. Gold Dog is sniffing at the air, although far less disturbed than either would have guessed.

Rori's house is the closest, and as they near the mountain range, it becomes clear that her house alone is the source of the smoke. Joe presses hard on the gas pedal, propelling them down that dirt road like that old truck had wings. By the time she realizes it's coming from the chimney, hear tears are past the point of no return. Of course, as whole new wave sets in the moment she spies Ryan's car in the driveway.

Aurora has the door open before Joe can even reach a full stop, and flies across the stone path with a black dog at her heels. Barely touching earth, she throws open the front door and rushes in to find her long-lost love tossing a log into their wood stove. Ryan melts at the very sight of her, and stands to meet her, face-to-face and heart-to-heart.

"It's a cold world without you, Aurora," he says, brushing the hair from her eyes.

"I've missed you too," she whispers into the crook of his neck. For a long moment, she and Ryan simply stand there, wrapped snugly in the comfort of their twenty-odd years.

"SIGNIFICANT GROVELING"

When Jeannine gets a call on her private phone, she knows it's only one of two people – Reardon or Dan. No one else has access to that line. Turns out the voice in her ear belongs to the former as opposed to the latter.

"Hey, Kid. What's your 20?" Reardon asks.

"Stuffolks."

"Really. Hmmm… Sure you know what you're doing?"

"Never had a choice," she replies with a smile.

"O-kay then…well, it appears you've already completed a good portion of your mission."

"How's that?"

"The Triad wants us to collect the nine, but in truth, they'd like the whole group," he shares, in hopes of coaxing her back into the fold.

"Apologies and safety guaranteed, I presume?"

"Of course."

"Well then, who's left after the shuffle?" she asks.

"Dan, I suspect…Zach, Ted, Stan, not sure about Lloyd. Lou and Riley. Roy's still got money, so he won't be around. Mitch, he's a good lad. He'll show. The *Hardy Boys,* on the other hand, may never get over 'collateral damage.' From the yelp, they may be seeking a new line of work, along with some therapy. Anyway, we should have plenty to round 'em up."

"I'll pass on the cattle analogy, thank you."

"Oooo, aren't we sensitive," teases Reardon.

"In light of what they've already been through, Sir, I think they deserve the decency of being treated as people."

"You're right. I'm sorry. Mea culpa," he pleads, acknowledging her line in the sand.

Locating Sean is a bit of a challenge, yet with the help of Elijah, they uncover the Dew Drop and a great plate of food. So, with significant groveling and a good dose of respect, Gold Dog and the group agree to share their expertise. Within hours, they're chauffeured to the complex, and within minutes reunited with the stones, as crows the world over take to the air.

"JUSTIN'S KEY"

As each of the original nine enters the glass room, a halo of light forms around the stones, and they continue to grow brighter by the second. Loretta wraps her arms around them and greets them as if they were Henry. The scientists are aghast when the Faithful applaud, weeping tears of relief at the sight of reinforcements.

Once the crystals are restored, Justin marches straight up to Julian, small suitcase in hand, and suggests they have a look at his drawings. For a moment the Director appears slightly bemused, clearly underestimating what is about to be revealed. Loretta's tribe are all nodding their heads, so he takes the little fellow by the hand, and escorts him up to a very large room.

Justin places the sketches in order while Lorna and Rosalie assist with the display. One by one, they hang them, as a room full of onlookers appears somewhat bewildered. Stretched nearly the length of one long wall are all the crayon drawings from his bedroom. They reference time; they reference space; they reference the known forces; yet most significantly, Justin's collection demonstrates a truly unique mathematical principle. As recognition slowly dawns in the scientists' eyes, they begin to notice that the equation has been replicated throughout every single dimension.

341

With all the elements in place, Justin taps on the microphone, just like the nice man said. It's a very large room from his particular perspective, and a whole lot of people are staring directly at him when the most penetrating smile creeps across his small face.

"These stones magnify the energy of human potential. They work on the polarity of fear versus faith," imparts the child who solves universal riddles like a good game of chess. Beyond astonished, the audience is positively speechless. Brains are whirling in every direction, busy absorbing a concept they had not yet considered.

"I gotta go the bathroom," he says into the microphone, and then runs across the stage toward his mother.

"A STATE OF DIVINITY"

For the next seventy-two hours, the entire complex is literally exploding with energy. The crystals are radiating like never before, and the staff is barely resting as their minds burst with tangential possibilities. While one segment explores physical properties, others are working with Justin, extrapolating data like water from a sponge. There were more drawings in his suitcase, and with what they've seen so far, lifetimes of study have been answered in crayon.

As each of the Nine share their stories, the scientists set about redefining their perceptions. *Fear*, under this definition, becomes an energetic force; it becomes a verb, indicating an action. Experiments conducted over the last several days using Justin's calculations have revealed that the energy of human potential can actually charge inert particles – majorana neutrinos - in either direction.

As the truth of realization is slowly absorbed, each individual begins a peaceful transformation, a genetic realignment, and an evolutionary leap toward human survival. Later examination will reveal an altered DNA structure, resulting solely from achievement of this heightened awareness.

Throughout the room, person after person moves into this *State of Divinity*, silently experiencing their connection with *All*. Yet there in the throes of wonder, poised on the brink of

343

potential alignment, each must choose to abandon their fear. From the moment she embraces her decision, Jacinda is awash with such a feeling of peace, the likes of which she's never known. *The truth is so ingrained we've overlooked it all the while,* she realizes, in light of the evidence that is now completely transparent at every level. *We're all exchanging energy...every thought...every action...is an interaction....* She slips off into the magnitude and the minutia of her thoughts, adrift in the serenity of knowing – and somehow it all just makes sense.

The stones, however, have begun absorbing fear at an exponential rate, which is baffling in light of the energy shift within the complex. The volcanoes resume constant spewing, and hurricanes are now mounting an angry assault that's headed straight for the Caribbean. Switching off the television, Emanuel turns to greet his arriving guests, who he has invited to join him for a chat.

"It certainly is *'Raining down,'*" Emanuel nods to the now darkened screen, "yet how exactly *'In the spirit of man?'* he asks Joe. "Forgive me. Please come in. Sit down. You'll join me for a cookie, eh?" the holy man suggests, smiling at Joe, and winking at the youngster.

The two men settle into soft leather chairs while Justin climbs aboard the oversized ottoman, also in service as a table for his cookies. After nibbling and sipping and enjoying the taste of chocolate, Emanuel turns to his guests and poses the question of the day.

"So what do you make of that statement, Justin, *'It will rain down in the spirit of man?'* Does it have any meaning to you?"

"It just means everybody," the boy answers.

"What about *'everybody?'"* asks Joe.

"Everybody. It means that the whole world is playing. All the kids. All the parents. Just everybody."

"You mean with the stones?" probes Joe, grappling for clarity.

"Yeah. You see, everybody's been scared for a really long time, but now it's time to learn something else. You tell them. Teach them how to do it," he directs Joe, with absolute faith that he *can* and *will* execute the appointed task. Scootching toward the edge of the ottoman, Justin drops down onto the floor. Turning to face Emanuel, he opens up another new door. "Someone taught them to be afraid, you know. It's always just been about the faith."

"LIFE'S FIRST BREATH"

Alone in his room, Emanuel struggles to assimilate the waves of information that Justin conveyed in those few simple words.

The spirit of man is just...everybody. It will rain down in the spirit of...everybody. And everybody's been scared for a really long time. And then something clicks deep down inside. *We have done this...My God, we've done this!* strikes him like a slap. *We have taught them! Governments use fear for control, corporations for profit, and the Church,* he grasps most painfully, *the Churches have taught us to fear God!*

Sickened by his realization, he cannot imagine feeling any more lost. Yet somewhere amid the ethers, among the spaces in between, he grasps Justin's final clue. *'The whole world is playing.' That's it! The stones are drawing energy from all over the world. Everybody! Everybody's fear! 'You tell them it's time to learn something else,'* blows through his synapses like life's first breath, just as Emanuel himself transcends into awareness.

"NEW BEGINNINGS"

Standing before a sea of cameras and reporters, microphones positioned like a halo around him, Wilhelm prepares himself to address planet earth. This is not his first appearance on the world stage, yet this realigned Willhelm feels a great deal more compassion. Citizens the world over are waiting – breathless – hovered between horror and despair, and they shall wait no longer.

"FEAR NOT!" he begins, "And all will be well in our world. It is a simple request, yet enormously powerful, and I'm here today to tell you that it's far more important than we've ever really known. Both religion and science now agree, fear itself is fueling these natural disasters. Your fear, my fear, our mothers' fear, and our fathers'. We have become a world driven by fear, and *WE ALONE* can choose a new direction.

"It is time to choose faith – in ourselves and in our potential. We are not alone, have never been alone and will never be alone, yet each of us is unique and magnificent," he delivers, as a single tear rolls down his cheek.

"We can save ourselves. We can stop the disasters. We can live respectfully, as one people. We can choose a new direction. Together we can save our world."

Across oceans and valleys, from mountaintops to city streets, cheers resound from the bedrock straight up through the clouds. As children wipe the tears of their mothers, and mothers remove weapons from the tired hands of soldiers, the violent winds subside, the lava recedes and a long-starving planet gets a taste of true healing.

Guardian crows fill the heavens, flying high above the earth, soaring aloft on great currents of faith. Through the infinite depth of their midnight eyes, they will be quietly overseeing our use of the gift. And from those depths, beyond the beyond, others will be watching too.

"We have the ability to change," Wilhelm continues, "To reach for a brighter tomorrow, for ourselves, for our children, for all those who have gone before us and all of those who will move beyond. We will align with our potential, with all that is possible, and together we will create a world for all people! And on this day, at this very moment, each of us holds the power to begin again."

THE END

EPILOGUE

According to modern science, a *neutrino,* meaning "small neutral one," is an elementary particle that usually travels close to the speed of light, is electrically neutral, and is able to pass through ordinary matter *almost* unaffected, "like a bullet passing through a bank of fog." This makes neutrinos extremely difficult to detect, yet every second of every day, approximately 65 billion neutrinos pass through each square centimeter of Earth.

Studies have revealed that it *is possible* for neutrinos to take on a charge as the result of what is called a *"Weak Interaction,"* one of the four known forces of the Universe. The better known forces include *"Strong Nuclear Reaction," Electromagnetism," and "Gravity."*

Weak Interactions have long been a hot topic among the world's leading physicists, including such earlier mental explorers as Einstein, Bose, Darwin and DaVinci. With fewer facts than theories, suppose for a moment that this lesser known force is being influenced, or charged, through a source we have yet to identify.

Imagine that we are already impacting those neutrinos, those minutest particles of our atmosphere, and let's define that source as *H-Factor Energy.* Evidence is accumulating that this energy may be tied quite directly to our choices and our intentions.

Twentieth century studies revealed that it's possible to bend a beam of light with the sheer force of one's will.

Energy healing is now an accepted alternative throughout much of the world, and is taught in nursing schools across the United States.

Though science has yet to define an appropriate vehicle to quantify the explanation, the effects of *H-Factor Energy* are becoming well documented.

So here we are, hovering on the brink of all that is possible – right where the realms of truth and fiction quietly align...

Stay tuned!

ALPHABETICAL CHARACTER REFERENCE

Aika (Aik) pronounced Ika (Ike): *Astrophysicist, Netherlands*

Alex: *Astrophysicist, Chile*

Aunt Mattie: *Cadence's aunt*

Aurora (Rori): *Stone Holder #2 followed crows from the desert*

Barry Nyack: *General Manager of the Hotel Stuffolks*

Beverly: *Jonas's lady friend (a/k/a "The Duchess")*

Bob: *TV Anchorman*

Brandi: *Levi's friend and confidant*

Bridgette: *Eleanor's partner*

Brogan Cantrell: *Newspaper reporter*

Cadence (Cady) Merriweather: *Heiress and Stone Holder #3*

Callie: *Drunken friend to Levi*

Carlie: *Sean's sister and Stone Holder #8*

Chad: *Mercenary*

Charlotte Merriweather: *Cadence Merriweather's Mother*

Commander Reardon: *Chief mercenary*

Daisy: *Sean's love interest and owner of the Dew Drop Inn*

Dan: *Lead mercenary at Loretta's farm*

Dr. Walter Fröenenberg: *Shift supervisor at laboratory complex*

Eleanor: *Hannah's mother, Bridgette's partner, Elijah's former lover*

Elijah: *Stone Holder #6 and a saxophone player*

Emanuel: *Church representative and founder of the Triad*

The Spaces In Between

Faithful: *Symposium volunteers sent to the laboratory complex*

Fatima: *Human Resources Assistant at laboratory complex*

Gold Dog: *Aurora's four-legged companion*

Grant Fontaine: *Loretta's Grandson, Mirabella's lover, Accountant*

Gretchen: *Wilhelm's Assistant*

Guillermo: *Laboratory staff*

Hannah: *Eleanor's daughter*

Harold Wexler: *TV Volcanologist*

Harry: *Grant's Doorman*

Henry: *Loretta's husband*

Jacinda: *Geophysicist from Lab Eleven*

Jeannine: *Mercenary*

Jennifer: *Food & Beverage Manager with the Hotel Stuffolks*

Jillian: *Levi's love interest*

Joe: *Aurora's friend*

Jonas: *Father of two daughters*

Julian: *Director of the laboratory complex*

Justin: *Four-year-old boy*

Juvie: *Feline friend to Elijah*

Kevin: *Mineralogist from Lab Eleven*

Lenore: *Human Resourses Assistant in laboratory complex*

Levi: *Farmboy and Stone Holder #4*

Levi's Mom: *Wise Woman*

Linda: *Motel owner's wife*

Lizzie Breslen: *Grant's Assistant and Stone Holder #5*

Lloyd: *Mercenary*

Lola: *Zeke's girlfriend*

Loretta: *Henry's wife, Grant's grandmother and Stone Holder #1*

Lorna: *Stone Holder #7*

Lou: *Mercenary*

Madeleine: *Triad Member representing the World Bank*

Maggie: *Cadence's Housekeeper*

Marlie: *Levi's friend*

Michael: *Cadence's lover*

Mirabella (Bella): *Grant's girlfriend and Stone Holder #9*

Mitch: *Mercenary*

Mr. Danielson: *Motel owner*

Mrs. Liefkowicz: *Tenant in Grant's Building*

Nancy: *Receptionist at Grant's office*

Neil: *Mercenary*

Old Astronomer: *Church Astronomer*

Patrick: *Carlie's husband*

Peggy: *Lizzie's sister*

Richard: *Human Resources Manager at laboratory complex*

Riley: *Mercenary*

Rosalie: *Justin's Mom*

Roy: *Mercenary*

Royce: *Laboratory staff*

The Spaces In Between

Ryan: *Aurora's husband*

Sam #1: *Levi's drunken friend*

Sam #2: *Floral delivery Driver*

Savannah (Zannah): *Elijah's house sitter*

Sean: *Carlie's brother*

Sophia: *Madeleine's Assistant*

Stanley: *Mercenary*

Stuart: *Levi's drunken friend*

Symposium Lady: *Wise Woman*

Ted: *Mercenary*

Vincent: *Jonas's intervention*

Warren: *Peggy's husband*

Wilhelm: *Triad Member representing world governments*

Zach: *Mercenary*

Zeke (Ezekiel Jones): *Levi's friend*